Shadows of Death

By the same author

A Safe Place to Kill

Shadows of Death

Nicholas J. Clough

ROBERT HALE · LONDON

© Nicholas J. Clough 2009
First published in Great Britain 2009

ISBN 978-0-7090-8886-8

Robert Hale Limited
Clerkenwell House
Clerkenwell Green
London EC1R 0HT

www.halebooks.com

2 4 6 8 10 9 7 5 3 1

Typeset in 10/12½pt Palatino
by Derek Doyle & Associates, Shaw Heath
Printed in Great Britain by the MPG Books Group, Bodmin and King's Lynn

Life itself is but a shadow of death and souls departed but the shadows of the living

Sir Thomas Browne, 1695–1682

Chapter One

Astrum

It wasn't just the strychnine that killed him, it was also the sleeping tablets.

There are better, less painful ways to die. The road to death begins with twitching muscles and the body starts to go rigid. Then painful jerking muscle spasms and difficulty breathing. There are up to ten of these attacks, the last few growing more violent and by then there is lockjaw, frothing at the mouth, bulging eyes and an arching of the neck and back.

Christopher Van Meer was a chemist. He recognized the symptoms but, by the time his consciousness broke through the Dexylamine, the eighth attack, the one that killed him, had started and it was too late.

In the distance, St Wilfred's Church clock was striking eleven when he went through the agony of death. In the final spasm his back arched suddenly upwards, then froze as the body muscles went rigid, leaving only the back of his head and his heels touching the mattress. At the same moment the lockjaw tightened the corners of his mouth – a pale, smiling, bulging eyed death mask. The body was still like that when Mrs Morris brought him his breakfast.

Pauline Morris was a dour, dispassionate, dependable woman with a heavy set, middle-aged figure and a face that looked as if it had been hewn from the local Yorkshire stone. Carrying Mr Van Meer's breakfast tray, she knocked softly at his bedroom door. There was no answer, but sometimes there wasn't if he had been working late into the night. She opened the door, walked to the curtains and drew them back. As light flooded into the room and she turned away from the window she saw the figure on the bed.

Most women would have dropped the tray and screamed, but Mrs Morris just stared at the body, put the tray down carefully on the bedside table and dialled the police on the mobile phone she took from her apron pocket.

Chapter Two

'Harrogate!'

Seven days before Christopher Van Meer died Thomas Daykin sat in his superintendent's office, drinking tea from the china Jarvis reserved for special guests. Daykin ignored the custard cream biscuits, arranged in a neat circle on a Spode plate; he had been putting on weight lately.

'Now calm down, Inspector,' said Superintendent Jarvis, 'it's not the end of the world and it won't be forever.'

'How long?'

'A couple of months' – he paused – 'perhaps a bit longer.'

'How much longer?'

Jarvis rubbed the back of his neck in a nervous gesture. Daykin knew him well enough to recognize the signs of bad news.

'It depends' – the rubbing got harder – 'on circumstances.'

'Why me? Why Harrogate?'

Mark Jarvis sensed a weakening in Daykin's voice.

'Well,' he said gently, leaning forward and putting on a concerned expression, 'Harrogate because they're short-staffed, a flu epidemic apparently. And you because you did so brilliantly in Leeds when we sent you there.'

'No,' said Daykin, flatly.

Jarvis said nothing, but turned his head to look out of the window. He knew that this would be difficult to sell to Daykin. Sometimes it was better just to let Daykin mull it over. He stared at the three misshaped larch trees on top of Skerretts Rise, all bent in the same direction, like children bowing from the waist against the wind in their faces. If Daykin didn't say something soon he would have to jump start the conversation.

Silence. Jarvis turned his head back to the room.

'Inspector, sometimes you have to put the Force and your brother officers before yourself. Don't you agree, Tom?'

8

Daykin felt his stomach sink. It was never good when Jarvis called him 'Tom'.

'Meaning what?' he said cautiously.

'If you don't go then someone else will have to, even me.' Jarvis smiled to show that he was joking. 'And if it's not me' – the smile faded – 'it will have to be Inspector Thompson.'

He let Daykin think about David Thompson, a married man with two children.

'And, of course,' said Jarvis, to hammer the point home, 'his youngest girl is in the middle of her GCSEs, Lord knows what moving schools will do to her studies.'

It was a killer blow and Jarvis knew it. But Daykin wasn't quite finished.

'All right, sir,' he said. Jarvis's smile reappeared, genuine this time. 'As long as I can take the dog.'

The smile disintegrated into a worried frown.

'Now, Tom, you know this is a country station and we tolerate your dog, but Harrogate is a town, they won't stand for you walking everywhere with that animal at your heels.'

It was Daykin's turn to look out of the window. Two could play that game.

'He goes or I stay,' he said eventually.

'I just can't see the top brass at Harrogate wearing it.'

'Then good luck in breaking the bad news to David Thompson,' said Daykin, getting up to leave.

'All right,' said Jarvis suddenly. 'I'll arrange for kennels for the dog.'

'And I commute.'

'If the dog is negotiable, that isn't.'

'It's only 50 miles.'

'As I said, they're short-staffed, you'll be working all hours. I don't want you burning yourself out by adding two hours or more to your working day.'

Daykin had won the first point, he knew that he had lost the second.

'All right.'

'That's settled then,' said Jarvis. 'I've arranged for a bed and breakfast for you. They take dogs.'

Jarvis wasn't anybody's fool.

'Clear your desk, you've got seven days to relocate your files. I'll call Harrogate and tell them to prepare an office for you.'

9

Chapter Three

The pace of life in Harrogate has never been more than a casual stroll and the people don't like change. That is why the town developed so slowly from a sleepy hamlet in the sixteenth century when the first spa well was discovered until just before the twentieth when, with the twin boosts of the railways and royal patronage, it grew into the largest town in the area. Public baths and a hospital opened and, to cater to the increasing tourism, large hotels sprang up on every main road. And there, in the late Victorian period, the changes in architecture ground to a dead halt. There are no towers of steel and glass, no multi-storey car parks. Even the shopping centres ape the genteel old buildings either side of the steep streets, punctuated by arcades and hanging baskets.

Daykin drove into the town from the east, along the main approach road, Knaresborough Road, as wide as a continental boulevard. To his right, was a battalion of hotels and the great green ocean of grass, bordered by beds of carefully planted flowers, called The Stray, rolled away to his left.

The police station, just off the roundabout at the end of Albert Street, is a large two storey building, stranded somewhere between Victorian colonial and urban red brick. The wide frontage with two rows of windows facing a large car park gives it the look of an army barracks.

Daykin turned his battered ten year old Renault into the car park and pulled to a halt in a space to the left of the front doors.

In the reception hall, a woman auxiliary sat behind a glass screen, typing slowly with two fingers at a computer keyboard. Daykin held his warrant card up to the glass. She stopped typing and stared at it.

'Inspector Daykin?'

Daykin nodded.

She looked at a sheet on the desk in front of her.

'You're late, Inspector.'

'Traffic,' said Daykin.

'Superintendent Wainwright has been waiting for you.'

'Then you'd better tell him I am here.'

She reached for the phone, dialled a number and spoke for ten seconds.

'Through the door,' she said, pointing to a plain wooden door beside the counter, 'along the corridor, up the stairs to the second floor. It's the door in front of you.'

Daykin stood in front of the wooden door and waited for the soft metallic buzz of the electronic lock release. He climbed up the two flights of stairs to a white door with brass fittings and a stainless steel nameplate.

Wainwright opened the door before he knocked. He was a large man, not tall, but broad-shouldered with a huge ball of stomach that overflowed the waistband of his trousers. He wore a short-sleeved designer shirt, showing muscular arms and an expensive watch. His full head of hair was cropped very close to his scalp. His big featured face broke into a smile.

'Inspector Daykin,' he said, in a deep accentless voice, shaking hands. If he was annoyed about being kept waiting, he showed no sign of it. 'You could be the answer to our prayers. Come in and sit down.'

He led Daykin into a large office, brightly lit by the sun streaming in through two tall sash windows. The deep pile beige carpet, Hessian wallpaper and furniture were all expensive.

Superintendent Wainwright sat at the far side of an antique knee-hole desk in the centre of the room.

He was too good a detective to let Daykin know that he was assessing him. He had read Daykin's personnel file. 'Very bright, hard working and well liked,' it said, 'but unambitous and insubordinate.' That sounded like Jarvis talking. Daykin coached the local police rugby team and had been a talented player in his youth, playing for Yorkshire and on the verge of the England team, until a badly broken ankle that didn't mend properly cut his rugby career short. Wainwright could see that when he was young, Daykin, tall and broad, could have been athletic but now the years that had started to rob him of his untidy shock of wavy hair had added weight around his stomach and chin.

Wainwright was fastidious about his own clothes and couldn't see any kindred spirit in Inspector Daykin. Creased corduroy trousers looked as if they had been bought when he wasn't the weight he was now, an old-fashioned tweed jacket had worn leather cuffs and elbow patches, the collar of his window-pane checked shirt stood off at odd angles and his tie was not quite knotted to the collar button. Even his

11

glasses looked twenty years out of date.

'I hear you've got a dog,' said Wainwright, putting on a pair of gold framed glasses and looking at some notes on the desk top.

'Yes.'

'Where is he now?'

'In the car, outside.'

'I don't want to be difficult, Inspector,' said Wainwright, pushing the glasses to the top of his forehead, 'but this is a town, not the countryside. You can't have him padding along behind you here.'

'I can't leave him at home.'

'Your superintendent said that you'd be difficult about the dog. Jarvis, isn't it?'

Daykin nodded.

'Yes,' said Wainwright, swinging his chair to look vacantly at the books in the glass-fronted bookcase at the far wall, 'I've spoken to him on the phone.' Something in his voice said that he didn't think much of Superintendent Jarvis. Daykin started to like Wainwright.

'Superintendent Jarvis says that he has arranged for a bed and breakfast that takes pets for you, so while you're on duty your dog can go in the kennels.'

'Kennels?'

'In the compound at the back of the station. They're for the police dogs. If you've got somewhere to go where it won't matter, you can take the dog. Otherwise you put him in the kennels when you come on duty and collect him at the end of your shift. Agreed?'

Daykin thought for a moment.

'Agreed. At least it won't be for long.'

Wainwright lost interest in the books and turned back to look at Daykin. 'What do you mean, it won't be for long'?' he asked suspiciously.

'Perhaps a couple of months, maybe less. Until the flu epidemic is over.'

'That's what Superintendent Jarvis told you, is it?'

Daykin took off his glasses and polished the lenses with the end of his tie.

'It's not going to be seven or eight weeks, is it?' he said as he put the glasses back on and blinked at Wainwright.

'In CID alone I've got two officers on maternity leave, two in hospital, one injured on duty and one idiot who decided to break not one, but both his legs in a motor-cross accident. Then half of what are left go home sick with flu.'

'How much over two months?'

'It will be four months, maybe five, if you're lucky.'

Daykin looked down at his shoes, as if deciding whether they needed cleaning. If he wanted time to think about four or five months in Harrogate, Superintendent Wainwright wasn't about to let him.

'Well, I'm glad we've sorted that out. I'll show you to your office, but before that I'll tell you about an easy case of a suspicious death you can take on, to bed you in. I've got the file here, so I might as well give you the details now.'

He reached for a maroon file on the top of the out tray on his desk and pulled his glasses back down to the bridge of his nose.

'I say suspicious death, but it's probably suicide,' he said, as he opened the file. 'Christopher Van Meer, forty-nine years old, owned a pharmaceutical company operating from one of those business parks on the outskirts of town. Was married but his wife died suddenly of a heart attack about six months ago. No children. He and his wife were, by all accounts, devoted to each other and he took her death very badly. Last night he apparently took a dose of strychnine large enough to kill a horse. His housekeeper, Mrs Morris, found him in bed this morning, arched like the Tyne Bridge.'

'Suicide note?'

Wainwright turned a couple of pages in the file. 'It doesn't say. Here,' he said, closing the file, 'you'd better take this with you.' He passed the file across the desk.

'Do you know Harrogate?'

'I've been here four or five times. Conferences, that sort of thing.'

'When the troops start coming back after they shake off this flu and can manage to struggle out of their nice, warm beds, I'll assign you a sergeant. You're going to need a bit of local knowledge. Until then, the best I can do is give you a map.' He reached into a drawer in the desk and pulled out a creased, well-thumbed A to Z. 'Here, take this, I'll buy another.'

He tossed the book so it landed on top of the file in front of Daykin.

'The house is one of those large ones in St Mary's Walk, you can't miss it, there will be a uniform standing at the front door and the crime scene investigators should still be there, so you will see their van parked outside.'

'I can see the office later,' said Daykin, getting up. 'Who do I see about Royston?'

'Royston?'

'The dog.'

'Ask reception as you go out.'

Daykin was opening the door when Wainwright said, 'The town centre is a nightmare of one-way streets. Until you find your way around, I'd take the main road round the town and cut off Otley Road on to Queen's Road; it's in the *A to Z*.'

Daykin went back down the steps to reception.

'Can you tell me where the kennels are?' he asked.

The auxiliary looked up from her computer.

'Why do you want the kennels?'

'Because I have a dog.'

She shook her head. 'You can't have a dog here.'

'I know, that's why I want the kennels.'

She sensed that this was not an argument she would win.

'Through the door you've just come through, down the corridor to the right of the stairs and out of the back door. The kennels are at the far side of the car-park.'

After leaving the dog, Daykin took Superintendent Wainwright's advice and drove round the edges of the town. In just under fifteen minutes he was parking his car in St Mary's Walk. As he locked the car door he looked up and down the street, then at the house.

It was the house of a man who cared about his home. It was an imposing building, standing square and proud in a well-kept garden. The walls, unlike its neighbours, which were shaded dark by years of soot laden air, had been cleaned. The blocks of Yorkshire stone, almost dimly glowing in the morning sun, were sandy grey and looked fresh from the quarry. The windows sparkled and around them the frames were painted unblemished white gloss. The rows of even slate roof tiles were without cracks or moss and the ornate terracotta chimney rose straight and vertical from the rooftop.

Across the front of the garden a low wall was topped by a row of gleaming black railings and the twin gates in the wall, as large and as ornate as council park gates hung from beautifully carved pillars. The gates were open, but tied between them was a plastic blue police tape. Daykin walked across the road and ducked under it.

As he strolled up the driveway he looked at the garden. The well-dug borders were crammed with flowers. The lawn was freshly cut in narrow regular stripes and manicured at the edges. A water sprinkler sprayed spirals of droplets across the surface of the lawn. It was a garden that could only be maintained by a professional gardener and Daykin could not help thinking that neither the house nor the garden showed that their owner had lost the will to live.

At the top of the wide steps, in front of the mahogany front door, was a bored-looking police officer. He stood, with his arms folded, slowly rocking on his heels and watched Daykin suspiciously as he walked towards him. As he started to climb the stairs Daykin showed him his warrant card. The officer nodded to him, but didn't unfold his arms. The door was ajar so Daykin side-stepped the officer and pushed it open.

Inside the house, he gently closed the front door and looked round the twenty-foot square oak-panelled hallway. In front of him was an ornate staircase which ran up twenty steps before splitting at right angles to a gallery that ran round the other three sides of the first floor. Daykin had just started looking at the grandfather clock that stood on the mezzanine where the stairwell divided, when a bald head rose suddenly over the balustrade on the gallery to his right.

'Who are you?'

'Daykin, Inspector. I've just been transferred here.'

The bald man's voice, full of aggression, softened instantly.

'Sorry, sir, I didn't recognize you.'

The head disappeared and Daykin heard a harsh rustling sound, backed by a regular soft padding noise, like a tiger walking through grass. As the man came down the stairs, peeling off a pair of latex gloves, Daykin saw that he was wearing the usual white plastic suit and beige sponge overshoes. As he descended, Daykin sized him up.

He was a middle-aged man, just less than average height and, from what Daykin could make out under the plastic, he kept himself in shape. He came down the stairs with the confident swagger of a fit man. The bald head wasn't fashionable shaving, it was natural.

'Sergeant Tennant, sir. Crime Scene Investigation,' he said, as he reached the bottom step.

'On your own?' asked Daykin.

'Short staffed, they've reallocated my team to the burglary and robbery squads for now.'

He looked round the hallway, as if hoping his missing team would appear.

'Where have they brought you in from?' he said, turning back to look at Daykin.

'The Dales. I'm stationed at Shapford.'

'The Dales? Still, there are worse places than Harrogate to be transferred to. They've probably told you we do things differently in the town, not the way you do it.'

'I've heard.'

'Well, sir, I've nearly finished, just a few things to label and bag,' he said, looking down at a holdall of exhibits. 'I'll be getting back to the station in about ten minutes, if that's OK with you.'

'What can you tell me about Mr Van Meer?' asked Daykin.

He suspected that Sergeant Tennant knew everything about everybody in Harrogate.

'Christopher Van Meer? Pillar of the local community. Ran a pharmaceutical company employing about thirty people. Lay preacher, was a local councillor for about eight years, sat on the committees of two charities. No criminal convictions, not even a parking ticket, no secrets, no scandals.'

'Not the sort of man to commit suicide?'

'No, except he took his wife's death very badly. People said he was . . . well, suicidal.'

'Did he leave a suicide note?'

Tennant shrugged. 'Some do, some don't. He didn't.'

The sergeant took a large tissue from his pocket and wiped the top of his head with it. Either he was hot or he thought it needed polishing.

'There was one thing.'

'Which was?'

'He was a chemist. He must have been able to get his hands on a lot of poisons which would take his life a lot less painfully.'

Daykin took his notebook out of his pocket, looked at his watch and made a few notes.

'Did he have any enemies?' he asked.

'Chris Van Meer? Funny you should say that, he was just about the only bloke in Harrogate who didn't. He ran a fair sized company, but his staff, suppliers, customers, even his rivals, didn't have a bad word for him.'

Daykin put the notebook away.

'I understand that a Mrs Morris found the body. Where is she now?'

'I thought I saw her go into the kitchen about five minutes ago.' Sergeant Tennant nodded towards a door at the far end of the hallway.

As Daykin passed the holdall he stopped, bent down on one knee and looked through the plastic envelopes. 'Anything interesting?' he asked.

This may be Daykin's case, but Sergeant Tennant was possessive about his exhibits. He almost ran to the holdall.

'I've got those in order, sir,' he said, hovering over Daykin.

'The post-mortem,' said Daykin, holding an envelope up to the light to look at it, 'when is it?'

'The pathologist didn't say, but he's pretty sure it's suicide, so he'll take his own sweet time.'

'Have you got his number?' asked Daykin, putting the envelope back into the holdall and taking his notebook out again.

Tennant reeled off the number from memory, at the same time gently grasping the handles of the holdall to move it out of Daykin's reach.

'Didn't you want to see Mrs Morris?' he prompted.

With some effort and a soft grunt Daykin got to his feet, thanked Sergeant Tennant and strolled towards the kitchen door.

'Lord save us from country bobbies,' said Tennant as he watched him go. But he said it softly, just in case Daykin's hearing was good.

The house was old and the kitchen had been designed to be run by a cook, supported by maids and footmen. Once the busy hub of a house full of servants, the room was much larger than a modern kitchen. It was bright, there were three large windows in the back wall, each protected by a row of iron bars for security. They looked out on to the back garden. This had been a servant's room, so there were no plaster cornices or carved wooden skirting boards. The walls were plain distempered plaster, the ceiling was low and the floor was stone.

The cupboards with plain wooden doors that had once lined the walls and held rows of crockery and piles of linen had gone, the coal fired range had been replaced by a modern gas stove and the large coppers that had once boiled the laundry had been unused for years and stood beside their replacements, a washer and tumbler-dryer.

On four massive legs in the middle of the room was a huge wooden table. In an area that had once been full of noise and bustle of busy people there was only now Mrs Morris. She sat at one end of the table, nursing a white mug with a yellow happy face on it. She was staring blankly into it. She didn't look as happy as it did.

She was a well-built woman, not fat, just broad. She had wide shoulders and strong hands that cradled the mug of tea. If there was strength in her build it was reflected in the large-jawed, square face. It was a face that could be trusted. A face that called a spade a spade and didn't suffer fools. Her hair, naturally chestnut but dyed two shades lighter was scraped back and tied in a short plait at the nape of her neck. On her face were touches of rouge and lipstick, but no other make-up. She wore a round-necked sweater under a matching cardigan and, over the dark-blue pleated skirt, a floral apron.

Daykin gently pulled a chair up to sit across the corner of the table from her and laid his warrant card on the table top.

'Mrs Morris? I'm Tom Daykin.'

She shifted her gaze from the tea to the warrant card, then to his face.

'I'd like to talk to you about Mr Van Meer,' said Daykin. He noticed that there was a far away look in her eyes and she didn't seem to be focusing.

'Would you like a cup of tea?' she asked, as if she hadn't heard him.

'That would be nice.'

She got slowly to her feet and walked to a cupboard on the wall. Sliding one of the glass doors open she took out a second happy face mug and poured milk and tea into it from a milk jug and tea pot on the table.

'Sugar?' she asked.

Daykin patted his stomach. 'Better not,' he said.

'Yes, better not,' she said vacantly.

Daykin sipped his tea and watched her over the rim of the mug. He waited patiently until he had almost finished his tea, then put the mug down on the table.

'Mr Van Meer,' he said, 'was he a good employer?'

'A what?' she said, the question forcing her back to reality.

'A good employer – Mr Van Meer?'

She pushed her tea away from her and, sitting straighter in her chair, clasped her hands in her lap.

'Yes, Inspector, he was a very good employer. I wouldn't have stayed with him all these years if he wasn't.'

'And you live here?'

'No, I have a flat in Harrogate. I work here full time, I arrive at six in the morning and leave after I've made the evening meal, usually about eight.'

'Long hours.'

'Mr Van Meer paid me well.'

'What will you do now?'

She looked round the kitchen as if saying goodbye to it already.

'This place will be sold and I'm too set in my ways to find other work; I'll retire.'

'I'm not trying to flatter you, but you look too young to get a state pension.'

'You asked if Mr Van Meer was a good employer,' she said, touching the side of the tea pot to see if the tea was warm enough to refill her mug, 'he was good enough to leave me something in his will.'

'Do you know how much?'

She looked at him disapprovingly. 'Mr Van Meer was too much of a gentleman to tell me and I wouldn't ask.'

'If Mr Van Meer was a widower without children, who inherits under the will?'

She must have thought about the inheritance because she answered immediately. 'He has a brother, Michael. I suppose the bulk of the estate, including this house, will go to him.'

She looked round the kitchen again. In the silence Daykin could hear the longcase clock on the stairs in the hall striking the hour.

'I've already asked the sergeant, but you will know better, did he have any enemies?'

She smiled for the first time since Daykin had come into the kitchen.

'Enemies? No, everybody loved Mr Van Meer. I don't know what people have been saying, but if anyone says that he had enemies, they'd better not say it in my hearing.'

She placed both palms on the table top and leaned forward, staring at him and daring him to go on. Daykin prepared himself. If the word 'enemies' set her off, the next one would send her nuclear.

'I wonder,' he began carefully, 'if you can think of any reason, unlikely or not, for Mr Van Meer to take his own life.'

'Mr Van Meer? Suicide? He was a God-fearing man who loved life, he would no more commit suicide than fly to the moon.' She paused, but only to take a breath. 'I know what they say, that he and his wife were devoted to each other and he couldn't live without her, but that's it, you see. He was so in love with her that he knew she wouldn't want him to kill himself. Besides,' she said, getting up, walking to a butcher's block by the windows and picked up a brightly coloured brochure then returning to the table and slamming it down, 'he was talking about taking a holiday in Cuba, said he wanted to see it before the Americans went back in and it gets commercialized and everything changes. You don't plan a holday if you are going to commit suicide, do you?'

Daykin looked down at the holiday brochure. She had a point.

'Has he had any bad news recently?'

'What do you mean?'

'Letters, phone calls, emails, anything that seemed to trouble him.'

'Now there you might have something, but not thoughts of suicide.'

She picked up the tea pot, got up and started to walk to the sink.

'More tea, Inspector?'

'Yes, please,' said Daykin, who didn't, but it would keep the conversation alive.

'There was a letter,' she said over her shoulder, as she emptied the tea leaves from the pot down the sink and rinsed the tea pot in hot water. 'He got a letter last Saturday, I brought it with the others to his study. I was clearing the coffee things away and I saw him open it. I remember it was a handwritten letter and after he read it he seemed, well, troubled.'

She wiped her hands on her apron, spooned fresh tea leaves into the pot from a silver caddy and poured boiling water over them.

'Where is the letter now?'

'Probably in the shredder. He was first person I ever saw use a shredder. He used to say that anyone who wanted to steal his identity would have to work very hard for it.'

'Did you notice the postmark?'

For the second time she looked at his disapprovingly.

'I am not in the habit of examining my employer's mail.'

She put the tea pot back on the table and sat down.

'There was one odd thing I did notice,' she said, as she poured milk and tea into the two mugs, 'whoever sent the letter got the name of the house wrong.'

'What do you mean?'

'The letter was addressed to Mr A.C. Van Meer. So they knew him well enough to know his initials.'

'A.C?'

'His first name was Arthur, but he hated it.'

'Sorry, you were saying?'

'The address of the house is Derwent House, 23 St Mary's Walk and the letter was addressed to Astrum, 23 St Mary's Walk.'

Daykin took out his notebook and wrote in it.

'That's very observant of you Mrs Morris,' he said.

She smiled again; she was beginning to warm to him. Picking up her mug, she took a short drink from it.

'Do you think he committed suicide, Inspector?' she said, as she put the mug down.

'Too early to say.'

'Not everyone whose wife dies, no matter how much they love them, commits suicide.'

'I know.'

Daykin put the notebook away again.

'Do you mind if I take a look around the house?' he asked.

'Take as much time as you like, Inspector.'

Daykin didn't think he would find anything. If there was something to find Sergeant Tennant, who had gone back to the station, would have found it. Everything in the house was so normal it verged on boring. Even the bed where the body had been discovered had been stripped and you would never know that a life had ended in this room a few hours ago.

In the study Daykin saw the shredder; the bin under it was empty. In the stationery rack on the desk were letterheads and envelopes labelled Trident Pharmaceuticals and the address he had been told was the one occupied by Christopher Van Meer's company.

On his way out, Daykin called into the kitchen to say goodbye to Mrs Morris, but the tea pot and the mugs had been washed and put away and she had gone.

Chapter Four

When Daykin got back to his car he sat in the driver's seat and read the file Superintendent Wainwright had given him from cover to cover. He took out his mobile phone and dialled the station. He asked for the telephone numbers of the pathologist, Michael Van Meer and Trident Pharmaceuticals. Then he asked to be put through to Sergeant Tennant.

'This is Tom Daykin,' he said, when the sergeant answered, 'what can you tell me about Michael Van Meer?'

'Michael is a gentle soul, married with three children. Lives in a semi to the west of town and works in the print room at the *Harrogate Advertiser* at their place on Beckwith Head Road.'

'Did he and Christopher get on?'

'Not really, but that's not what it sounds like. They were chalk and cheese. Apart from their parents, they didn't share anything. Chris was running a successful business; Mike has been stuck all his working life in the print room. Chris liked fine wines, opera and gourmet food. Mike's idea of a good weekend is rock climbing, canoeing and finishing off with six hours of fell walking. They only met about twice a year; when they did they got on fine, but you wouldn't see them going out for a drink together.'

'Mike didn't care about money, then?'

'Hell, no. If what you're thinking is that he killed Chris for his money, think again. Whatever Mike gets out of Chris's estate he'll give at least half of it away. Probably to a spina bifida charity, his middle child suffers with it.'

'Not a candidate for murder then?'

'Look, sir, don't try to make this into something it's not. Chris Van Meer committed suicide. End of.'

'Will it take you long to find out how the strychnine got into his system?'

'Depends how busy the forensic lab is.'

'Take a guess.'

'I want to get this wrapped up as quickly as you do, sir. Ten days, if I push them.'

'See what you can do.'

Daykin closed the phone. Perhaps Sergeant Tennant was right, a simple suicide of a grieving man. It was just that Mrs Morris seemed so sure that it wasn't.

He opened the phone again and dialled the pathologist's office. The post-mortem was at nine the following morning. He told them he didn't need to be there, but gave them his mobile number to let him know the results. He phoned Trident Pharmaceuticals to get directions to their factory. By now it was going on towards lunchtime. He drove back to the station and walked through the building to the kennels at the rear. They smelt of damp hay and disinfectant. Royston was lying in the corner of the compound on his own, as out of place as a civilian in an army barracks. Daykin took him to the car and they drove to the great green expanse of The Stray.

Daykin walked and the old English sheepdog, its white mop top of hair bouncing around on its head and the wind ruffling its grey coat, ran in front of him and in circles round him with the enthusiasm of a prisoner on the day of his release. After forty minutes Daykin began to walk back to the car and the dog fell into step beside him. As Daykin opened the car door he looked down at the dog. The dog sat down, its large pink tongue hanging out of its mouth, and watched him from behind the veil of hair.

'All right, Royston, you can come with me, but no misbehaving.'

The dog jumped into the back seat of the car and lay down, panting gently.

Daykin drove out of town along the Knaresborough Road and after two miles saw the large sign for Compass Point Business Park on his left. The sign, likes its twin facing the opposite way at the other side of an impressive entrance, was about twenty feet high with blue writing on a pale grey background. In the twelve-inch high slats, which could be removed as they came and went, the names of the tenants were listed. Near the top, in unit 8, was Trident Pharmaceuticals. It had started to drizzle as Daykin pulled into the entrance.

The architect had spent time thinking about the design of the park. At either side of the entrance, behind the signs, pale blue walls curved invitingly from the road into the business park. On each wall was the park's emblem, a large circle crossed by two lines and, on top of the vertical line, an arrow head. As the wide entrance drive narrowed,

Daykin could see that it ran round the business park in a circle. Surrounding the circle, between the lawns cut with the precision of a golfing green, were two- and three-storey buildings, mainly manufacturing and warehousing. In the centre of the circle, on its own island of grass, was a squat four-storey office block.

Daykin parked his car in one of the four tarmacked spaces in front of unit 8 and looked through the windscreen at the building. It looked as if it was about twenty years old, still modern but starting to show its age. The frontage was mainly smoked glass but the dividing strips of wood were fading and, in places, the varnish had lost its gloss. It was one of the smaller buildings, only two flat-roofed storeys high. He got out of the car.

'Won't be long, Royston,' he said, but the dog ignored him. It had found an empty soft drinks can and was pushing it round the rear foot well with its large black button of a nose.

He strolled, hands in pockets, across the pavement, now glistening with rain, to the glass and stainless steel revolving front door.

The reception area was what designers call minimalist. The two walls that weren't smoked glass were pure shining white, matching the polished marble tiles on the floor. The only light that didn't struggle through the dark glass windows came from concealed spotlights in the high ceiling.

In the centre of the room, sitting at a desk that looked like a trestle table, was a receptionist. She wore black. Daykin walked over to her. She watched him, a smile on her face that was just short of warm. He put his warrant card down on the white desk.

'I'm Tom Daykin. I'm investigating Mr Van Meer's death. Can I speak to a director of the company?'

The receptionist picked up her phone and pushed a button. 'Mr Rees? There's a police inspector here about Mr Van Meer.' She put the phone back down. 'Mr Rees will be straight down.'

Daykin stood near the window, there wasn't anywhere to sit, and polished his glasses with the end of his tie. Within two minutes a large white panel opened in the far wall and a thin man with sharp features and oversized glasses came through it. He wore the standard middle management grey mass-produced suit, heavy, black rubber-soled shoes, a beige shirt and a dark red tie. He looked to be in his middle fifties, but his deeply lined face and sallow skin perhaps made him look older than he was.

'Can I help you, Inspector?' he asked in a thick Welsh accent.

'Is there somewhere we can talk?' asked Daykin, looking round the almost empty reception.

'Yes, of course, my office,' said Rees, turning round and walking back to the panel he had come through. It had closed automatically behind him and he pushed one side of it. A hidden catch unlocked and the panel opened. Through the door directly in front of them, was a glass wall, behind which was a laboratory, stretching to the back of the building. Inside it about twenty men and women in white lab coats were working at benches. The area, matching the reception, was completely white, the only colour coming from the flames of the Bunsen burners and the stainless steel of the laboratory equipment stacked in racks against the left-hand wall.

Rees walked to a narrow lift and pushed the button to open the doors. They went in silence to the first floor and to one of the office doors.

The minimalist interior designer who furnished the office would not have been pleased if he saw it now. There was the same white trestle table desk and the wall behind it was divided into two-foot squares to act as a bookcase. Box and lever arch files filled the squares, some standing upright but most lying on their sides or leaning at angles. The army of box files did not stop at the wall. Half of the floor was covered by them. The desktop was almost filled with untidy piles of paper, coffee rings, half empty packets of mints and a diary, used as a coaster for a nearly full bottle of vodka. Seeing Daykin look at it, Rees opened a filing cabinet drawer and put the bottle away.

'Not expecting visitors, see,' he said defensively.

Daykin sat down in one of the stainless-steel chairs with black leather seats and looked at the framed certificates on the wall. All were for accountancy and business administration.

'What's your position in the company?' he asked.

'I'm a director of the company, effectively the financial director.'

'And shareholder?'

'Yes.'

'What's the structure of the shares?'

Rees didn't answer at first. He took his time settling himself into his chair and rearranged some of the papers on the desk.

'I thought you'd come here to talk about Chris Van Meer?'

'Just a bit of background. Shares?'

'Chris held ninety-five per cent, I had five.'

'So effectively he owned the company?'

'You could say that, yes. It's a pharmaceutical company, he understood what went on in the labs and what would sell in the market.'

'And you?'

'I took care of the running of the business. The sign on my door says financial director, but I'm really the office manager. I do everything from ordering paperclips to arranging long-term loans.'

'Is the company healthy?'

'Very. Growth of an average of twelve per cent for each of the last five years and a better sales to profit ratio than almost anyone in the industry. We have a very strong bottom line.'

'What happens to Mr Van Meer's shares?'

'There's a clause in the company Articles of Association: in the event of one shareholder dying, the other can purchase his shares.'

'So you become sole owner of the company?'

'If I can raise the money. It also presents a problem: I'm not a chemist, so I'll have to hire someone who can oversee the laboratory.'

'Or sell the company.'

'That wouldn't give me much money by the time I'd repaid the loan to buy the shares and would leave me out of a job. At my age I won't get another one easily.'

'Does the word "Astrum" mean anything to you?'

'Astrum? No, never heard of it.'

'Mr Van Meer, was he suicidal?'

'No, far from it. He and his wife were very close, but he was dealing with her death. He and I talked about expansion of the company next year, he asked me to look for a larger building to house the laboratory.'

'Can I take a look at his office?'

'If you want, but it won't tell you much.'

They made their way from Rees's office to the one next to it and when Rees opened the door Daykin saw what he meant. The furniture in the two offices was identical, but this one was just as the designer meant it to be. The desk was clear of papers, the only object on it was a white phone to one side. The squares on the back wall were nearly empty, there were framed photographs in two of them and in another a butler's tray holding a kettle, a blue mug with the emblem of Yorkshire Cricket Club on it, a teapot, milk jug and an ancient brass-bound wooden tea caddy.

'I told you you wouldn't find much,' said Rees from the doorway as Daykin walked round the room. Even the wastepaper basket was empty.

'Looks like the office of a man who is going home to kill himself and wants to leave everything neat and tidy,' he said.

'No, it was always like this. Chris Van Meer was a creature of habit.

He came into the building at exactly seven-thirty each morning and, unless he was in the lab, was working at his desk until six. At half-past one he ate a sandwich he brought from home, usually tuna and sweetcorn, and read the *Guardian* for thirty minutes. When he went home he would shower and change and then watch the seven o'clock news on Channel 4 until eight, then he and his wife, when she was alive, would eat the evening meal and be in bed by ten.'

'This routine, was it common knowledge?'

'It wasn't a secret.'

Daykin looked at the two photographs. One was of a middle-aged couple, almost certainly the Van Meers, taken in what looked like the South of France. The other was of a group of young men, taken about thirty years ago by the style of the clothes. Daykin could just make out a much younger Christopher Van Meer at the right of the group, who were all smiling into the camera with the total confidence of youth.

'Who are the people in the group photograph?' he asked over his shoulder.

'Search me, I never asked. I think that once he said something about Cambridge, but I wasn't paying too much attention.'

Daykin lifted the lid of the tea caddy. It was nearly full of dark, almost black, tea-leaves.

'Tea lover, was he?'

'That's an understatement; I've never seen anyone drink so much tea. About eight of those mugs a day.'

'It looks an unusual tea.'

'It is; a tea merchant in Harrogate made it up for him. It's a blend, but mainly Assam I think. Once a month a van would arrive and deliver four packets of it.'

'It does sound a lot.'

'He used to take one or two packets home, so I think he drank just as much there.'

'It can't have been good for him.'

'Better than alcohol. He never touched that.'

Daykin took out his notebook, jotted a few sentences in it, then put it back in his pocket.

'Thanks, Mr Rees, that's all for now.'

'What happens next?'

'I get reports from the pathologist and forensic scientist and if it looks like suicide, I send a letter to the Coroner's office.'

'And if not?'

'Believe me, you don't want that. Lots of CSI policemen spending days stomping all over your building and looking through every cupboard, desk and file for days.'

They walked back to the lift.

'Mr Van Meer,' said Daykin, as they waited for it, 'did he have a laptop, I didn't see a computer in his office.'

'No, Chris and computers didn't get on. He could see the advantages, but never got to grips with the technology. He did things the old-fashioned way. If he had to do any arithmetic, it was pen, paper and a calculator. He hand wrote everything, from memos to draft letters.'

'But there was a computer at his home.'

'That would be his wife's. She had been a research scientist and I guess she got into computers early.'

The lift doors opened.

'Thanks again for your time,' said Daykin.

'From what you say, Inspector, let's hope it was suicide.'

'We'll see,' said Daykin, as the lift doors closed and ended the conversation.

Chapter Five

Daykin dropped the dog off at the kennels and, as he passed the reception desk, the woman behind the glass screen looked up.

'Superintendent Wainwright is looking for you.'

'Is he in his office?'

'When he rang me ten minutes ago, he was.'

He climbed the stairs and knocked on Wainwright's office door. Wainwright opened it.

'Hello, Tom,' he said, standing in the doorway, not inviting Daykin in. 'Suicide, was it?' Before Daykin could answer he said, 'I've got an office to show you, tell me on the way.'

They strolled along the corridor and Wainwright said, 'So, tell me it was suicide.'

'A man who has lost his wife and is grieving for her takes strychnine last thing at night.'

'There's a "but" coming, isn't there?' asked Wainwright, as they turned the corner to walk down the stairs.

'He wasn't depressed and was making plans for the future.'

'So what's the answer? You don't think someone bumped him off, do you?'

'I don't know, I'm waiting for the pathologist and forensics.'

'Wrap it up as suicide if you can, Tom. Best for everyone.'

They reached the door of the office and Wainwright opened it.

In the Force pecking order, it made sense that if a superintendent had a large, two-windowed, second-floor office at the front of the building, an inspector could only expect a small, one-window office at the back. That is what Daykin got. In the middle of the room were two desks facing each other.

'You were due to share with Inspector Meredith, he's the berk who fell off his motor-cross bike, so you have this to yourself for a while.'

The tops of both desks had only a single telephone on them so

Daykin sat down at the nearest one.

'Hurry the pathologist and the lab boys along, Tom, I've got other work you can be doing,' said Wainwright, as he left.

Daykin sat and stared at the two empty desks. The phone on the desk in front of him looked like it needed cleaning, but he picked it up and dialled 0, holding the earpiece away from his face.

'Sergeant Tennant,' he said, when the operator answered, 'is he in the building?'

'Room 105.'

Daykin walked out of his office, looking at the number on the door as he shut it – 115, Tennant couldn't be far away. He turned right, the numbers started going down and he found room 105 just along the corridor. It was an office the same size as Daykin's, but Tennant had been at the station long enough to make sure that he didn't have to share with anyone. As Daykin walked in he was putting a file back in the top drawer of the filing cabinet.

'Christopher Van Meer's bedroom, what did you find in it?' asked Daykin.

Tennant shrugged. 'Not too much, the only things I sent away for tests were on the bedside table. An empty water glass, a bottle, milk jug, some tea in a brown paper package and a mug.'

'With a Yorkshire Cricket Club white rose?'

'How did you know that?'

'Lucky guess.'

'I phoned the lab,' said Tennant, walking back to his desk, 'they say the earliest result will be next week.'

'Thanks,' said Daykin, and returned to his own office. He sat at the desk, took off his glasses and polished them with the end of his tie.

'It's the tea,' he said to himself, 'and if it's the tea I don't have to wait until next week.'

He got up and went out to his car. He drove back to Compass Park Business Park.

'Can I see Mr Rees?' he asked the receptionist at Trident Pharmaceuticals.

'I'm afraid he's gone out to a meeting.'

'That's all right, I'm going back to Mr Van Meer's office, I know the way.'

It took him three pushes at the panel before it opened. He took the lift to the second floor and went into the office. The butler's tray, the mug, jug and tea caddy were still there. He opened the caddy and looked inside. It was empty. He cursed softly to himself and almost ran out of the office. Near the lift was a flight of stairs he hadn't noticed before and he ran down them two at a time, to the reception area.

'Where's the tea that was in his caddy?' he asked the receptionist.

'What tea in what caddy?'

'The caddy in Van Meer's office.'

'I think Mr Rees told the cleaner to throw anything perishable away.'

'Where would she throw it?'

'There's a bin at the back of the building.'

'How do I get to it?'

'Go back to the laboratory, there's a door to the left. Follow the corridor round the building until you reach a pair of blue doors. That's the back entrance. The bin is by the loading bay.'

Daykin strode quickly out to his car and got a pair of latex gloves and an evidence bag, then followed her directions.

The loading bay was a strip of concrete, stretching about forty feet along the back of the building and built up five feet from the ground level so that goods could be wheeled straight on to the back of waiting lorries. Over it was a sloping plastic corrugated roof that let the light in and kept the rain out. To the right of the bay was a bin area. Daykin groaned loudly. The bin was an industrial sized heavy-duty plastic one, about six feet tall. He walked to the end of the bay so that he could look down into it. He groaned again, it was full.

Walking down the ramp at the end of the loading bay he stood facing the large plastic bin. He pulled on the latex gloves and, jumping so that he gripped the lip of the bin, pulled it down on to the tarmac. The top layer of rubbish spewed out. It was mainly cardboard boxes and paper. He gently kicked some of it around to see what was underneath. Most of the food, waste from the laboratory and used tea bags were in plastic bin liners and he bent down to rummage through them, ignoring the smell that was getting worse the further into the bin he searched.

Then he saw it. About half a pound of fresh leaf tea in a clear plastic bag. He carefully lifted it out of the pile of rubbish and put it into the evidence bag. He pushed as much of the rubbish back as he could and used all his strength to push the bin upright. He threw the last of the cardboard boxes into it, peeled the gloves from his hands and threw them in, sealed the evidence bag and strolled back through the building to his car.

He put the bag of tea-leaves on the roof and stood by the driver's door, looking at it. Pulling his mobile phone out of his pocket, he dialled the forensic science laboratory in Wetherby. He asked for Dr Stevens.

'Stevens,' said a voice.

'Charlie, it's Tom Daykin.'

There was a pause at the other end of the line. It lasted so long that Daykin said, 'Charlie?'

'Still here, Tom. What favour do you want this time?'

'What makes you think I need a favour?'

'I have friends who invite me out for meals, friends who call to say that they have a spare ticket to an international, even friends who want me to go on holiday with them. You are the only one who rings because you need a favour.'

'It's just a small favour, Charlie.'

'It always is. What is it this time?'

'I need to know if some tea I got is poisoned with strychnine.'

'If I tell you it's not, will you drink it?'

'It's serious, Charlie.'

'I'm really busy, Tom.'

'It's really serious, Charlie.'

Another long pause.

'When do you want it?'

'Tomorrow.'

'Not a hope in hell!'

'I'll bring it round this afternoon. With a bottle of single malt.'

'Glen Elgin?'

'I can get the exhibit and the Scotch to you in about an hour.'

'OK, and Tom?'

'Yes.'

'Next time, make it a social call, will you?'

After Daykin made the round trip to Wetherby, there was nothing he could do until the following morning so he went to Superintendent Wainwright's office.

'You said you had some other work for me, sir.'

'Van Meer's case is finished?'

'No, I'm waiting for a forensic report, it will be here tomorrow.'

Daykin spent the rest of the day working on files and closed the last of them at six. Using the *A to Z* he found the bed and breakfast Jarvis had booked for him. On the doorstep, the landlady and the dog eyed each other suspiciously.

'I've put a dog basket in the room,' she said as she let them in.

If Mrs Byron had ever owned an old English sheepdog, the basket she left in the room wasn't bought for it. Royston, over seven stone in weight and, on his hind legs, four feet tall, could just about sit in it.

Daykin took the blanket out of the basket and laid it on the floor. He filled the dog bowls he had brought with food and water and went down to diner.

Dinner was not good. There were no other guests and he ate alone in the dining room. The only dish on the menu was macaroni cheese which tasted of cornflour. He took the dog for a walk, found a pub that would let Royston in and spent the next two hours, the dog at his feet, drinking three pints of beer and reading the evening paper. He was back in the bed and breakfast and he and the dog were both asleep by nine.

Chapter Six

It was earlier than he expected when he got the call from Charlie Stevens. He was drinking a mid-morning mug of tea when the phone rang.

'What made you think I'd find strychnine?' asked Stevens. He had always started conversations abruptly ever since Daykin had first known him, which must now be over twenty years.

'You did?'

'A good lacing all the way through the sample.'

'How many cups would he have to drink to kill him?'

'Even if he was a big, fit young man, one cup would finish him off.'

'Thanks, Charlie.'

'Thanks for the bottle. Tell you what, I'll ask Lisa to lay out an extra place at the table one night – are you on for a home-cooked meal?'

'Anytime, Charlie.'

Daykin put the phone down, leaned back in his chair and polished his glasses with the end of his tie. He had been sitting like that for five minutes when there was a knock on the door and Superintendent Wainwright walked in.

'Any news?'

'Yes, sir. Not good.'

Wainwright sat down heavily in the chair at the other desk.

'Tell me.'

'Christopher Van Meer drank a lot of tea and ordered a special blend from a shop in Harrogate. It was delivered to his office, but he took some of it home. If you wanted to poison him you could either break into his home, very risky with the eagle-eyed Mrs Morris, or take the easy option and poison the tea before it arrived at the office.'

'Where does that leave us?'

'If Christopher Van Meer wanted to commit suicide he would have made a cup of tea at home, slipped some strychnine into it and drunk it. He wouldn't lace four packets of tea with it at work, then take one home.'

Trevor Wainwright pushed his glasses on to his forehead and rubbed his eyes. 'Oh God, Tom, just what I didn't need right now.' He held out a hand. 'Give me the files I sent down to you, I'll reallocate them.'

He took the files and seemed to get up with more effort than he sat down. At the door of the office he stopped and looked back at Daykin.

'Find the bugger who did this as quickly as you can, Tom. And in case I forget to tell you, thank God you're here.'

Daykin sat at the desk thinking, who would want to kill a man who didn't have any enemies?

He found a piece of paper in one of the desk drawers and wrote down a list of things to do. He hadn't bothered to ask for any help; he knew he wouldn't get any. That would make the routine jobs, like house-to-house enquiries a time-consuming chore. He folded the paper and put it in his pocket. Time to get started.

The start of a murder enquiry is all activity. An incident room is set up, people are sent out to ask questions, make searches, programme computers, collate information. The incident room is like Waterloo Station at rush hour – officers bumping into each other, coming in and going out, machines rattling, shouted conversations and a bustling urgency. This was not like that. One man and, occasionally, his dog. Alone. Daykin wasn't looking forward to it.

He spent most of the rest of the day in his office, on the phone. The pathologist told him what he already knew: Christopher Van Meer had died of strychnine poisoning. Sergeant Tennant didn't have anything in writing, but someone at the forensic laboratory had told him that the strychnine had showed up in a tea cup on Van Meer's bedside table. He spoke to Michael Van Meer about his brother. Christopher had always been the ambitious one. A degree at Cambridge followed by eight years at one of the international pharmaceutical companies, working his way up to senior research manager. Then his own company which had struggled and nearly went down until they found a new slimming formula. It had been sold under licence to an American company and was the foundation of Trident Pharmaceuticals' healthy balance sheet.

Shortly after six, Daykin decided to pack up for the day. He collected the dog and drove back to the bed and breakfast. He ate alone again. Macaroni cheese again. He decided to look for a flat.

Chapter Seven

Pluvia

It was going to be the sort of day Daykin hated. He hadn't liked the dull routine of door-to-door enquiries when he was a young copper and age and experience hadn't diluted that dislike. Today would be knocking on doors, asking the same questions, getting the same answers and building a box file of completed questionnaires. The day did not work out as planned. He dropped the dog off at the kennels and went through reception to his office to collect the paperwork. At the glass-fronted counter he stopped to tell the support staff where he would be for the rest of the day.

'You've got a visitor,' she said, nodding to a man sitting on one of the plastic chairs by the front door.

Daykin looked at him. He sat with his legs stretched out, reading the paper. Whatever he was reading made him frown with concentration. Every few seconds he circled something on the page with a red pen. He was a slim man, somewhere between athletic and skinny. His hair was a pale ginger, the colour hairstylists call strawberry blonde, and it fell untidily forwards from the crown of his head, the sides long enough to cover his ears, to an uneven fringe on his forehead. His eyebrows and eyelashes were the same colour as the hair and his freckled face had the tanned, lined, weatherbeaten look that trawlermen have. He was casually dressed in a white T-shirt, faded denim jeans, battered deck shoes without socks and a black corduroy jacket.

'Can I help you?' asked Daykin.

The man looked up suddenly, his concentration on the newspaper broken. He folded the paper carefully and slid it into his jacket pocket.

'Are you Inspector Daykin?'

Daykin nodded. The man put his hand into the inside pocket of his jacket and pulled out a warrant card.

'Sergeant Hudson, Scarborough Police Station,' he said, getting up.

'What brings you here?' asked Daykin.

'I came to speak to Christopher Van Meer.'

'You're a bit late.'

'So I heard.'

'What's your interest in him?'

'I'm looking into a suspicious death in Scarborough and he might be involved.'

Sergeant Hudson put his warrant card away and smiled an easy, relaxed smile. Daykin decided to take the conversation to his office, so they climbed up the stairs and settled themselves, facing each other at the two desks.

'This suspicious death,' said Daykin, 'who was he and how did he die?'

'Robert Miller, a record producer. He fell over the side of his yacht about five weeks ago.'

'Fell, or pushed?'

'People fall overboard all the time, but Miller was a good sailor and a strong swimmer. He went over only half a mile from shore in a quiet sea. The boat had a sea ladder but even if he couldn't get back on board it was an easy swim to shore for him. Maybe pushed.'

'Was he on his own on the boat?'

'Yes, anyone else on board would have tried to rescue him, or at least radioed the RNLI.'

'So how do you know he was only half a mile from shore when he went overboard?'

'A charter captain was bringing his boat into the harbour. He saw the yacht and heard a splash as if something heavy had gone into the water. He reported it to the coastguard as soon as he docked.'

'What time of day?'

'That's something else. Miller left port half an hour before dusk – that's an odd time to go for a sail.'

'Did the captain see anything odd about the yacht?'

'He could tell the anchor was up, it was riding the waves. And the sails were furled.'

'Could Miller have sailed it alone?'

'It was a thirty-one foot Pacific Seacraft. It needs a crew of at least two, but he was an experienced sailor so, yep, he could have handled it alone, at a pinch.'

Daykin took a faded blue check handkerchief out of his trouser pocket, took his glasses off, breathed on the lenses and polished them.

'So maybe he was on his own on a yacht and it was dark. What happened to the yacht?'

'The coastguard sent out a boat with a marine searchlight. They found the yacht drifting about a mile down current from where it was last seen. There was no one aboard, so they towed it back to port. Miller's body was washed up just south of Flamborough Head six days later.'

'Any sign he'd been hit with anything before he went in to the water?'

'If you've ever seen a body that's been in the water for six days, you'll know that the pathologist couldn't do much with what we gave him. All he could say for sure is that he was alive when he went overboard and he drowned.'

'Any reason for him to take his own life?'

'Not that I've found. Money wasn't a problem, the pathologist didn't find any terminal illnesses; no love affairs gone wrong. A man who had everything to live for.'

'Meaning?'

'After university he went to work for EMI as an electrical engineer. He got into record production and after eight years left to set up his own company. They have offices and a studio in Wardour Street in Soho. He produced a number of top recording artists and made a mega fortune. About five years ago he decided to semi retire. He went back to his roots; he came from Scarborough. He bought a house on the cliffs over South Bay, built a recording studio and made a few quality records with artists he liked and some new talent. He was, by all accounts, very happy.'

'Did he live alone?'

'Mainly. He had a few relationships, but nothing lasted very long.'

'Anything else you can tell me about Robert Miller's death?'

Terry Hudson took out his notebook and flipped through several pages.

'No, that's about it.'

'Then let's get a cup of tea and we'll talk about Christopher Van Meer.'

'We couldn't make that a pint of beer, could we?'

Daykin looked at his watch.

'It's nine-fifteen in the morning! Tea.'

They walked back along the corridor and down the stairs to the canteen. Apart from two uniformed officers writing in their notebooks, the only person in the cafeteria was a tired looking young woman in a white overall and dark bags under her eyes, arranging cups and saucers for the rush of people that might never come.

'I'll get these,' said Daykin. 'Sugar?'

'Three please, Tom, and tell her not too much milk.'

Daykin brought the cups to the table and sat down.

'Why did you want to speak to Van Meer?' he asked.

'Because Robert Miller died five weeks ago. Christopher Van Meer wrote to him and, by the date on the letter, Miller must have received it a couple of days before he died.'

'Do you have the letter?'

'At forensics. But I have a photocopy.'

Sergeant Hudson took three folded pages of paper from his inside jacket pocket and passed them across the table. Daykin unfolded them and smoothed the creases with the palm of his hand. The photocopy was of expensive, custom-made notepaper with an address at the top right hand corner in copper plate writing that Daykin guessed was embossed on the original.

'Ignore the first two pages,' said Hudson, 'it's all about families and the weather. The interesting stuff is on the last page.'

Daykin turned over the first two pages and, pushing his glasses back on to the bridge of his nose with his forefinger, began to read.

I suppose you've heard about poor old Dominic. I know that at our age we are all like ripe fruit, but we're falling off the tree a bit too frequently. I'm very worried about you, me and the others. I think we should all get together sometime before long to talk about what we should do. You and I are not too far apart, but people like Silus and Darius are down south, so somewhere in the Midlands? We could travel down together. Let me know what you think.

Regards,

CVM

Daykin read the page twice.

'Do you know if Miller contacted him?'

'I went to Van Meer's house early this morning and' – he looked down at his notebook for the name – 'Mrs Morris gave me Van Meer's telephone numbers. I checked Miller's phone bill up to the day he died. There were no phone calls to or from Van Meer. I don't know if Miller wrote back to him.'

'And you're certain this letter is from Van Meer?'

'I showed the copy to Mrs Morris, she recognized the handwriting.'

Daykin sipped his tea and watched Terry Hudson tear the tops off three paper sachets of sugar and pour them into his tea. He looked round for a teaspoon then, taking a pencil from his pocket, he stirred his tea with it. When he had finished he sucked the pencil and put it back in the pocket.

'Does the name "Astrum" mean anything to you?' asked Daykin.

'Astrum? I've seen it somewhere in Robert Miller's letters.' He paused. 'Yes, it was a nickname Van Meer used.'

'A nickname?'

'Yes, something a bit childish: he'd call himself Astrum and Miller was Pluvia. Haven't a clue what it means.'

'Star and rain,' said Daykin.

'What language is that?'

'Latin.'

'You speak Latin?'

'It's a long story.'

Daykin drank the rest of his tea.

'How are your staffing levels at Scarborough?'

'OK, why?' asked Hudson suspiciously.

'You think you've got a murder and I know I have. And the victims knew each other. We may have a serial killer. You and I need each other.'

'And your plan is?'

'I've got some house-to-house to do, we can split it and see what we've got by the end of the day. I'll get my boss to square it with yours. Agreed?'

Hudson shrugged, it seemed more neutral than agreeing.

'You'd better book yourself into a hotel in Harrogate tonight. Phone your wife and say you won't be home.'

'She won't be too interested – she ran off with her yoga instructor three years ago.'

'If you've finished your tea, I'll give you half these forms, and we'll meet back here' – Daykin looked at his watch – 'at four-thirty.'

The house-to-house was as uninteresting as Daykin remembered from when he was a beat constable, but at least he only had half of it to do. He walked most of the streets round Christopher Van Meer's house, asking questions and filling in forms. At just after four he called it a day, got back in his car and drove to the station.

Terry Hudson was in the canteen on his second cup of tea, his pen hovering over the paper again.

'How did you get on?' asked Daykin.

Hudson held his hand up for several seconds, then circled something in the paper with his pen.

'Sorry, Tom,' he said, 'the last horse in an accumulator at Doncaster tomorrow.'

'The work they pay you for, how did you get on?'

Hudson folded the newspaper, pushed it into his jacket pocket and pointed to a pile of completed questionnaires. It was about one-third the size of Daykin's pile.

'Anything interesting?' asked Daykin.

'No, the usual. Didn't see anything, didn't hear anything.'

'Then before we pack up for the day, I've got a phone call to make and we should take a look at Van Meer's study.'

'Haven't the CSI been through that?'

Daykin ignored the question.

'Now we know he was writing to people, we need to take a look at his correspondence.'

'People?'

'The letter you've got says "the others": you don't think he only wrote to Miller, do you?'

Daykin left Hudson in the canteen with his tea and his newspaper, went back to the office and called Superintendent Wainwright. The superintendent was more than happy to have an extra officer, an experienced detective sergeant, and said that he would call the superintendent in Scarborough and arrange Hudson's secondment for as long as needed. Then Daykin went back to the canteen. By now Terry Hudson was on his mobile phone to his bookmaker. Daykin waited for him to finish.

'We both know where the house is,' he said, 'why don't you drive?'

Hudson put on a pained expression.

'To tell you the truth, Tom, my back's playing me up, can you drive?'

At the house the attitude of the constable at the door had gone from bored to stupefied. He nodded again as Daykin and Hudson walked up the steps.

'Is Mrs Morris here?' asked Daykin.

'She was this morning, sir. She said that the solicitors had told her to tidy up, close the house and let them have the keys.'

'So it's locked?'

'No, she said I might need the loo, so she'll collect the keys when I finish my shift.'

Daykin opened the front door and made his way to the study he had seen to the right of the kitchen. The door was closed but not locked.

In the Victorian house the study was a surprise. The Scandinavian pine on every surface could have looked out of place, but whoever fitted it had built it to blend into the room. And the pine worked well with the hardware, the fax machine, photocopier and video phone. Even the Bang and Olufsen hi-fi looked as if it belonged.

'You take the desk; I'll go through the filing cabinet,' said Daykin.

The desk, a solid thin sheet of pine on pencil-thin black legs, with the look of a wallpapering table, had only one slim drawer and in thirty seconds Terry Hudson had finished his search and was looking over Daykin's shoulder.

Christopher Van Meer's filing cabinet was a reflection of the man, neat, organized and tidy. The top drawer had files on his business and Daykin skimmed through them quickly, shut the drawer and opened the one under it. Filed neatly in a row in the drawer was correspondence. Van Meer had a horder's mind; he kept copies of correspondence with everyone from his travel agent to his wine merchant. At the back of the drawer was a thin file labelled *Pluvia*. Daykin took it out, laid it on top of the files in the drawer and started reading.

It was the chronicle of a friendship. The letters started fifteen years earlier and were the story of two lives through jobs, houses, relationships, marriages, cars, illnesses, deaths and families. When he had finished Daykin knew more about both men, but not why they died so suddenly within five weeks of each other. He looked up from the papers and turned his head to look at Terry Hudson.

'Anything?' he asked.

'There wasn't much in the drawer so nothing unless you want to know how much he paid to charities last year or what his council tax bill was.'

'Nothing Van Meer and Miller had in common?

'No.' Hudson paused. 'I read something in Miller's papers that they both went to Cambridge University, but different colleges and probably at different times.'

'How do you know?'

'There was something from Pembroke in Miller's papers and I've just seen a yearly subscription to some magazine at Trinity College in the drawer.'

'It's the only thing we've got, so why don't you cancel your hotel here tonight and go back to Scarborough.'

'Why?'

'Because I think we should both spend a day going through Miller's house.'

'I'll get off then,' said Hudson.

'I'll see you at your station at nine. Don't be late.'

'Wouldn't dream of it, Tom.'

Wainwright wasn't pleased when Daykin told him that he was going to Scarborough, but there wasn't much choice. He gave Daykin two days to find what he wanted in Scarborough, then he had to be back full time in Harrogate. Daykin went to the local newsagents, bought a copy of the evening paper then sat at his desk with a large mug of tea and looked for flats to let.

Chapter Eight

Daykin kept to the A roads, bypassing York and taking the A64 directly into Scarborough. Despite the traffic he made the fifty miles from town to town in just over an hour.

He stopped outside Scarborough and checked the map. The station was on Northway, a short main road in the town, running across the headland between North Bay and South Bay.

The view of Scarborough was not the one which they show on the postcards. A watery sun struggled to break through high clouds and the sea, slumping on to the beaches in small apathetic ripples, was more brown that Mediterranean blue. There were people on the beaches, but there weren't many and they all wore coats. It was one of those days at a British seaside town when only those determined to enjoy themselves went to the tourist areas, and the cafés cooking hot meals did a far better trade than the deckchair sellers.

Daykin pulled the battered Renault into a space outside the five storeys of red-brick police station at ten minutes before nine o'clock. Terry Hudson was standing on the front step inhaling deeply from an untipped Capstan full strength. He was a man who took his vices seriously.

'Morning, Tommy,' he said cheerfully, as he stubbed the cigarette out with his heel.

'Let's get one thing straight,' said Daykin. 'On duty I'm "sir". I don't know what it's like in Scarborough, maybe you call the chief constable "Ronnie", so I'll allow the occasional lapse. But nobody, not even my mother, calls me Tommy. Understood?'

'You're the boss, Tom.' The smile hadn't slipped on Terry Hudson's face.

'Let's go and take a look at Robert Miller's house. It's your patch, you drive.'

Hudson pulled a face.

'Oh yeah, bad back,' said Daykin, turning back to the Renault.

Terry Hudson directed Daykin on Northway and along a road sloping gently uphill away from the town to the cliff tops above South Bay. Occasionally he looked over his shoulder at the dog sitting on the back seat, a snow-white veil of hair hanging over its face, broken only by the large black nose. The dog ignored him.

After twenty minutes they turned off the road to a narrow country bridleway, so narrow that small lay-bys were cut into the hedges every few hundred yards to let two cars pass each other. The road curved right towards the cliff tops and just when Daykin thought that Terry Hudson was going to plunge them like lemmings over the edge, Hudson said, 'Here it is.'

Across a gap in the hedge, hanging on a heavy roughcut stone pillar, was a five-bar gate. It was an impressive gate. Well made, the wood shining with teak oil, the hinges and metalwork matt black and the joints fitting snugly together. And, judging by the two chains locked with heavy brass padlocks, a gate designed not just to look good, but to keep people out. Hudson saw Daykin looking at the chains and, rummaging through his pockets, produced a small keyring.

'Keys,' he said, holding them up. He got out of the car, unlocked the padlocks and swung the gate open.

Through the gateway, the bridleway narrowed to a single dirt track. Daykin drove carefully along it, avoiding most of the potholes. They crested a shallow rise and then he saw it.

It was an old, two-storey farmhouse, painted a rich terracotta, the paint beginning to fade from the battering it took from the cold westerly winds that blew across the moors and the salt-laden squalls that funnelled up the cliffs from the sea. It stood about twenty yards from the cliff top, facing west to catch most of the late morning and afternoon sun.

Painting the exterior terracotta when, for most of its life it had been whitewashed, was not the only change the late owner had made. The deep mullioned windows were double glazed, the stable door at the side of the house looked newly hung and painted and, standing discreetly at the back of the house, was an impressive triple garage. The barrel tiles on the roof had been recently laid and, as there was no chimney, Daykin guessed that there was an expensive central heating system. Terry Hudson took the keyring out again and flipped his notebook to the back page where he read a six figure number out loud.

'Burglar alarm code,' he said.

As Hudson got out of the car the dog jumped from the back seat and, using the front passenger seat as a trampoline, was past him and bounding around on the front lawn like an overgrown lamb.

'The forensic team may still have work to do; they wouldn't want him in the house,' said Hudson, screwing his eyes up as he watched the dog.

'They've still got work to do after five weeks?'

'Sometimes,' said Hudson lamely.

Daykin nodded towards the dog.

'He sees this as a day out for the three of us. He'd feel left out if we went inside and he didn't. He'd sulk. Trust me, you won't like it if he starts sulking.'

'On your head be it,' said Hudson, and walked to the front door of the house.

Daykin followed him. It was quiet here, but a wind had sprung up, stirring the sea into life and he could hear the regular rhythm of the waves crashing against the cliffs twenty yards behind and 200 feet below them.

Terry Hudson used the keys on the two locks in the front door.

'The outside is imitation Tuscan, the inside is Tate Modern,' he said, at the sound of the second lock disengaging.

He opened the door and moved quickly to the cupboard under the stairs where he pushed the numbers into a key pad and the high-pitched screeching that had started when he opened the door stopped suddenly. Daykin was sure that he saw Terry Hudson breathe a sigh of relief. In the silence there was only the distant sound of the waves again.

Daykin looked round the room they were in. All the interior walls had been knocked down, the only intrusion into the sixty-foot square space was an open tread wooden staircase leading to the first floor. The floor had been laid with old wooden planking, each plank about a foot wide and dark with age. The walls, uniformly painted matt beige, were covered in modern art, and on pedestals, and lit by spotlights, around the room were small abstract bronze sculptures. All the furniture was fashionable. A glass dining table surrounded by six tall black and chrome chairs stood in one corner and in front of the Victorian fireplace was a large flat-screen television and two leather sofas facing each other across a low table.

They both stood for a few moments, looking round this cathedral to artistic arrogance.

'If you were wrapped up in this stuff,' said Daykin eventually, 'would you want to commit suicide and leave it all behind?'

'Depends how much money you have. If you have enough, this is just mundane.'

'Terry Hudson,' said Daykin, 'you're a philosopher.'

'What do you want to see?' asked Hudson, slightly embarrassed.

'Did he have an office?'

'In the recording studio.'

They walked through the kitchen to the back door. The kitchen, from the floor tiles through the cupboard doors and the work surfaces, the dishwasher, hob and oven, even the double sink, had the look of being unused.

'The last time I was here,' said Terry Hudson, holding up the keyring and frowning at the number of keys, 'I opened the oven door. The instruction manual was still in it.'

Hudson found the key he needed, opened the back door and they walked from it across a yard to an outbuilding. The yard, laid in a pattern of cobbles, radiating from a large wrought iron drain cover at its centre, was enclosed by the house, the outbuilding and, on the other two sides, high walls topped with metal spikes. The building that faced them was low with a barrel-tiled roof matching the one on the main house but, by the lightness of the mortar and the freshness of the stonework, it was newly built. Hudson unlocked the door with the first key he tried. As he opened it he reached to his right and flicked on a switch. The room was instantly bathed in a bright light from twenty downlighters in the ceiling.

It was on two levels. The walls of the main area were lined with acoustic tiles. High stools, microphones and music stands stood around the floor as if they had just been abandoned. On the upper level, fronted by a glass wall, was the recording booth large enough to seat three people. Unlike the main room, it was dimly lit.

'Where's the office?' asked Daykin.

'At the back of the recording booth. Follow me.'

They climbed four steps and walked through the recording booth, a small room with a large mixing table. At the back of the room a door stood open. It led to a small windowless room. The only furniture was a reproduction antique desk, three chairs, a filing cabinet, another flat-screen television attached to one wall and the opposite wall covered with framed gold discs.

'Are we going to find anything?' asked Daykin.

'I dunno, Tom, I haven't been in here, there didn't seem much point.'

'But you've been in the recording studio.'

'What makes you say that?'

'You know where everything is, including the light switch.'

'Fair point,' said Hudson, shrugging his shoulders.

'You take the filing cabinet this time, I'll take the desk.'

The desk didn't hold much, a couple of dozen invitations to the VIP enclosures at a number of rock concerts and a leather-bound address book. Daykin looked under 'V'. He knew he'd find Christopher Van Meer's details, but just wanted to make sure. He leafed through the other pages; the book was nearly full of names, addresses and telephone numbers. Daykin tucked the book under his arm.

Terry Hudson had the easier job. The bottom two drawers of the three drawer cabinet were empty.

'Anything?' asked Daykin.

'Not so you would notice. He seemed to belong on the rock 'n' roll lifestyle and short on the clerical side.'

Terry Hudson closed the drawer and turned round to face Daykin.

'I'll tell you one thing, even working part-time he was making shed-loads of money. Bastard.'

Daykin looked round the room. For the first time he noticed some photographs on the wall by the television set. He walked over to look at them. Most of them were of people he vaguely recognized as rock stars, standing next to a short, sun-tanned man with a mop of black hair, the length and style of the hair altering as the years went by.

One photograph stood out from the rest. It was of a group of young men and Daykin leaned forward to take a good look at it. A very young Robert Miller, with long hair and a beard, was recognizable from the other photographs.

'Come here,' said Daykin quietly. Terry Hudson moved to stand beside him.

'That is Robert Miller,' said Daykin, pointing to Miller. His finger moved to the man on the right of the group. 'And that,' he said, 'is Christopher Van Meer.'

'Looks like a bunch of students,' said Hudson. 'So they did know each other at Cambridge.'

Daykin took the picture off the wall and turned it round. On the back, in fading blue ink, was written 'The Greenrush Club, Cambridge'.

'Who the hell are The Greenrush Club?' asked Terry Hudson.

'Some student club at Cambridge. Now ask yourself if any of the other' – he counted quickly – 'ten men in this photograph are dead.'

As Daykin put the photograph back on the wall Terry Hudson

groaned out loud.

'We're going to bloody Cambridge, aren't we?'

'You know you really want to. But first let's take a look at the boat. Where is it?'

'In dry dock.'

Robert Miller's boat had been put in dry dock so the CSIs could take their time going over it. Daykin and Hudson spent two hours opening drawers and doors, looking in dark corners and under bunks. It was a fine boat with sleek lines, polished wood and brass, white, neatly coiled ropes, huge sails and state of the art electronics. They finished the search on the deck where Daykin prowled around every inch, looking at everything like a prospective buyer.

'How tall was Miller?' he said eventually, leaning gingerly against the guard rail.

'About five foot five, why?'

'These rails must be four foot six; they'd come up to his shoulders. He couldn't fall over the side accidentally – he jumped, or was pushed.'

'And you don't think he jumped.'

'He'd just completed an expensive house project. He had enough money never to have to work again, no issues of being depressed. No signs of drugs or sex either, but he had rock 'n' roll and that seems to have been enough for him.'

Terry Hudson, who was starting to lose interest, looked around the deck of the boat.

'Seen enough?' he said.

'For now. Let's go and talk to the crime scene investigator then the pathologist.'

'Can't we go for lunch first?'

'I've only got forty-eight hours.'

Chapter Nine

Standing on a table by the wall in the crime scene investigator's office were six cardboard boxes. Each box was stacked with the exhibits in clear plastic bags. Daykin emptied the boxes in turn on to the table top and rummaged through each one. He sat down at the desk and pulled a filing tray towards him. In it were three reports, from the CSI, the pathologist and the coastguard. He picked up the top one, leaned back in the chair and read it, slowly and carefully, while Terry Hudson looked at clouds racing across the sky and thought about who would win the 3.30 at Goodwood.

When he had finished, Daykin looked at the telephone number on the front of the pathologist's report and dialled it.

'Dr Samuels?' he said, when the phoned was answered.

'This is Samuels.'

'Tom Daykin, North Yorkshire Police, Doctor. Do you remember performing a post mortem on Robert Miller?'

'The man who went over the side of his yacht about five weeks ago?'

'That's him. Have you anything to add to your report?'

'No. He drowned. That's all I can say. How he got into the water I can't tell you.'

Daykin thanked him and put the phone down.

'No need to see the pathologist now?' said Terry Hudson, turning from the window.

'No, let's head back to Harrogate.'

'Why?'

'Because you need to pick your car up, I want to meet you outside the station at six tomorrow morning.'

'Oh God, we are going to Cambridge, aren't we? Why so early?'

'I have to get back by tomorrow night. That's when I report to Wainwright.'

'So,' said Hudson, strolling to a chair on the opposite side of the desk, 'Robert Miller, murder or suicide?'

'Murder.'

'Why so sure?'

'If he wanted to commit suicide, he could have done that at home.'

'One last sail in his expensive yacht?'

'It was dusk, an odd time for a sail, especially his last.'

'Just a quick sail round the bay?'

'The coastguard says there was hardly any wind.'

'Enough for a slow sail round the bay?'

'The sails were furled.'

'Moor just offshore and watch his last sunset?'

'The anchor was up. Anyway,' said Daykin, getting up, 'he had no reason to commit suicide. Someone killed him.'

They drove back to Harrogate where Terry Hudson unlocked his car and drove straight back to Scarborough. Daykin sat in his office for forty-five minutes, scanning the property section of the paper before going out to look at two flats he had marked.

Six in the morning was not Terry Hudson's favourite time of day and when he stood at the front door of Scarborough Police Station, drawing deeply on a cigarette, he was annoyed. He didn't want to be here just before dawn, he felt sick with fatigue and the horses had cost him a lot of money yesterday. He had made a cup of tea for breakfast and the milk was off. It was only five days past its sell-by date so what were the supermarkets playing at? His mood didn't get any better when he saw how cheerful Daykin was. Or that he had brought the dog.

They were half an hour into the journey before Terry Hudson spoke.

'Do you know where we're going?'

'We go down to the York by pass and pick up the A1. Down to Huntingdon, then the A14 to Cambridge.'

'You've been there before, then?'

'Once, a long time ago.'

Thomas Daykin was not a man who talked easily about himself, except to his close family. If he had not been so shy he would have told Terry Hudson that the only time he had ever been to Cambridge was when he was eighteen years old and his father had driven him there in the old Land Rover that was the family's only vehicle. He had been a very bright pupil at school. It was a local grammar school but he would have been one of the very best pupils at a large comprehensive. He had been awarded a scholarship to Jesus College and he and his father went to look round the town and to arrange rooms at the college. Three days later his father died. He suffered a massive heart attack on the high fields he farmed above the town of Shapford. He had been dead for ten hours before they found his body.

The only boy in a family of four children, the need to support the family meant that Daykin had to find a job, and quickly. The image of an academic life in Cambridge evaporated on the morning of his father's death. He applied to join the Police Force, sold the farm and bought a house the family could share. His mother still lived there.

If Cambridge had a rush hour, they missed it driving into the outskirts just after 9.30.

'There's a street map in the glove box,' said Daykin, 'see if you can find Parkside Police Station.'

'Which area is that?'

'Parkside. The name of the station is a bit of a clue.'

Terry Hudson opened the glove box and pulled out a dog-eared owner's manual, a half-empty packet of wine gums and a creased insurance policy before he found a map of Cambridge.

Parkside Police Station is two storeys of 1960s brick and windows with what seems like a top floor someone added as an afterthought. It stands in the south of the city on a major road, looking like a budget hotel. Daykin parked his car at the roadside and walked into reception. Terry Hudson stayed by the front door and lit a cigarette.

'Inspector Foster,' said Daykin.

'Chief Inspector Foster,' said the man behind the glass screen.

'Since when?'

'Don't worry mate, only last week.'

Daykin pushed his warrant card under the glass. The man hardly glanced at him.

'Is he expecting you?'

'He is.'

'Take a seat, pal.'

Rank didn't seem to impress him.

Daykin was reading a nine-month-old magazine when Hudson came into the reception area.

'Who are we waiting for?' he asked, sitting down next to Daykin, leaning over to look at the magazine and breathing the smell of stale cigarette at him.

'Chief Inspector Bill Foster.'

'Do you know him?'

'We used to play rugby together.'

The door to their right opened and a man Hudson guessed was Bill

Foster walked in. He thought about it later and tried to remember any men he had met who were larger than Foster. He couldn't. He must have been at least 6 feet 8 because he had to bow his head to get through the door. He was, Hudson judged, in his mid-forties and, although he carried a bit of excess fat, it wasn't much in what must have been a frame that turned the scales at going on for 270 pounds.

'Hello Bill,' said Daykin, getting up, 'this is the sergeant I was telling you about, Terry Hudson.'

'Hello Bill,' said Hudson.

'He and I,' said Foster pointing at Daykin, 'have got drunk together, fought in pub brawls and cried over the graves of each other's families. We've known each other for twenty odd years. He calls me Bill – he's earned the right. You haven't. You call me sir. Understood?'

Terry Hudson nodded, it seemed the best thing to do.

Foster turned back to Daykin.

'Do you need an office, Tom?'

'We won't be here long enough, what we do need is some local knowledge.'

'Coffee?'

'Great.'

Foster led them to a first-floor cafeteria and ordered three coffees. When they sat down he unfolded a map of Cambridge city centre on the table.

'You're here,' he said, pointing at an area near the foot of the map, 'where do you need to be?'

'Trinity and Pembroke,' said Daykin.

'Go into town, past the railway station to the next major junction. First left, first right on to Tenniscourt Road. Pembroke is a couple of hundred yards on your left. Then follow the one way system round the Corn Exchange and turn right up Trinity Street. The college is on your left at the top.'

'We have to be back in Yorkshire tonight,' said Daykin to Terry Hudson, as he drained his coffee cup, 'why don't I drop you off at Pembroke and I'll take Trinity?'

Daykin and his father hadn't had a close relationship. They didn't go to the pub or football matches together and, before he died, Daykin hadn't realized how much he would miss him. After he had left Terry Hudson at Pembroke College he drove round the streets of Cambridge and the memories of the only day his father and he had spent alone together came back to him like long-lost snapshots.

As he walked up to the main doors of Trinity College, Daykin could see that his path was blocked by a man in a suit, standing with feet apart, hands behind his straight back and watching Daykin with a steady stare. Daykin hadn't seen anyone wear a bowler hat for years, but this former soldier was wearing one. When they were six feet apart Daykin stopped and took out his warrant card. The gaze shifted briefly from Daykin's face, to the card, and back again.

'What can I do for you, Inspector Daykin?' he said in a soft voice, hardened at the edges by a thick Midlands accent.

'I'd like to see what I can find out about a student who was here about thirty years ago.'

'In trouble, is he?'

'The worst sort. Someone has killed him.'

'Then you'd better come with me, sir.'

The bowler hat and the man underneath it did a smart about turn and strode at a fast pace up the corridor. He stopped at a heavy, dark wood-panelled door. It was a very old door and screwed to its centre was a very old brass plate with the word 'Registrar' engraved on it.

'The Registrar should be able to sort you out, Inspector,' said bowler hat, knocking and opening the door for him. Then he was gone, leaving only the rhythm of his own footfall on the marble floor hanging in the air as he marched back to the college entrance.

Inside the room, standing behind a wide counter, a middle-aged woman sized Daykin up as he entered. She looked at the untidy hair, the crumpled sports jacket and the creased corduroy trousers and decided that he was a new lecturer.

Daykin, who had kept the warrant card in his palm, showed it to her.

'We don't get many police officers walking in here, Inspector,' she said. 'What can I do for you?'

'A student called Van Meer who was here about thirty years ago was killed recently, I need some information about him.'

'Then you may be lucky. We're transferring our files to computer and have already gone back forty years. Van Meer is an unusual name, so we shouldn't have much trouble in tracing him.'

She turned a computer screen round so that Daykin, by leaning on the counter top, could see it and she began typing at the keyboard. Within seconds two names came up on the screen: Rupert and Christopher Van Meer.

'Christopher,' said Daykin.

She highlighted the name and pressed a key. Within a second the history of Christopher Van Meer at Trinity College filled the screen.

Daykin read quickly, he would look at it more closely later. Graduated with a First in chemistry almost exactly thirty years ago. A good, hard-working student with no real interest outside his studies, except membership of the Union, the backgammon society and a dining club, not one of the famous ones, one too unimportant to be named. There was a small footnote at the bottom of the screen, some figures and letters.

'What does the last entry mean?' asked Daykin.

'That's the bursar's code for a student who has been arrested, but not charged with anything. It looks like it was in his last year. Drunk and disorderly, celebrating the end of his final exams probably.'

'Any other details of the arrest?'

'Sorry, the original files have been destroyed, I can't tell you anything that's not on the screen.'

'Can I have a print out?'

'I don't see why not.' She pressed two keys and a printer under the counter rolled out a single sheet of paper.

'Thank you Mrs—' said Daykin, folding the paper and turning back to the door.

'Archer. I hope you catch him.'

Daykin thought that she had misunderstood.

'Sorry?'

'The man who killed Christopher Van Meer, I hope you catch him.'

'I'll try my best, Mrs Archer.'

Chapter Ten

Daykin got into his car and dialled Terry Hudson's mobile number. It was switched off. He called Parkside Police Station and asked for Chief Inspector Foster.

'Bill, have you heard from Sergeant Hudson?'

'Not a word.'

'Then he's either doing a very thorough job, or he's finished early and gone to the pub.'

'My money would be on the pub.'

'Mine too. He's not the sort to go looking for one with a gourmet bar menu, a pint is a pint. What's the nearest pub to Pembroke?'

'As you come out of the main doors, there's the Red Lion almost directly in front of you.'

The Red Lion was an old public house with deep bay windows either side of the door. Daykin saw Terry Hudson from the road, he was sitting at a table in one of the windows, the light making it easier to read the paper. Daykin walked through the door and watched Hudson from the doorway. He sat at a small round table, a nearly empty pint glass at his left elbow. With the pen in his right hand he was working down the card on the racing page. Daykin walked to the table to stand over him. If Terry Hudson was embarrassed, he didn't show it.

'Hello, Tom. Just taking a short break.'

A puzzled look crossed his face. 'How did you find me?'

'It wasn't difficult.'

'Pint?'

'Too early for me.' Daykin sat down. 'What have you got?'

Terry Hudson took out his notebook and opened it on top of the newspaper.

'Robert Miller wasn't a very good student. Too much time drinking this stuff' – he pointed to the glass of beer – 'chasing women and playing tennis. He was one of the stars of Pembroke College and nearly got a Blue for it from the university.'

'When did he graduate?'

'Almost exactly thirty years ago. I saw the certificate.'

'So he and Van Meer were contemporaries. Did he get a good degree?'

'No, a Two Two in electrical engineering. And he was almost sent down twice.'

'What for?'

'There's a strange thing. The first time is on his record: he was found in one of the rooms in Girton College. That was an all female college.'

'I know. And the second time?'

'All I can say is that it was in his final year. There's nothing on his file. Someone with a lot of clout at the college had had the records wiped clean.'

'Did you find anything to show he knew Van Meer?'

Terry Hudson shook his head.

'Do you want another beer? I'm going to have a coffee. I've a phonecall to make then we'll go back to Pembroke.'

'Why?'

'Because the only common link is that they both got into some trouble in their final year. So far I don't have enough to tell Wainwright.'

'I think we're wasting our time,' said Terry Hudson, draining his glass and holding it up for Daykin.

'Maybe, but it's my call, not yours.'

Daykin went to the bar and ordered a beer and a coffee. Then he phoned Bill Foster again.

'Bill, do you have a hi-tech unit in the town?'

'What do you need?'

'Someone who can reconfigure information that has been wiped from a computer.'

'There's a young kid called Matthew, he's a genius with computers and, as a bonus, he's a pleasant young man, not a geek.'

'Can you tell him to meet me at the registrar's office at Pembroke College in thirty minutes? If he can't, call me.'

They sat at the table for twenty minutes, then walked to the college. At the registrar's door Terry Hudson opened it without knocking.

'Morning again, ladies,' he said cheerfully.

The three women in the room looked at him with emotions from curiosity to indifference.

'What can I do for you now, Sergeant?' asked one.

'To tell you the truth, Mrs Hartley, I'd finished, but my Inspector here thinks he may be able to get a bit more information out of you than I could.'

Everyone in the room looked at Daykin. Only Terry Hudson was smiling.

'Mrs Hartley . . .' began Daykin, although he was not sure what to say. He was saved by a knock on the door behind him and a young man strolled in, carrying a large holdall by a strap over his shoulder.

'Inspector Daykin?' he said lowering the holdall to the ground. 'I'm Matthew Nelson, you've a computer you want me to look at?'

He was young, he couldn't have been long out of his teens, and he was casually dressed in a leather bomber jacket, jeans and tan Timberland Premium boots. He had an open face and a ready smile. He stopped chewing gum to speak, but when he had finished the sentence, the chewing started again.

'Can you bring back information that's been wiped off a computer?'

'Retrieval? That depends on who wiped it, if he knew what he was doing, if you've still got the hard drive and what software he used.'

'Have you still got the computer, Mrs Hartley?' asked Daykin.

'I don't know when the information disappeared, Inspector, but we've had these computers for about seven years.'

'That should be OK,' said Matthew Nelson, kneeling down to unzip the holdall. 'I've got a laptop with some new software in here, let's see what it can do.'

He pulled an aluminium coloured laptop from the holdall and grabbed a handful of cables. He opened the laptop on the desk next to Mrs Hartley's PC tower, connected the two computers and started typing. Everyone else in the room stood round watching him. There wasn't anything else to do.

'Has anyone tried to reconfigure this file?' he asked.

'I did, twelve months ago,' said Mrs Hartley.

The young man tutted softly, like a plumber looking at someone else's work.

After ten minutes Nelson hit the desk top with the side of his fist and leaned back violently back in the chair.

'Goddamnit!' he shouted at the computer screen. He turned round to look at Daykin.

'Garbage,' he said. 'Whoever wiped the file was good. He used software that wiped the hard drive, then overwrote it with rubbish. It does that three times.'

'Anything else you can do?' asked Daykin.

'No, that part of the file is scrubbed clean, all I've got is a date.'

He pointed to a date in February thirty years ago near the top of the screen.

Daykin took a note of it, thanked everybody in the room and left to walk back to his car. On the way he rang Chief Inspector Foster.

'Bill? Where are old files kept?'

'How old?'

'Thirty years.'

'At headquarters in Huntingdon.'

'I'm coming back to the station now. Can you get an archivist on the phone?'

'Not a problem.'

'One date isn't much for all our efforts this morning,' said Hudson, as they drove towards Parkside.

'It ties our two men together.'

'How come?'

'We know that Van Meer was arrested in his final year, that he was at Cambridge at the same time as Miller and you saw Miller's graduation certificate, the date is in his final year. They had to be arrested for the same offence.'

In fifteen minutes they were in Bill Foster's office and Bill Foster was putting an archivist on the speaker phone. Daykin recited the date to him and after two minutes he said that there was a file and it could be emailed to Cambridge. Bill Foster looked at the computer on his desk and at Daykin.

'Don't look at me, Bill, I'm a Luddite. If you want the email opening, you will have to do it.'

Foster sat down at the desk and within 30 seconds they were watching sheets of paper falling in a neat pile on the printer tray.

Daykin and Hudson took about ninety pages with them to an empty office where they split the pile and began reading. An hour later they knew why Christopher Van Meer and Robert Miller had been arrested.

Cambridge is full of clubs and societies, from anti-war protestors to Zen Buddhists. One of the very small clubs, one that hardly anyone had heard of, was The Greenrush Club. It met once a month during term, and was a club with three rules. There were only ever twelve members, no two of them could come from the same college and no two of them could be reading the same subject. The aim of the club, it said in its charter, was 'the pursuit of hedonism'.

At their February meeting thirty years ago the club had booked a meal in a private room above the White Hart pub near Silver Street Bridge. There was beer before the meal, wine with it and port afterwards. Then there was a stripper. A member called Signum had booked her and during her act, when she got down to her G string, the lights went out. She was grabbed by three men, she was sure it was three, who manhandled her to the ground and raped her in turn.

When the lights came back on all twelve men in the room were standing in a group at the far end of it from her and she couldn't say which of them had done it.

As soon as she got dressed the dancer caught a taxi to Parkside Police Station to report the rape, but her first problem was, in the days before DNA, she couldn't identify anyone. Her second problem was some stupid police work. The police arrived at the room above the pub mob-handed and stomped all over the crime scene. Then, instead of trying to isolate the culprits, they arrested everyone and carted them off to the station. In the time the police took to get them there, the twelve prisoners had got some very good advice from someone. When they were booked in they were polite and co-operative, but when it came to interviews none of them said a word. The police knew a rape had been committed, but had no way of deciding, let alone proving, which three of the men in the cells were guilty.

After a month there was still no forensic evidence, no witness statements, no admissions and no other evidence. The police wrote to all twelve, saying that they weren't taking any further action.

Two days later, the dancer, Kim Nixon, stormed into the station, swearing vengeance on everyone from the suspects to the officer in charge of the case.

Daykin reached for the phone on the desk and dialled Bill Foster's extension number.

'Bill? Are there any officers who dealt with the Kim Nixon rape still at the station?'

'After thirty years? The two main men were Inspector Craddock, he died last year, and Sergeant Perriman who retired ten years ago.'

'Is he still around?'

'I think so. Do you want me to see if I can get a phone number?'

'Please. I've got the old addresses of the suspects, can someone see if any of them appear on the Police National Computer?'

When he put the phone down Daykin looked at the list of addresses. 'We've got to get back to Yorkshire soon,' he said. 'There's one address here – Joshua Swanson lived in Grantham. It looks like it might be his parents' address, so let's set off now and take a look at it on the way.'

'Why?'

'Grantham, it's only a short detour.'

Chapter Eleven

Lucere

'I wonder,' said Terry Hudson, when he got bored with watching the road signs on the A1 go by, 'what those stupid names are for.'

'The same reason The Greenrush Club only ever had twelve members.'

'And for those of us who don't speak in riddles?'

' "Astrum" and "Pluvere" are "star" and "rain". There's an old folk song called "Green Grow the Rushes, O". Do you know it?'

'I'm not a fan of folk songs, Tom.'

'There are twelve verses which number upwards.

One is one and all alone.
Two lillywhite boys.
Three rivals.
Four gospel makers.
Five symbols.
Six proud walkers.
Seven stars in the sky.
Eight April rainers.
Nine bright shiners.
Ten commandments.
Eleven who went to Heaven.
Twelve apostles.

'So?' said Hudson.

'So your man Miller was Pluvere, the April rainer and Van Meer was Astrim the star in the sky. And the man called Signum, that was his club name, means "symbol".'

'Why the stupid Latin names?'

'I don't know, because they were naïve, because they thought it made the club sound mysterious or sophisticated. All I know is that is why there could only ever be twelve of them.'

'OK, so which ones committed rape?'

'From twelve thirty-year-old Latin names, how the hell do I know?'

It was the type of house couples spend all their working lives to pay for and when they have, they don't want to leave. About fifty years old and architect designed, it stood in an acre of well-tended gardens. It was a fine, solid house with carved stone on the lintels and round the three chimneystacks.

It was dusk when Daykin drove his car through the gateway and as they came to a stop outside the front door, spotlights, triggered by motion sensors, bathed the driveway in a harsh sodium light. Daykin got out of the car yawning and stretched to loosen the muscles after two hours' driving. He walked to the front door and pressed the button of the house bell. The door opened almost straight away and standing in the frame, lit from behind by the hall lights, was a tall, gaunt man in a cardigan and tartan carpet slippers. His shirt was white, the collar starched, his tie a sober maroon and his trousers navy blue pinstripes. He looked as if he had just come home from the office and replaced his suit jacket and shoes with cardigan and slippers. He probably had. Daykin produced his warrant card and held it up to the light.

'Tom Daykin, North Yorkshire Police,' he said.

There was no reaction from the doorway, not even surprise.

'An inspector calls,' he said eventually.

There was a dull resignation in his voice and look of sadness in his eyes.

'Are you Mr Swanson?' asked Daykin.

'I am. And what brings a policeman all the way from North Yorkshire to ask me that?'

'It's about your son Joshua.'

'Is it now?' This time there was surprise. 'Well, you'd better come in.'

He stood aside and pointed them to his study through a door to their left. There was little studious about the room Swanson called his study. There were bookshelves, but few books, there was no desk, no computer, no newspapers or magazines lying on the side table. Just three ancient armchairs and a pervading musky sweet smell.

When they sat down Swanson stretched his long legs out, then lifted them so that the soles of his slippers rested on the front of the random stone fireplace.

'Now,' he said, selecting a pipe from a cherrywood circular rack by his chair, 'what was that you were saying about Josh?'

He clamped the stem of the pipe between his teeth and looked at both of them with the same emotionless stare they had seen at the front door. He pulled a twist of dark tobacco from a small brass barrel beside the pipe rack, rubbed it unhurriedly between his palms then forced it into the bowl of the pipe with his thumb. All the time his eyes never left their faces.

'Your son,' asked Terry Hudson, 'where is he now, we'd like to speak to him.'

'Why do you want to speak to him?' asked Swanson, taking a box of matches from his cardigan pocket and lighting the pipe, his staring eyes disappearing in a cloud of acrid blue/grey smoke. The room was suddenly full of the musky sweet smell that had been, up until then, only in the background.

'Something that happened a long time ago, in Cambridge,' said Hudson.

Swanson took the pipe from his mouth and examined the glowing tobacco in the bowl.

'My son is dead.'

'How?' asked Terry Hudson, patting his pockets for a cigarette packet. After two hours in a smokeless car and a difficult witness to interview, he needed the nicotine.

'Two summers ago. Josh took a holiday to the Philippines and didn't come back, at least not alive.'

Terry Hudson put a cigarette in his mouth, lit it and inhaled deeply. He took a tiny strand of tobacco from his lower lip and put it in the ashtray on the table beside him. Swanson watched him, letting him finish before he continued.

'He ate his evening meal at a restaurant in Davao and went back to his hotel. During the night he developed severe stomach cramps. The hotel called a doctor, but it was too late. The autopsy showed food poisoning.'

'Was his wife all right?' asked Hudson.

'Josh never married, too busy working. He had read mathematics at Cambridge and when he went down he got a job with a merchant bank in the City. He worked long hours, but became very successful and very rich. That kind of success can only be bought at a price. So no wife, no children, no hobbies and no friends outside work.'

'Not even his old Cambridge friends?' asked Daykin.

Mr Swanson drew on his pipe and let the smoke trickle out of the corner of his mouth.

'Funnily enough, I think he still kept in touch with some, if not all, of them.'

'Funnily enough?'

'Yes, I believe there was some problem in his last year at Cambridge, I think some of them fell out quite badly.'

'Did you hear anyone call him by any nickname?'

'Nickname? No, unless you mean Lucere. I haven't a clue what it means; I didn't have a classical education.'

'Shine,' said Daykin, 'it means shine.'

'Does it?' said Swanson, although he didn't appear to be interested. He took a small silver smoker's penknife from his pocket and used the flattened end to tamp the tobacco down in the pipe. A spark fell out and drifted down to his feet. His slippers and the rug round them were pitted with tiny black burn marks.

'He was in a club at Cambridge,' said Daykin, 'called The Greenrush Club. There were twelve of them and they all had names like that. Did he ever talk about it?'

'No. Except whatever they fell out about had something to do with a club.'

'Did your son ever tell you he was afraid of something or someone?' asked Hudson.

'I don't think that merchant bankers lead the sort of lives that puts them in fear of violence.'

'I don't suppose you have any of your son's papers?' said Daykin.

Swanson shook his head firmly.

'My wife took Josh's death very badly. We received his personal effects from the estate agent who sold his house. She sent it all to a charity shop. His office sent his paperwork. She made a bonfire of it in the back garden.'

The pipe had gone out, but he didn't appear to notice and kept sucking at the stem thoughtfully.

'She wouldn't even have a photograph of him in the house, that's the only one.'

He pointed to a photograph hanging on the wall in a mirrored frame. A young man in a graduation robe smiled out, flanked by two proud parents. Daykin recognized his face from the group photo in Van Meer's office.

'Is your wife in?' asked Terry Hudson.

The sadness which had been in Swanson's eyes earlier, but had left when he talked about his son, returned.

'I don't think she would want to speak to you,' he said softly. 'You see, I'm a travel agent. I booked the trip when my son went to the Philippines, my wife has never really forgiven me.'

Chapter Twelve

Signum

Daykin had never been afraid of the dark. He was up an hour before dawn the following morning and took the dog for a long walk round The Stray. When he got to the police station, Royston, either fed up with canine company or wanting to get warm, started misbehaving badly as they walked towards the kennels. When he was in this mood there was no arguing with him, so Daykin took him up to his office where the dog settled itself in the corner.

After five minutes there was a knock on the door and Superintendent Wainwright walked in.

'We've got a meeting, Tom. Remember?' He looked at the dog, but said nothing.

Daykin straightened a sheaf of papers and put them into a file.

'Whenever you're ready, sir.'

'My room, ten minutes then.' said Wainwright. He looked round the room.

'Where's Sergeant Hudson?'

'He'll be along.'

'What do you mean, "he'll be along"? This is a meeting, not a family picnic.'

He turned to walk out of the door. As he was closing it, he shouted over his shoulder, 'And put that bloody dog in the kennels!'

Ten minutes later Daykin got up to walk to Wainwright's office. Terry Hudson met him in the office doorway.

'Morning, Tom. Coffee?'

'We haven't time, meeting in Wainwright's office.'

'He doesn't know I'm late, does he?'

'He was in my office ten minutes ago, asking where you were.'

'No coffee then?'

'It wouldn't be your best idea.'

Terry Hudson looked behind Daykin.

'What's the dog doing here?'

'Don't you start.'

Wainwright was waiting for them. If Hudson had missed his morning coffee, Wainwright hadn't. It sat on the desk in front of him, a small cup of black sugarless liquid. The rumour was that it was Turkish coffee but only his secretary, who made it for him, knew for sure.

For the next fifty minutes they talked about The Greenrush Club, Cambridge, rape and that at least three of the twelve were dead. Then they talked about motives, club members and how they were going to contact them. When they had finished, Wainwright leaned forward, his hands clasped and his forearms resting on the desktop.

'So, we could have a serial killer who is bumping off, one by one, members of a club that disbanded thirty years ago, or it could all be a coincidence.'

'That's about the size of it, sir,' said Daykin.

'What do you want me to do?'

'Give me five more detectives and two weeks I'll be able to tell you which it is.'

'Come on, Tom! You know how short-staffed we are! Not a hope in hell!'

'I can't do this with just Sergeant Hudson, sir. If it is a coincidence, we lose a couple of weeks. If it isn't and we just sit here, treading water, the Press are going to crawl all over us.'

'Two weeks?' said Wainwright.

Daykin nodded.

'Sergeant Hudson, how is your staffing in Scarborough?'

'Not bad the last time I looked, sir.'

'Your superintendent, Coles isn't it?' said Wainwright, writing on a pad. 'Look, Tom, I've got some officers coming back from sick leave tomorrow. I can't promise anything, but I can give you two of them and if I can persuade Superintendent Coles that this is sort of a joint investigation there's a chance he may send three more. That's the best I can do. See what you can unearth before tomorrow. That's all.'

They went back to Daykin's office and then they had a bit of luck. The phone rang as they walked in.

'Chief Inspector Foster,' said the operator. Daykin pressed the speaker phone switch.

'Tom, you asked me to check The Greenrush Club members on the

PNC. I can tell you exactly where one of them is.'

'You're not going to turn this into one of your guessing games, are you, Bill?'

'No. Clive Ellington, got five years for fraud at Winchester Crown Court last July. He's serving at Her Majesty's Prison, Rudgate.'

'Five years is a long time.'

'Big fraud, four million quid went missing, it was a Ponzi scheme and it's not his first time.'

'Police officers won't be his favourite group of people, he may not talk to us.'

'If you were serving five years you'd talk to anyone, Tom, just to relieve the boredom.'

'Thanks, Bill,' said Daykin and he put the phone down.

'Ponzi scheme?' asked Hudson.

'High yield bonds. You promise the punter thirty or forty per cent yield on his investment, tell him some fancy story about the difference in international exchange rates, then you get his money, you pay thirty per cent of it back and say it's interest. He tells all his mates, they give you a few million to invest and you disappear. It works on greed.'

'Ever been to Rudgate?' asked Hudson.

'Once, about eight years ago. It's not far from here, Wetherby. See if you can get us a visit this afternoon, will you?'

'Couldn't we just sit here and do some paperwork?'

'There's not much to do right now, besides, the troops may arrive tomorrow.'

Daykin got up to leave.

'Where are you going?' asked Terry Hudson.

'To raid the stores. By the way, I can't have this office to myself, you've just about made that other desk yours, make it more permanent.'

Thirty minutes later, Daykin was back, carrying a large cardboard box which he put on the floor by his desk. Terry Hudson leaned over to see what was in it, but the top was covered by an unrolled flip chart.

'How did you get on?' asked Daykin.

'They took a bit of persuading, but we can get in at two this afternoon.'

'I've organized for us to have an incident room on the top floor, let's get it ready. We'll set off in about ninety minutes.'

The trip to Wetherby was pleasant enough, the sun was shining and they stopped at a pub for lunch. The Brewery had invested a lot of money in the outside appearance of The Royal Standard, but hadn't matched the investment in the interior, or in training the staff. Daykin and Hudson ordered lunch from a wipe clean menu that no one had bothered to wipe. When the food came it was somewhere between average and inedible. Daykin, who was driving and didn't like breathing beer on prison inmates, ordered mineral water. Terry Hudson who wasn't driving and didn't care about beer fumes, downed two pints.

Rudgate is an open prison, at the opposite end of the scale from the grim London Victorian buildings and the modern high security prisons. They went through the minimal security checks and were sitting in a small visiting room within fifteen minutes of parking the car.

As he came into the room, Daykin recognized him straightaway from the group photograph. His hair was now grey and cut a lot shorter, he carried about thirty pounds more weight but had the same clear blue eyes and the flattened nose, broken in some juvenile sporting accident, or childhood fall.

He strolled towards them, a sweater draped over his back and tied in a loose knot across his chest. He smiled and offered his hand, the same way he must have met his victims at Henley or Ascot.

'Inspector Daykin,' he said in a cultivated voice as he sat down and gracefully crossed one leg over the other, 'we haven't met. You're not with the City of London Force, are you?'

'North Yorkshire.'

The smile broadened slightly.

'Sorry to waste your time, I haven't done anything in North Yorkshire. Must be someone else.'

He started to get up raising his hands, palms upwards to show how sorry he was.

'It's about The Greenrush Club, Mr Ellington.'

Clive Ellington stopped and turned back to face Daykin.

'Good God, there's a name from the past,' he said casually, but the smile had gone and they had his interest.

'We need your help.'

'The sort of help, Inspector, that gets to the Parole Board?'

'I can't make any promises. Let's see where the conversation takes us.'

'Yes, let's,' said Ellington. 'What, just for the sake of argument, do you want to know?' he said, as he sat down again.

'Why don't you start with who else was in the club,' said Daykin, getting out his notebook.

'Before this goes any further, no notebooks.'

'Why not?' said Hudson, opening his book on his knee.

'Because, Sergeant, this is a prison. It may be an open prison, but if some of the inmates think I have been giving the police information, they may decide I need a lesson in the most painful place you can be hit with a baseball bat.'

'Who has a baseball bat in prison?' said Hudson.

'You would be truly amazed at what gets smuggled into here.'

'Do you remember Christopher Van Meer, Robert Miller and Joshua Swanson?' asked Daykin.

'Not my favourites in the club but, yes, I do.'

'They're all dead.'

'Death and taxes Inspector, the only two inevitables of life. And we're none of us exactly in the first flush of youth.'

'I believe that some of them were murdered.'

'Do tell. And you think I had something to do with it?' Ellington made no effort to hide the mockery in his voice.

'We believe that the deaths have something to do with The Greenrush Club and, as you're first member we've found alive, I'd like you to tell me about it.'

Clive Ellington uncrossed his legs, got up and walked to the small window that looked out on to farmland. He watched a distant tractor ploughing the far field, its path marked by a flock of bickering seagulls, a tiny distant moving mosaic as they flew up into the air then landed on the freshly turned earth.

'The Greenrush Club,' said Ellington, talking to the window and looking through it as if looking at his own youth. 'I'd almost forgotten it existed. I was only in it for a short time before it disbanded. I joined at the end of the first term of my last year and it went belly up about three months later.'

'How did you come to join?'

'There were only ever ten of them, or was it twelve? Anyway, someone at Hughes Hall got sent down, so the club was one short. They advertised for a new member by putting up notices in most of the colleges – they had some rule about no two members being in the same college. I answered the advert out of curiosity, really. You can't move in Cambridge for all these pathetic little societies catching butterflies or building a scale model of the Empire State Building out of matchsticks, that sort of thing. But this one looked a bit of a laugh.'

'Did you know anyone in the club?'

'Not before I joined, no. Oh, I see, you want me to tell you about the other members.'

Ellington walked back to his chair and sat down slowly. Then, just as slowly, he crossed his legs and smiled. He was mocking them again, silently this time.

'I may get this wrong,' he began, 'but ignoring Van Meer, Miller and Swanson whom you already know about, and me, I was number five. Let's start with number one, Solus, Darius Moore. Reading theology at Clare. You'd think that someone reading theology would be as dry as old sticks, but Darius was always smiling, always laughing, a real joker. I often wondered why someone reading theology had joined a club devoted to hedonism. Never did find out.

'Next was Albus, Jerry Merchanto, our resident Yank. He was over in Cambridge on a Rhodes Scholarship reading . . . do you know, I can't for the life of me remember what he was reading. I think he went back to the States, probably a multimillionaire debenture broker on Wall Street now. Should have kept in touch with him.'

'What part of America was he from?'

'Hartford, Connecticut. I remember that, "prettiest piece of greenery God ever created" he used to call it.'

He smiled at the thought for a few seconds.

'Then,' he continued, 'there was Aemular, Paddy Freeman. Patrick Josiah Freeman, rugby Blue, reading philosophy at Sidney Sussex. I don't know what else he could do, but he could drink alcohol like a man with hollow legs.

'Dominic Lucas was Evangelium, the brightest and best of all of us. What a brain! Reading economics at Queens'. Graduated with a First, so he's probably made a fortune and retired to some private island by now. He was so obsessed by money that he made us all put five hundred quid in a pot. Said he'd make a fortune for us. Five hundred pounds was a lot of money for students thirty years ago, but we all believed in him, so we all stumped it up, begged, stole or borrowed it. I suppose it's worth a lot of money now, but I don't think any of us found out what happened to it.

'Amulatio, Francis Sheppard. Uncle Frank we used to call him, he was about ten years older than the rest of us. I think he was at St John's. He was certainly reading Greats because he used to bore the rest of us senseless as dinner. We ran a book on how soon after the soup arrived he would start. Who gives a toss what Greats did, if I wanted to know, I'd have read Greats myself. I couldn't warm to Francy, he wasn't clubbable.

'So who's left? Imperium, Peter McDonald, Big Mac. We called him that because he was a little runt of a guy, can't have been more than five foot four. "Balls" was the other thing we used to call him. Someone found out he was born without a scrotum, his balls never dropped, poor guy. He was reading history at Christ's, but he wasn't interested in it, he just liked the university life. After he went down he took a short service commission in the army.

'Then there was Caelum, Silus Cunningham, pompous prat that he was, reading law at Peterhouse. Sounds like a great sweaty, fat barrister, doesn't he? That's exactly what he is. When I got my last sentence I thought about asking him to represent me, just for old times' sake, but, to tell you the truth, I couldn't stand the thought of all that condescending arrogance. Surprisingly, he's about the only one who keeps in touch.

'Finally, Discipulus, John Hastings. Jack the Lad. Reading French at Downing. Couldn't give a flying fuck about anything or anybody, couldn't John. Massive chip on his shoulder about something; he never did say what it was.'

'What happened to them, what are they all doing now?' asked Daykin.

'How the hell should I know? When the club folded we all went our separate ways. Haven't seen hide nor hair of any of them since then.'

There was silence in the room and Ellington uncrossed his legs.

'Is that it?' he asked.

'Tell us about the rape when you all got arrested,' said Terry Hudson.

'Bloody coppers!' said Elligton. 'You never leave things alone, do you? It was a poxy stripper thirty years ago: it wasn't the sodding great train robbery.'

'Just a couple of questions, Mr Ellington, then we'll let you go,' said Daykin.

'Go, Inspector Daykin? Have you any idea just how tedious it is in here? Talking to you two is at least better than lying on my bed staring at the ceiling or trying to communicate with some brain dead cons in this place.'

'The allegation of rape?'

'I wouldn't tell you which three it was, even if I knew. What I do know is that it wasn't me and it wasn't Miller, because he was gay.'

'Who was the girl?'

'The stripper? Just some local slag. Don't ask me her name, I didn't even hear it. I don't know who booked her. All I can tell you is that when she left she was screaming and swearing like I'd never heard before or since. She sounded a bit foreign, but she knew Anglo Saxon swear words I didn't.'

'Can you think of any reason why anyone would want to murder members of your club?'

'No, I can't. But I can tell you this: it would have nothing to do with some slapper from the back streets of Cambridge.'

'Anything else,' asked Daykin, looking at Hudson. Terry Hudson shook his head.

As they got back into the car Daykin said, 'We'd better start making notes of what he said.'

'It'll do later, Tom,' said Terry Hudson, taking a small dictaphone from his pocket, 'I was recording him.'

Hudson settled himself into the passenger seat.

'Some useful stuff,' he said.

'Depends how much you believe.'

'How so?'

'He lied to us. He said Miller was gay, you told me that he wasted his time at university chasing women. He said he didn't know who booked the dancer. His number was five, that's Symbol in the rhyme. Symbol is Signum – he booked her. If he did book her, I don't believe he didn't know her name.'

Daykin started the car.

'Let's head back to Harrogate and call it a day. With luck Wainwright will have organized some cavalry to help us tomorrow. Then we'll see if the maths works or not.'

'The maths?'

'Twelve middle aged men. We know that three are dead and one is alive. If we find all the others are alive, you could just about accept that a quarter have slipped off the dish. Maybe four of them at a pinch. Any more than that and its too much for coincidence. So that's the maths. Two more dead and we have a serial killer. With extra help, we may know tomorrow.'

As they neared Harrogate, Hudson said, 'Any plans for tonight, Tom?'

'Flat hunting.'

'Great, a house-warming party!'

'Right now that would be you, me and Royston.'

'I can get some people.'

'If they're like you, forget it.'

That night Daykin liked the first flat he saw. It was near the town centre, it had forecourt parking, they accepted pets and it was well furnished. He hoped that his luck would hold at work the following morning.

Chapter Thirteen

Solus

When Terry Hudson arrived at the station the following morning the office he and Daykin shared was empty. On the middle of his desk was a yellow Post-it note: *Room 305 ASAP.*

Hudson climbed the stairs to the third floor, found room 305 and opened the door, which had a stainless steel sign in the holder which said Incident Room.

He saw what Daykin meant by raiding the stores. Two trestle tables ran at right angles to each other, a dozen chairs were stacked in two piles, the flip chart was facing them on a stand, a computer had been set up at another, smaller, table and on the trestle tables were packets of pens, telephone message pads and spiral notebooks. The cardboard box was at Daykin's feet as he wrote on the flip chart. When Hudson opened the door, Daykin turned round to look at him, so did Royston, who had taken up residence in the corner of the room, by the radiator.

'Expecting company?' asked Terry Hudson, as he looked round the room.

'The guys from Scarborough arrived half an hour ago, Wainwright is giving them his welcome lecture. He's taken a man from the burglary squad, Martin Brown and a woman from the stolen vehicle squad here in Harrogate. They're sitting in on the lecture and they'll all come up here together soon.'

He looked at a piece of paper on the table. 'What can you tell me about Davis, Franson and Schmidt?'

'Bob Davis is one of the lads, great at parties. Fancies himself more than a bit. You will have to watch him, he's not above cutting corners to get a conviction. I'm not surprised my superintendent has unloaded him on you, he's a ticking time-bomb. Sarah Fanson is all right, she's just made CID and she's a bit enthusiastic, but that will soon rub off.

She's a career policewoman, she'll outrank you one day. Good old Frazer Schmidt, his grandfather was German and everyone calls him Fritz. He's a bit of a geek, good with computers, but if you're looking for hard work, he's your boy.'

'I had a word with the custody sergeant,' said Daykin. 'Martin Brown is serving out the last nine months of his twenty-two years. He was always a plodder, now he's a disinterested plodder. Lots of local knowledge, but I don't think that's what we need. Bridget Cooper has passed her sergeant's exam and is waiting for a vacancy before she moves back into uniform. A good copper, but she's married with two children and her husband works away a lot. He's a heating engineer for a construction company, so she struggles to balance the family and the job.'

'A mixed bunch,' said Hudson. He may have said more but just then the door opened and Superintendent Wainwright walked in, followed by three men and two women.

'This is Inspector Daykin,' said Wainwright, as the group fanned out into the room, 'he's in charge of this case. You will take your orders from him and from Sergeant Hudson.' He turned to go. 'Good luck, Tom,' he said. The custody sergeant had said that Wainwright was a very good judge of character. Daykin hoped that he was just wishing him luck.

'Grab a chair and sit down,' said Daykin. He waited until they were all seated, the three Scarborough detectives at one table, the two from Harrogate at the other.

'I don't know how it works in Scarborough or Harrogate,' he began, 'so to make it easy we'll play by my rules. Sergeant Hudson calls me Tom, but he's a sergeant and set in his ways. You will call me sir.' He took seven hardcover A4 notebooks from the cardboard box.

'Leave your notebooks at home, you won't need them. On this case these will be your notebooks. They're called diaries.'

He placed one in front of each of them and passed another to Hudson.

'Every piece of information you get, no matter how trivial, goes in there and every evening we'll talk about what you've got. I want you here at eight-thirty in the morning and you don't leave before six. If you're following a live lead, you stay until you've finished. Sergeant Hudson will draw up a rota for days off, don't expect too many. Any questions so far?'

Five heads shook from side to side, some less enthusiastically than others.

'Here,' said Daykin, striding to the flip chart, 'is what we've got so far. Twelve members of a club called The Greenrush Club thirty years ago in Cambridge.'

On the chart were twelve names, starting with Darius Moore at number one and ending with John Hastings at number twelve. Red lines had been drawn through the names of Van Meer, Miller and Swanson. A blue star had been drawn next to Ellington.

'The red lines show the three men who have died, the star shows we traced and interviewed Ellington. Within forty-eight hours I want a line or a star against all these names. There are seven of us and eight names, so I'll take two, the rest of you take one each. Fritz?'

A thin, pale-face topped by untidy blond hair looked up.

'You're good with computers, you collate all the information we get. Any problem?'

The face shook briefly, then looked down again.

'We've been given six telephones, a fax machine, a computer and the use of two cars. Get the details of your man from Sergeant Hudson. If the man is dead we need to know how, when and where. See if there was an inquest and, if so, what that found. If he's alive contact him and find out when we can see him in person. Remember, if he's alive he maybe either the next victim or a suspect. Let's get started.'

'Look, Tom,' said Terry Hudson, 'some of these maybe really easy, why don't you just take one name for now and let's see if any of the others can take a second name.'

'OK' said Daykin. 'Who have you got for me?'

'Why don't you start with number one, Darius Moore?'

Daykin sat down at the table and, taking one of the spiral notebooks, wrote down everything he had heard about Darius Moore.

At that same moment a man in a black Armani shirt and hand-cut cashmere trousers looked down on the four men working on two cars parked on the floor below him. Although it was a warm day and the sun shone through the skylights the sliding garage doors were pulled shut. It was a typical workshop on a small industrial estate in the suburbs of Middlesbrough. The ground floor was a vehicle repair area and up the left hand wall a set of metal stairs led to an office on the first floor. It was in the office, looking down on the ground floor that smelt of paraffin heaters and exhaust fumes, through a picture window that the man took a cigar from his mouth and turned back towards another man, who was sitting on a sofa, reading the sports pages of one of the tabloids.

'I had a visit from the police yesterday,' he said casually.

The other man looked up from his paper.

'They didn't find anything?'

'No, we had a tip off from the guy in the police intelligence department, so everything was kosher when they arrived. I even made them a cup of tea.'

'You will have to keep him sweet: he's worth it,' said the man on the sofa, his eyes going back to the newspaper.

'I've already had Eddie slip him fifty quid.'

The man at the window put the cigar back in his mouth and glanced down at the shop floor.

'I want those cars out of here by midday.'

'They will be; by then they'll be in Newcastle.'

Dennis Bradley saw himself as a businessman. He had earned enough money to buy a six-bedroomed house in the country between Middlesbrough and Guisborough, to drive a Rolls Royce and take three holidays a year to five-star hotels in places like Bermuda and Dubai. He had three main sources of income: this garage, where stolen luxury cars were brought to have their identities changed before being shipped abroad, the people who worked for him regularly couriering drugs from London to the North-east, and he collected debts. Not the bad debts of finance companies, the debts that were difficult to collect, debts owed to drug dealers, bookmakers and loan sharks. He bought the debts at a large discount and the ways he collected the money were nothing to do with courts or attachment of earnings. The debtors found a way to pay, or they were hurt. Badly.

Bradley rolled the cigar to the side of his mouth so that he could talk around it.

'I've bought a couple of debts from that bookmaker in Scarborough, what's his name? Butcher?'

'Do you want me to take care of them?' said the man on the sofa.

'One of them won't be a problem. Some bloke who works in the accounts department of the local council. He had a very bad run on the greyhounds, a ten grand bad run. I'll give you his details. Send Eddie and a couple of the boys round to persuade him to pay up.'

'Are you sure he's good for the money?'

'He'll have to get creative with his bookkeeping at work, won't he?'

'What about the other one?'

'That's more difficult. Some geezer owes Butcher fifteen grand. He's a copper, a detective sergeant called Hudson.'

'How did Butcher let him run up a debt like that?'

'Maybe he figured he would need a favour one day. Anyway, I want something a bit more subtle than Eddie and a baseball bat. See if you can get Garvey on the phone.'

Ten minutes later the other man got up from the sofa and walked to the window, holding out a mobile phone.

'Garvey,' he said.

Bradley took the phone, walked to his desk and stubbed out the cigar in the ashtray.

'Ray,' he said, 'I've got a job for you, a bit of debt collecting.'

'Who, where and how much?'

'Name of Terry Hudson, he lives in Scarborough and he owes me fifteen grand.'

'What's in it for me?'

'Fifteen hundred.'

'Is he going to be difficult?'

'There's a complication, Ray. He's a copper.'

'I'm not going after a copper for fifteen hundred.'

'Two grand, then.'

'Three.'

'Come on, Ray, I've bought this debt, if I give you three grand, there's nothing in it for me.'

Garvey thought it over for a few seconds.

'All right, two grand, but you owe me.'

'There's plenty more where this one came from, Ray,' said Bradley and he read Terry Hudson's details over the phone.

As he switched the phone off, the man on the sofa said, 'You buy those debts for about twenty-five per cent of face value.'

'This one was tricky, I only paid ten per cent for it, but Garvey doesn't need to know that.'

Daykin finished reading the notes on Darius Moore and reached for the phone. After three calls he was given the number of Church House, who keep all the records of anyone ordained into the Church of England. Darius Moore had been ordained and sent as the curate to a parish church in a village near Guildford. After two years he was given his own inner city parish where he made a name for himself as a priest who mobilized the local community against drug dealers. His firebrand style led to the church authorities offering him the post of Assistant Dean at Salisbury Cathedral. Three years of increasingly aggressive theological arguments with the bishop led to them nearly coming to blows one day. After some pressure, Darius Moore resigned from the cathedral staff and from the Church of England. That was all

Church House could tell him.

Daykin sauntered over to where Schmidt was sitting. 'Can you find a man called Darius Moore on that computer?' he asked.

Frazer Schmidt sat down at the keyboard, logged into a search engine and typed in the name of Darius Moore. One of the entries gave the name of the Church of Enlightened Reality. Schmidt typed in the name and a website appeared on the screen. Someone had taken a lot of time and trouble designing the website. Colour photographs of the church appeared and then dissolved at different points on the screen, verses from the Bible, in a rainbow of different colours, rolled upwards as a background and then, starting as a tiny white light at the top right hand corner and slowly expanding to fill the screen, was a picture of a man, standing in a pure white suit in front of a congregation, his feet together and his arms outstretched like the risen Christ. Daykin thought he must be Darius Moore. He looked closely at the image. The man wore all white, suit, shirt, tie and shoes. As if to highlight the whiteness of his clothing, his face and hands were deeply tanned and his hair, worn long in waves that swept over his ears and the collar of his suit, was jet black.

'The Church of Enlightened Reality calls to all those who seek the ultimate truth,' said one of the messages on the screen. Daykin thought it might be a good idea to heed the call. He walked over to the end of the table where Terry Hudson was writing in his new book.

'I've found Darius Moore,' he said.

'Alive?'

'Yes, living and preaching near Reading.'

'Preaching?'

'We'll talk about it later. I'm going to Reading.'

He picked up the nearest phone and dialled the number that he had taken from the computer screen and written in his diary.

'Church of Enlightened Reality,' said a female voice, with the trace of an American accent.

'Can I speak to Darius Moore?' asked Daykin.

'Bishop Moore, well, no. He's counselling some of his flock right now.'

'This afternoon?'

'I'll check his schedule.'

She pronounced 'schedule' as 'skedool'. Definitely American.

'Bishop Moore has a slot free at two o'clock,' she said after a pause.

'I'll see him then,' said Daykin.

He collected the dog and drove to the bed and breakfast where he packed an overnight bag and told Mrs Byron that he might be away for the night. He had told her that he was leaving at the end of the week, so she didn't seem to care.

The drive to Reading was uneventful and Daykin arrived in the town centre by one. The church was to the north-east, towards the village of Dunsden Green. He drove to the village and asked the locals about the church. It had been going for ten years. An area of countryside of about thirty acres had been bought and a large modern church with a steep sloping roof and a bronze cross above the door, twenty feet high, and floodlit at night, had been built. Over the next few years other buildings had appeared, until they were hidden by a ten foot high wall that ran round the whole area. There were lots of local rumours about what went on behind that wall, but the people who came to the church in their hundreds each Sunday appeared normal enough. At 1.45 Daykin finished his cheese sandwich and coffee in the Dunsden café and drove the short distance from the village to the church compound.

He saw the cross first, it stood at the apex of the roof, directly over the wide stained-glassed windows of the church frontage. Then he saw the walls that ran round the compound in a high barrier, broken only by a pair of black gates, decorated with a pattern of small gold crosses. By the gates in a concrete guard house with a large glass window stood a man in an anorak and, although it was a dull overcast day, a pair of mirrored sunglasses. He stepped forward, a clipboard in his right hand, as Daykin stopped his car in front of the gates and wound the window down. The man waited patiently as the window descended in a series of pauses and jerks. He leant forward to look inside the car and seemed to stare suspiciously at the dog in the back seat, Daykin couldn't tell what was happening behind the sunglasses.

'Name,' he said, turning his attention to Daykin. Daykin looked back at two small identical images of his own face.

'Daykin,' he said 'here to see Bishop Moore.'

The man looked at his clipboard.

'Just a minute,' he said, and went back to the guard house where he made a phone call. Then he came back to the car and gave Daykin a clip-on badge that had VISITOR in red capital letters across it.

'Wear that at all times. Straight down, first car-park on the right, the Bishop's office will be in front of you.'

He went back to the guard house, the gates opened electronically and Daykin drove through.

Inside the compound it was a sanitized world. Grass lawns were mowed and edged, brick work, paint and windows were spotlessly clean and there was no sign of any litter. He parked his car and strolled to the plate-glass door in the building in front of him. There was a buzzer. He pressed it and a metallic voice, which he recognized as belonging to the American woman, answered. She released the lock and he walked into a reception area. It was a room of concealed lighting, soft music and tasteful antiques.

Behind a Georgan bow fronted desk sat a woman in a lilac suit with a white corsage on her lapel. She smiled broadly at Daykin as he walked in.

'Bishop Moore is expecting you, Mr Daykin. I'm sure that he won't keep you but a few minutes.'

She moved a well manicured hand towards a pair of leather Chesterfield sofas. Daykin sat down on the nearest one and picked up a magazine from the rack. He was only five lines into the first article when a door at the far side of the room opened and the man Daykin had seen on the website stood in the doorway. He was dressed again in white, this time in a high-necked mandarin jacket.

'Inspector Daykin,' he said in a low, mellow voice. Bishop Moore must have been making enquiries about Daykin, who had not told anyone he was a police officer and hadn't shown his warrant card. The bishop stood aside to usher Daykin into his office.

Everything in the office was large. The picture window looked out on to rolling lawns that led down to the school. The mahogany desk was the size of the bridge of a destroyer, and a suede-covered sofa was placed next to the low table on which were carefully arranged a stack of expensive and professional produced church brochures. Daykin sat down at one end of the sofa and Moore took a seat at the other. As they sat down they had a chance of taking a long look at each other. Moore was dressed in a well cut white suit. Daykin, now that he was close to him, could see that the suntan and the hair colour both came out of a bottle. The Patek Philippe watch, the heavy gold bracelet, the Bishop's purple that bordered the large cross that hung from his neck and the way he wore his glasses, on the top of his head like Italian men wear their sunglasses in the shade, all spoke of vanity.

Darius Moore saw an overweight, slightly scruffy, middle-aged man with untidy hair and rumpled corduroy trousers and sports jacket. He watched Daykin take off his glasses, breath on the lenses and polish them with the bottom of his tie. Moore's gardener was better dressed than this man.

'How can I help you?' asked Bishop Moore, leaning forward to move a brochure in the display half an inch to the right.

'I believe we can help each other.'

'Belief is a good thing to have.'

'I lost mine some years ago, but I think I've got it back.'

'You haven't come all this way to join our community, Inspector?'

He not only knew Daykin's rank, he knew where he had come from.

'No, I've come to ask what you can tell me about The Greenrush Club.'

Bishop Moore leant forward again and pushed the brochure back to its original position. This time it was a quick, nervous gesture.

'The Greenrush Club? Strange name, I can't say I've ever heard of it.'

'Cambridge, thirty years ago. You were Solus.'

Too much detail for Darius Moore to keep pretending he didn't know what Daykin was talking about. If he was embarrassed at being found lying, he didn't show it. He smiled the same easy smile that was on the website, looking directly into Daykin's eyes. His teeth were white and even against the tanned skin and framed by the neatly trimmed goatie beard. It was sort of smile that he practised for hours in front of a mirror.

'The Greenrush Club, of course, I had almost forgotten it. Not a time of my life of which I'm particularly proud, but we were all young and if you can't be stupid when you're young, you never can.'

'Hedonism.'

'I'm sorry?'

'Hedonism, not stupidity. The club was for selfish pleasure.'

'There may have been some high-spirited fooling around, but that's all.'

'A girl was raped.'

The smile was gone now and under Darius Moore's bland expression there was a hint of malice.

'In my experience, nothing valuable is ever found if old coals are raked over.'

'Nixon, her name was Kim Nixon. Three of you raped her, the others knew it was happening and no one said a word.'

'At least you will agree that loyalty is a noble emotion.'

'Not when it leaves an innocent girl violated.'

'Innocent? That little whore?'

'Don't tell me, she was gagging for it.'

'Don't be ridiculous!'

'Did you rape her?'

'No.'

'Who did?'

Bishop Moore, close to losing his temper, took a few seconds to bring himself under control.

'Loyalty, Inspector, is as long lasting as it is noble.'

Daykin got up and walked to the picture window. He watched a gardener straightening the edges of the lawn with a half moon spade.

'Do you still contact any of the other members?' he said.

'Silus Cunningham occasionally writes and Chris Van Meer, but then it's only an exchange of emails every three months or so.'

'Mr Van Meer is dead,' said Daykin, turning round to see the reaction.

'Dead?' For the first time Darius Moore's façade disappeared completely and all that was left was a well dressed, confused and frightened man.

'He was poisoned. I'm almost certain he was murdered.'

'But. . . .' Moore was stumbling for words. 'Why?'

'Maybe something to do with Kim Nixon. Robert Miller and Joshua Swanson are also dead, we're trying to trace the others.'

'You're not telling me I'm the only one left alive?'

'No, we've seen Clive Ellington, he's still with us, but we do need to find the others urgently.'

'The only other one I know anything about is poor old Francis Sheppard who fell off a mountain some years ago. They never recovered his body, but if he'd been alive he'd have turned up by now.'

'Anyone else?'

Moore didn't need time to think.

'No, we all drifted off our separate ways when we went down. To be honest, we didn't have much in common except the club and when that folded we had nothing to tie us together.'

He sat deep in thought for a few seconds.

'Except Chris. I liked him, I'm sorry he's gone.'

There was a sadness in his voice and Daykin believed him.

'Tell me about the night of the rape,' Daykin said, moving back to sit on the sofa.

'As I said, it was a long time ago.'

'Do you know which of the twelve raped her?'

'Yes, I do. I heard them talking about it just before she arrived. But before you ask again, Inspector, I wasn't telling the police then and I'm not telling you now, even if they turn out to be dead.'

'So you weren't one of them?'

'No, we all struggle with our own demons, but the sins of the flesh aren't one of mine.'

They both sat in silence for sometime whilst their demons danced at the front of their minds.

'Help me,' said Darius Moore, eventually, 'you said you could help me.'

'Tomorrow I'll know for sure, but I think that several of your club members have died suddenly in the last few years. You could be in real danger. I'd like you to come into protective custody. I guarantee you will be protected.'

Darius Moore looked round the office and out of the window.

'I'm well protected here, look at the walls and the security guards.'

Daykin knew that to Bishop Moore this was as much a business as it was a ministry, its profits would fall without the guiding hand of its managing director. He took one of his cards out of his pocket and put it on the table.

'It's an open offer,' he said, getting up. 'If you change your mind, give me a call.'

Chapter Fourteen

Albus, Imperium and Discipilus

At exactly nine o'clock the following morning Daykin stood in front of the flip chart and picked up a red and a blue marker.

'Darius Moore, Solus,' he said, marking a blue star by the name, 'alive and well and living in Reading.'

He moved his hand to the next name on the list.

'Who has Jerry Merchanto?'

'Me, sir,' said Bridget Cooper. She shuffled the papers in front of her, nobody liked being first.

'Dead or alive?'

'Dead, sir.'

'When and how?'

'He fell from the top of a forty-floor office block in San Francisco ten years ago.'

Daykin scored a red line through Merchanto's name.

'Fell or was pushed?'

'Probably fell, sir. After Cambridge he went back to Connecticut for a few years where he worked in marketing, then he was head-hunted by a California company and moved to San Francisco. He did well for a few years, then got into financial problems. It's not clear if it was drugs, gambling or something else, but the inquest decided that it all eventually got on top of him and one night he went to the roof of his office block and threw himself off.'

'No suspicious circumstances?'

'Neither the SFPD or the San Francisco Coroner thought so.'

'Next, Patrick Freeman?'

'That would be me, Tom.'

'Alive or dead?'

'Alive, living in Manchester, but there's a kicker.'

'Which is?'

'Nine months ago he was the victim of a hit and run. The driver was never caught, but it's left him in a wheelchair.'

'Go and see him as soon as we've finished here,' said Daykin, marking a blue star beside Freeman's name.

'What, today?'

'It's a fine day for a drive across the M62. Dominic Lucas?'

'Dead, sir,' said Frazer Schmidt.'

'What happened?' asked Daykin, drawing a red line across the name.

'Long story, I'm afraid. Before he left Cambridge he was so bright that they invited him to stay on as a don, but he left to join a city firm of stockbrokers. Maybe eight years later he and two others started their own firm, dealing in the futures market. They made a fortune, he married his secretary, bought a large house in St John's Wood and everything was rosy.'

'But he died?'

'A lot of brilliant men have idiosyncrasies. His was he hated flying, hated travel of any sort. So, while his wife jetted off to the Seychelles or Rio he stayed at home and worked. He went into work on Christmas Day most years.'

'Bah humbug,' said somebody.

'Mrs Lucas started to worry about him and eventually persuaded him to buy a holiday cottage in Surrey. I say holiday cottage, it was a four-bedroomed house just outside Guildford with a swimming pool, sauna and tennis court. That was where he died.

'His wife was off for a few days' shopping in Paris. She made him promise to go down to Guildford for the weekend. The pathologist said that it was some time on the Saturday night, he must have disturbed a burglar and there was a fight. Dominic Lucas wasn't a big man, he had poor eyesight and you wouldn't call him fit. When his wife got back to St John's Wood and he wasn't there she called Guildford. After a few hours of no reply to her calls, she phoned the Surrey police. They found him battered to death at the bottom of the main stairs.'

'Suspect?'

'They started the usual investigation but no, it's still an open case.'

'Ellington we know about,' said Daykin, looking down the list, 'Francis Sheppard?'

'That's me, sir,' said Sarah Fanson.

'Dead or alive?'

'Dead, presumably.'

'I know. Tell the others.'

'Twenty years ago he went mountaineering in the Alps. He was an experienced climber, but went out alone on a day when the weather deteriorated. He didn't come back to the hotel and hasn't been seen since. Twelve years ago he was officially pronounced dead.'

'Any suspicion that he was murdered?'

'No, just another climbing accident in bad weather. They'll probably discover his perfectly preserved body in about ten years' time.'

Daykin hesitated, but then drew a red line through the name.

'Peter Macdonald?' he said.

'Macdonald's mine, sir, and he's dead,' said Bob Davies.

'How?'

'Shot between the eyes.'

'When?'

'After university he was at a loss what to do with himself. A history degree qualifies you to teach history and not much else. He didn't fancy teaching so, to give him three years to decide what to do with the rest of his life, he took a short term commission in the army.

'Thirty years ago was the height of the troubles in Northern Ireland. He joined the Argyle and Sutherland Highlanders. Macdonald's a good name to have in a regiment like that. Within a year he was in Belfast. He came through his first tour of duty without a scratch but, with just two weeks left of his second tour, he took a foot patrol out into West Belfast. By now the terrorist snipers were targeting the officers. Just off the Shankill Road he caught one in the middle of his forehead, died instantly.'

'Anyone claim responsibility?'

'The Provisional IRA.'

'Who has Silus Cunningham?' asked Daykin, as he drew a red line through Macdonald's name.

There was silence.

'He's the only one we haven't checked, sir,' said Martin Brown. 'I had John Hastings.'

'For God's sake tell me he's alive'.

'Afraid not, sir, accidentally electrocuted, apparently.'

Daykin drew another red line. 'Tell me about it.'

'He left Cambridge with a first class honours in French and, a bit like Macdonald, didn't want to teach and had a degree that wasn't much use for anything else. Then someone told him they knew a manager of a British development company who were building a hotel complex near Bordeaux and they needed a French speaker. He got the job and in the next nine months learned a lot about commercial development. He also met David Rosenthal who eventually became his partner.

'Rosenthal was a genius at finding vacant land, ripe for development, raising finance on it and putting all the licences in place. Hastings was the construction side, organizing the building contractors and leasing the property out. They were a great team and they were on their third major development, an office block in Birmingham city centre, when Rosenthal went to see his doctor about chest pains he was having. He was told that he had a congenital heart defect and that he had to immediately stop the lifestyle he had been living. That wasn't David Rosenthal's way. He worked eighteen-hour days, ate mainly fatty foods and smoked sixty cigarettes a day. Within a year he was being shown round a disused factory by the owner when he suddenly clutched his chest and keeled over.

'Hastings tried to carry on, but the way the finances were structured they needed a steady flow of development and when Rosenthal died the production line of new work died with him. Finance wasn't John Hastings's strong point and as quickly as it was up and running, the company folded, taking Hastings into bankruptcy.

'After a couple of years he discharged the bankruptcy and went back into development, starting small this time. He bought old houses and renovated them into student flats, doing most of the work himself to save money. One wet Monday evening he was drilling through a wall when he hit a live cable that shouldn't have been there. End of story.'

'How long ago?' asked Daykin.

Martin Brown looked at the note in his new CID diary. 'A good fifteen years ago.'

Daykin looked back at the flip chart. 'Right,' he said, 'let's look at what we've got.' He turned the flip chart to a new page. 'Three groups,' he said, starting to write. 'Dead by accident, suicide, or unknown killer; Merchanto, Lucas, Sheppard, Swanson, Macdonald and Hastings.'

'That's a lot, sir,' said Bridget Cooper.

'It is, but it happens.'

Daykin, who had written the names on a list, started a new one. 'Alive: Moore, Freeman, Ellington and probably, Cunningham.' His hand moved to the right of the page. 'Dead by serial killer: Van Meer and Miller.

'Two problems. First, how do we protect the four who are alive?

Second, who killed the last two? I'm going to try to contact Silus Cunningham, I want you to concentrate on locating the four who are alive and see if you can persuade them to let us give them some police protection. Ideally move them to a safe house until we can find the killer. I also want you to see if you can find Kim Nixon. Finally, work on the same members of the club as you were before, see what else you can find out about them?'

'Which is more important?'

'Protecting these four. Get started. Terry, are you off to see Freeman?'

'On my way, Tom.'

Chapter 15

As Terry Hudson got in his car and started the journey to Manchester, a Volvo motor car pulled to a halt in the road where he lived in Scarborough and the driver unfolded a map and started to read it.

Ray Garvey was very careful. The Volvo was a few years old, painted a neutral colour and neither very dirty or newly washed. It was not the sort of car that would attract any attention. He looked over the top of the map at the house where Hudson lived. A large Victorian semi-detached divided, by the number of bells on the stone pillar by the front door, into flats. He had checked the back of the building first. One back door, a narrow flagged path leading down the back garden from the door to a gate and, through the gate, a litter-strewn alleyway, just wide enough for one car. If his target was going to run, Garvey liked to know where he was going and how to cut off his escape. He would corner Hudson with the car in the alley. Garvey looked slowly up and down the road, using the rear view and wing mirrors. No obvious problems. He carefully folded the map and got out of the car.

He was a small, muscular man with a crew cut of steel-grey hair. He was dressed casually in a black waterproof jacket and grey jogging trousers. He looked like he had just come from the gym. He had. He made his way across the road to the house, strolling casually, not glancing to left or right. Anyone watching him would think he was a friend or family visiting one of the tenants.

A small cardboard square above the fourth door bell down said 'T. Hudson'. The name had been written in blue roller-ball ink and had smudged. Garvey rang the bell several times, then took a small brown notebook from his pocket and wrote down the number of the flat and the house. He rang each of the other bells several times, starting at the top and working his way down slowly. He got to number 8 before the front door opened. The young man who opened it was in his early twenties, taller than average and wearing a baggy sweatshirt and oversized jeans to try to camouflage his seventy pounds of excess weight. He had a round face with the early signs of the heavy jowls that would develop in middle age. His hair was combed forward and gelled up at the front, and around his chin was the dark hair of the beard he was starting to grow. He looked at Garvey with soft, trusting blue eyes.

'Have you come to collect the sofa?' he asked, opening the door a fraction more to show Garvey an old damask-covered sofa standing in the hall.

'No,' said Garvey pleasantly, 'I'm looking for Mr Hudson in flat 5.'

'He's not in.'

'I know. I rang the bell a few times. Do you know where I can find him?'

'I'm not sure, sometimes he's here, sometimes he's not.'

'Look,' said Garvey, glancing up and down the street as if someone might hear, 'you look like someone I can trust. It's a bit embarrassing, but Mr Hudson owes my boss some money and we really need to collect it. Cashflow, you understand.'

'Who do you work for?'

'It's a fair chunk of money, Mr Hudson will know who he owes it to.'

'How can he get in touch with you?'

'To tell the truth, I'm out and about a lot. I'll make sure I get in touch with him. Tell Mr Hudson this, will you? I'm here asking politely for what he owes, but my boss's patience has just run out. The next time I see him I'd like him to have the money or be able to go and get it for me. Will you tell him that?'

'I don't know when I'll be seeing him again. We're not exactly friends, we just say hello if we meet on the stairs.'

'I know you will do me the favour of trying to contacting him,' – Garvey looked at the name above the bell of flat 8 – 'Mr Woods.' He smiled. 'Remember, I know where you live.'

When Garvey left, Todd Woods went back to his room. Ten minutes later his bell rang. He was not a religious young man, but for five seconds he closed his eyes and prayed it was the man coming to collect the sofa.

Chapter 16

Caelum

It didn't take Daykin long to locate Silus Cunningham, or to find out that he was still alive. He phoned the Senate of the Inns of Court, who keep records of all barristers. Silus Cunningham, Queen's Counsel, was now deputy head of chambers and practising admiralty law in Hare Court, one of the monkey puzzle of streets that run through Lincoln's Inn Field. Daykin called the chambers' number and the receptionist put him through to Cunningham.

'This will have to be quick, Inspector, I'm due in the Royal Courts of Justice in ten minutes.'

'The Greenrush Club,' said Daykin.

'Good God, that's a name from the distant past, what do you want to know?'

'Are you still in touch with any of the other members?'

'After university we all drifted off in different directions, as people do. Nobody kept in touch much, except me.'

'You, Mr Cunningham?'

'Defect of personality, I suppose. I was the secretary of the club and kept all the records. I still send a circular every December, telling the members what I've been up to for the last year – at least I send it to those who are left.'

'Who do you know to be dead?'

'Poor old Jerry Merchanto committed suicide, Fran Sheppard went missing in the Alps, Josh Swanson died in the Philippines, Big Mac was shot in Belfast and Paddy Hastings was electrocuted. I think that's it.'

'You'd better take Dominic Lucas, Christopher Van Meer and Robert Miller off your list.'

'Lucas, Van Meer and Miller? All three of them? How?'

'Mr Lucas disturbed a burglar in his holiday home, Mr Van Meer was poisoned and Mr Miller drowned.'

'But that brings our numbers down to four out of twelve. We're only in our 50s, that's incredible!'

'We believe that Van Meer and Miller were murdered. We are concerned for the safety of you and the other three surviving members.'

'Why on earth would anyone want to harm us?'

'It may be something to do with a girl called Kim Nixon, who was the victim of a multiple rape shortly before the club broke up.'

There was a long pause.

'I told them that this wasn't over, it would come back to haunt us. I just didn't know it would be in this way or would take so long.'

Another pause.

'You don't think there's anything suspicious about the deaths of Jerry, Dom or any of the others, do you?'

'It's something we're looking at. Did all the people in The Greenrush Club get on together, any bad feeling?'

'No. Oh, yes, there was one incident. We had a ten-year reunion in Cambridge. Most of us were married by then and brought our wives. Bob Miller met Paddy Freeman's wife for the first time. I don't know if the marriage was on the rocks anyway, but she ended up leaving Paddy and going to live with Bob. Paddy was furious, threatened them both.'

'The night of the rape, did you rape her?'

'Do we have to reopen thirty-year-old wounds?'

'I'm afraid so.'

'I said nothing that night, I haven't changed my mind.'

'It was you who told everyone to keep quiet?'

'There's no point in denying it. I was in my last year studying law and I spent the previous summer working in a chambers which specialized in criminal law. I learnt a lot there, especially what a powerful weapon silence is. I told the others to keep quiet for two reasons. We were all about to start our careers and nobody wanted his life ruined by a criminal conviction and the inevitable lengthy prison sentence. Additionally, it was a time when students and police were, more or less, sworn enemies, so the others didn't take too much persuading.'

'Do any of the members contact you?'

'The yearly missive generates two or three replies, normally, but not always, from the same people.'

'Anyone else ever ask you about the other members?'

'Hardly ever. In the last ten years I think I've been contacted about three times. Once was a young woman, called Johnson or something, doing a Ph.D. in international finance and trying to get in touch with Dom Lucas. There then was a finance company trying to trace Clive Ellington and some solicitors asking if anyone had heard from Fran Sheppard.'

'How do you contact the others?'

'Some by letter, most by emails.'

'Can you give me those details?'

'What's your email address?'

'I'm a Luddite, Mr Cunningham, computers baffle me.'

'Give me your fax number.'

Daykin opened his diary and read the fax number of the machine in the incident room.

'Forgive me, Inspector, I have to go. I'll fax you the details.'

'And your safety, Mr Cunningham?'

'Sorry, Inspector, no time.'

The phone went dead.

Daykin didn't put the phone down, he pushed a button that connected to one of the other lines and dialled Cambridge Police Station, where he asked for Chief Inspector Foster.

'Bob? I need a favour.'

'What do you need, Tom?'

'Can you get hold of the old rape file of Kim Nixon and send it to me?'

'Give me the details.'

'And can you ask an officer to spend a day or two trying to find her?'

'I'll see what I can do.'

Daykin got up, but only walked as far as the table where Martin Brown was sitting. He sat down opposite him.

'How's it going?' he said.

Brown stopped pretending to be busy and put his pen down.

'OK, sir. You?'

'Tell me a bit more about John Hastings, where did he die?'

Martin Brown reached for his diary. He had written 'M. Brown' in neat script at the top right-hand corner of the cover. Some school habits are hard to break.

'At a house in Reading, sir,' he said, looking down at the page.

'Reading?'

'He thought it was a developing market.'

'Thanks,' said Daykin, getting up.

'Is that it, sir?'

'For now.'

Daykin went back to his seat and pulled a phone towards him, thinking that it was a coincidence that Hastings and Moore should both settle in Reading. He got the number of the Reading Coroners Office from directory enquiries and called them. They would still have some details of a twenty-year-old inquest on computer and could email them to him. He asked them to fax them.

Daykin hated the coffee in the canteen, so he collected Royston from the kennels and strolled with him to a local coffee shop where he bought a large cardboard mug to take away, then sat on a bench on The Stray and watched the dog pad around the grassed area for thirty minutes. By the time he got back to the station and put the dog in the kennels the forty pages of fax message from Reading were stacked on the table. He spent most of the afternoon picking through the dry bones of a twenty-year-old inquest.

John Hastings was a man without enemies, not even an estranged wife. The live cable had been hidden behind the wall for so many years that the conduit pipe had rusted through. Hastings was using a drill with a metal casing, one hand on the pistol grip and trigger, the other guiding the drill bit by cupping it over the top of the casing. When the tip of the drill hit the live cable it made a perfect connection and Hastings was electrocuted efficiently and instantly.

The Coroner was in no doubt that it was an accident and there was no evidence to disagree with him. Daykin marked up the papers, placed them into a file and put the file into the cabinet in the corner of the room.

'Get everyone together,' he said to Bridget Cooper. 'We'll see how much more we know now than we knew this morning.'

Five officers pulled up chairs in a semi-circle around the table Daykin was using.

'I'll start,' he said, when the noise of scraping chairs and shuffling died down.

'Darius Moore, graduated from Cambridge and went into the Church of England. With the speed of a politician on acid he got himself promoted through the parishes to Assistant Dean at Salisbury Cathedral and was aiming for Bishop, at least. Then he had an argument with the authorities and left to set up his own church. Becoming bishop was easy – he just appointed himself. Now he runs a thirty-acre church complex near Reading giving some Christian fundamentalist doctrine to the people who are desperate to hear it. He probably pockets most of the weekly collection. He's very much alive and arrogant enough to refuse any protection. I'll keep on at him to see if I can persuade him that this is serious as he could be the next victim.

'Clive Ellington, also alive, but not doing quite as well as Bishop Moore. After a life of swindling the needy and the greedy out of their money, he got a five-year stretch for a Ponzi fraud which he's serving in Rudgate. He thinks he's safe because he's in prison. I've tried to explain that prisons are designed to keep people from getting out, not getting in and, because whoever is doing this knows where he is twenty-four hours a day, he's possibly the most vulnerable. He doesn't want protection, he shares his arrogance with Moore.

'Christopher Van Meer, killed by strychnine poisoning, the latest one to die. The poison was put in his tea. He drank endless cups every day, so it had to get him sooner or later. Widowed, no children. Owned a successful company, so, fairly wealthy.

'Robert Miller, record producer to the stars. He went into semi retirement in his home town of Scarborough and his main hobby was sailing. One evening he fell over the side in calm waters and, if alive and conscious, could have got back on board or swum to shore. I believe he was murdered.

'Joshua Swanson, successful businessman who didn't take much time off work. He went to the Philippines where he died of food poisoning. He could have been murdered, but the smart money says this was just a tragic accident.

'Finally, Silus Cunningham, distinguished barrister-at-law, secretary of The Greenrush Club and, although he's a bit cagey about it, probably keeps in touch with all the others who are still alive. He's going to send me their addresses, so keeping an eye on them may be easier after today.

'Right, Bridget, who do you have?'

'Jerry Merchanto, sir. He was a high-flying salesman until he discovered alcohol and cocaine at about the same time. His work started to suffer and word is that he was on the point of being fired. A cocktail of bourbon and cocaine affects people differently and they say it made Jerry depressed. One night he made his way up to the roof of his office block and threw himself off. The San Francisco's Coroners Office say that there were no suspicious circumstances, nothing to show it was anything but suicide. He never married and had no children. He has two sisters, living in Connecticut. Sir?'

'Yes?'

'I could get a lot more information locally, would the Force pay for a trip to San Francisco?'

'Put it in writing, I'll pass it by Superintendent Wainwright.'

'Forget I said anything, sir.'

'Fritz?'

'Dominic Lucas, sir. Financial whizzkid. At public school he began investing in silver, just when the market started rising, then it took off. When it peaked, just about the time he went into the sixth form, he moved into gilt-edged stocks, about six months ahead of a major surge. At university, having already made his first half million at school, he formed an investment club which paid its members five hundred per cent on their investment by the time he graduated.

'After that his job was just an extension of what he had learnt at school and Cambridge. He was a combination of a man who was prepared to put in the long hours and who had an instinctive feel for the market. Give him a thousand pounds for a year and he'd give you back five thousand, even after he'd taken his cut of thirty per cent.

'The Surrey Force sent me the files on his death. It wasn't pretty, but it was simple. He disturbed a burglar who hit him with what was probably a weighted cosh, then kicked him to death. The pathologist said the culprit was about six feet tall, almost certainly male, and right handed. That's about all he could say and no one was ever arrested, let alone charged.'

'No suspects?'

'Not even a hint of one.'

'Did you find anything about investments of five hundred pounds each made by The Greenrush Club?'

'No, sir, I didn't see anything like that.'

'Sarah, Francis Sheppard?'

'Oh, gosh, yes,' said Sarah Fanson, 'Fran Sheppard. A pretty uneventful life. Married late, one daughter, but he and his wife separated when the girl was two. History repeating itself really, as his own parents divorced when he was young. He had a half-brother and two half-sisters to his mother's second husband. His own wife remarried a' – she looked at her notes – 'Doctor Jackson, some kind of scientist.

'After his divorce he did some research on Homer for a publishing house and then drifted into teaching English to Russian students at a private school in St Petersburg, where he learnt Russian. After that he went to work for Reuters in their Vienna office, translating Russian news stories. That's where he discovered mountain climbing. He was pretty good, too. Within three years he'd climbed Mont Blanc and been part of a team that got to the top of the Matterhorn.

'By now he was experienced enough to go out on his own, free climbing without ropes. That was the death of him. He did everything right, good equipment, let the hotel know where he was going and when he was setting off. He must have been halfway up when the wind suddenly changed direction, bringing a major snow storm in from the west. He was due back at the hotel by four. By the time they raised the alarm at seven it was too dark and too treacherous to look for him. The following morning they sent out a mountain rescue team, but all they found was one boot and an ice axe.

'That was twenty years ago. Eight years after that he was declared dead. There wasn't any estate to speak of, his daughter got nothing after the probate fees had been paid.'

'Bob,' said Daykin, 'what about Peter Macdonald?'

'Nothing much to add, sir. I checked with army records. A routine patrol were about to head back to barracks when a lone sniper shot Macdonald from a neighbouring rooftop. It was a Catholic area and if anyone knew anything they were either too loyal or too scared to say anything. The IRA put out a bulletin, the usual stuff, one of their freedom fighters had taken the life of a soldier of the occupation.

'The Intelligence Services were told by an informant that the gunman was Eamon Stokes. By then he was serving time in the Maze. Before they had time to interrogate him he was stabbed to death by another prisoner in an argument about politics.'

'Politics?'

'The real IRA had split from the provos, Stokes had joined them and there's a chance that he was killed as, if he ever got out, he would be too dangerous.'

'No doubt that he killed Macdonald?'

'The Royal Ulster Constabulary say that they weren't looking for anyone else.'

'That leaves John Hastings. Martin?'

'Nothing much to add, the Coroner's verdict was straightforward accident.'

Daykin looked hard at Martin Brown. What Terry Hudson had said about him just serving out his time must be right.

'OK,' he said, 'let's wind it up for today. First thing tomorrow Sergeant Hudson will fill us in on Patrick Freeman and I want you to contact all the remaining ones, Moore, Freeman, Ellington and

Cunningham and persuade them to have some protection. After that we will need all the help we can get trying to trace Kim Nixon. See you at eight-thirty.'

Chapter 17

Aemular

Terry Hudson did not have a good journey. From Harrogate to the motorway he followed an old car driven by an older man in a flat cap. Hudson hated drivers who wore caps. The ones who wore cloth caps moved too slowly and the ones who wore baseball caps drove like idiots.

Half way across the M62 the traffic ground to a halt. For the next six miles all three lanes moved at a maximum of five miles an hour. Then, as he got to the outskirts of Manchester, it started to rain.

'Bloody Manchester,' he said to himself, as he turned on the windscreen wipers.

He had looked up Freeman's road in an *A to Z* and, driving up the road, he found Freeman's house, it was the only one with a ramp for a wheelchair running beside the front steps.

Hudson climbed the steps and rang the doorbell. He waited and was about to ring the bell again when a voice sounded through a small loudspeaker to the left of the door.

'If you're selling something, I'm not buying, if you're collecting for charity I already gave, and if you're a Jehovah's Witness I don't believe.'

'Mr Freeman?'

'How do you know my name?'

'I'm a police officer.'

'Show me your warrant card.'

Terry Hudson looked around and saw a small camera bolted on to the stonework and angled down, covering the front step. He took out his warrant card and held it up to the lens.

'North Yorkshire. What do you want?'

'To speak to you about Cambridge.'

'Cambridge was long ago and far away.'

'It's raining out here.'

'It usually is.'

Terry Hudson raised his voice.

'If you want me to ask about your private life so the neighbours can hear, I'll start right now.'

Hudson waited, he didn't have anything else to do. After forty-five seconds the door handle, set 9 inches below normal, turned and the door began to swing open. Patrick Freeman slowly moved the wheelchair backwards, pushing the door open with a rubber-tipped walking stick and all the time glowering darkly at Terry Hudson from behind round-framed tinted glasses.

He was a man who had found his personal look somewhere in the 1970s and had settled there. His hair was long, covering his ears and almost down to his shoulders. He wore denim jeans and jacket, desert boots and a tie-dyed T-shirt. His face, sallow as if he spent most of his time indoors, was framed by long sideboards and a drooping moustache.

'You'd better come in,' he said, spinning the wheelchair around and moving away from Hudson down the hallway. 'And shut the door,' he said over his shoulder.

Hudson followed him into the kitchen. Somewhere in the heart of the house a Grateful Dead album was playing. The kitchen reflected a house occupied by both able-bodied and handicapped people. About half the cabinets were set low on the wall, there were two sinks, one only about a foot off the floor. The floor was rough-surfaced tile, to stop wheels skidding on a wet surface. The light switches were all set low in the walls and half the power points were at normal height, half in line with the light switches. All the kitchen appliances, including the matching stainless-steel kettle and toaster, were on the lower work surfaces and Hudson noticed as he came through the door that, like one from a restaurant into a commercial kitchen it was spring loaded to swing both ways and had a large porthole cut low in it, to see if anyone was on the other side. The bottom twelve inches of the door were covered by a metal kick plate.

In the centre of the kitchen Freeman turned his wheelchair around again to face Terry Hudson.

'So what do you want to know?' It was more a demand, tinged with bitterness and anger, than a question. Hudson started on neutral ground.

'The Greenrush Club,' he said. 'Why did you join and how long were you a member?'

'You come all the way from Yorkshire to ask me about some stupid student club that disbanded thirty years ago?'

'If it wasn't important I wouldn't be asking about it.'

'It's not important to me. I'm sorry you've wasted your time. See yourself out.'

Terry Hudson would have happily closed the diary he had just opened and left, but that feeling was not as happy as his fear of having to face Daykin in the morning. He cocked his head towards the sound of the music.

'So you're a Dead-head,' he said.

Patrick Freeman looked at him suspiciously. 'If you like the Dead,' he said, 'what's your favourite track?'

'Maybe "Casey Jones", but when I really think about it, "Golden Road" was Garcia at his best.'

'What about "Truckin'"?'

'Great, but I thought it was too long and lost the beat a bit in the middle eight.'

Freeman reached into a leather pouch that hung from the left arm rest of his wheelchair and pulled out a small metal tin with a print of a cannabis leaf on it. He saw Terry Hudson looking at it as he opened it.

'Don't worry, it's just Golden Virginia. I only smoke the wacky baccy when the depression gets too bad.'

He opened the tin and took a packet of cigarette papers from it. Opening the paper, he teased some tobacco from the mound in the centre of the tin and gently laid it along the length of the paper, using the finger and thumb of his right hand very patiently. He started to roll the paper round the tobacco. Hudson took a packet of Capstan from his pocket.

'Try one of these?' he said.

Patrick Freeman looked at the packet. 'No, thanks, I tried those once; they made me cough and go dizzy for ten minutes.' He smiled for the first time since the front door had opened.

They both lit their cigarettes, inhaled and blew smoke upwards towards the ceiling at the same time. Now there was a common bond in music and nicotine.

'The bloody Greenrush Club,' said Freeman eventually, 'what a pile of cack that was.'

Terry Hudson thought about writing in the diary, but decided it might interrupt the flow that had just started.

'How so?' he said.

'I can't believe I got into such a pathetic bunch of people. I was at the end of my first year at Sydney Sussex. I'd had a friend called Phil Myers, Mill Fires we used to call him. He was finishing his third year and going down. He was a member of Greenrush and said that, as I was studying philosophy at Sussex, there was a spare place for me in the club. They only met a few times a year. It seemed like a good idea and Phil had enjoyed it, so I joined.'

'Did you enjoy it?'

'I was eighteen years old, my first year away from home, an all-male crochet club would have seemed good to me.'

'Tell me about the rape of Kim Nixon.'

Patrick Freeman, who was putting the cigarette to his mouth, paused.

'I don't want to talk about that.'

'As I said, its important.'

'To who?'

'Both of us.'

'Why?'

'Because I need to know and you may just stay alive.'

'Alive?'

'Haven't you noticed how many of the club aren't with us anymore?'

'I get those sanctimonious round robin letters from that prat Silus every year. I know that Jerry, Fran, Josh, Peter and John have gone, but so what? We're not exactly young. Out of twelve, five is a bit much, but it's not front-page news, is it?'

'Dominic Lucas?'

'What about him?'

'Dead. Chris Van Meer?'

'Chris?'

'Dead. Bob Miller?' Silence.

'Dead. So that's now eight out of twelve. Sound a bit more unusual?'

'It happens.'

Patrick Freeman wasn't convincing either of them.

'Eight out of twelve dead and you've been hit by a car and nearly died. Tell me about that.'

Freeman wheeled the chair three feet to a worktop and stubbed his cigarette out in an ashtray, although it was only half finished.

'When I went up to Cambridge,' he began, looking directly at Terry Hudson, 'I was about as right wing as you get. That's why the club appealed to me, your spare time devoted only to personal pleasure. But

103

when I went down, life changed. Some people discover religion, I discovered Communism and, as a bonus, it was fashionable. I joined the Young Communist League and soon my spare time was for meetings and marches. I even got myself arrested once.

'I mellowed over the years, but still hated everything The Greenrush Club stood for and despised most of the people in it. I haven't kept in touch with any of them and wouldn't want to.

'In the League I went from job to job as a full-time activist and, about eight years ago, started working for Greenpeace in Manchester. You can't, in all conscience, work to save the planet and pour carbon into the atmosphere by driving a car. So I got myself a bike. I didn't have many long journeys to make and if they were less than 20 miles, which they usually were, I rode. I got really fit.' He reached for the tobacco tin again. 'Not like you see me now.

'What made my accident even more stupid,' he continued, focusing on rolling the cigarette, 'was that I took some courses on cycle safety and danger awareness. One evening I was cycling home from work on a road I'd ridden a thousand times, when a car hit me from behind, threw me twenty yards and put me in hospital in traction for three months.'

'Did you see the car?'

'And take its number plate while doing forced somersaults in the air? I didn't even see the make or colour of it.'

'Was it deliberate?'

'The police accident report couldn't say. It could have been a mistake by the driver; maybe he was drunk, or he could have tried to kill me. In any event, he didn't stay around to find out how I was and he has never been traced.'

Terry Hudson wrote a few notes while Freeman took a very long pull on the cigarette and drew the smoke deeply into his lungs.

'We believe that the girl who was raped may have something to do with the recent deaths. Tell me about the night of the rape,' said Hudson.

This time Patrick Freeman didn't pause.

'It started just like any other meeting. Someone had organized a private room above a pub. I didn't know that there was going to be a stripper until halfway through the meal. I heard Hastings, Miller and Macdonald talking about it, how they were going to turn the lights off. Why didn't anyone stop them? Well, we'd started drinking in the pub before we went up for the meal, most of us had a skinful and, to be honest, a lot of that night is a bit hazy.

'All I know for sure is that when the girl had finished her act the lights did go off. There were some sounds of someone being held down, muffled shouting, then a sort of thrusting, scrambling sound that must have been someone having sex, or more than one person because it started, paused, started again, paused again, started, then stopped.

'Miller ushered us all to the end of the room then someone, I think it was Macdonald, turned the lights back on. The girl was lying naked on her back in the middle of the room, her legs apart. Nobody was in any doubt what had just happened. She seemed dazed, bewildered and she got slowly to her feet like a wounded animal. Then she picked up her clothes which were lying all over the floor and got dressed. I remember her wincing in pain as she did so. And, as she put her clothes on, she gradually recovered her spirit, and began shouting and swearing at us, all of us standing there at the end of the room in a group. She came towards us, but Ellington picked up a silver candlestick and told her if she came any closer he'd cave her head in with it. So she spat at him, full in the face, and left, saying she was going to the police.

'When she left, drunk as we were, there was a major argument. Darius Moore was saying that there were three who were guilty, but there were nine who were innocent, so why should they suffer? Merchanto was going on about being deported and Lucas said that he had a career to think about. But Cunningham was a rock. He wasn't the best liked of us, too pompous for most, but he argued that we were a club, we owed a duty of loyalty to each other, all for one, one for all, that sort of thing. He said that if we stuck together there was nothing the police could do. I remember one of those loyalty things; we all stood around in a circle and put our right fists into the middle. Childish, but he made us do it. We were drunk.

'When the police arrived there was a code of silence, our own little Mafia. And it worked. If they could have got one of us to talk three of us would have gone to prison for a very long time. But we stayed silent, bastards that we were.'

'So you think it was John Hastings, Robert Miller and Peter Macdonald who raped the girl?'

'Think? I was sure of it then and I'm sure of it now.'

'Would you give a witness statement?'

'After thirty years? Against three men who I grew up with and who are all now dead? Not in this lifetime, Sergeant.'

Terry Hudson looked through his notes.

'I think that's all I have for now, Mr Freeman, except one thing: we'd like you to come into protective custody.'

Patrick Freeman, who had let the cigarette burn during his narrative, stubbed it out.

'You see this room? Since my accident I've been experimenting in helping the disabled. It's not just my kitchen, its my laboratory. I'm not going to leave all that because some copper thinks a mad erotic dancer is trying to bump me off.'

'Well,' said Terry Hudson, closing his book, 'if you change your mind I'll leave my card.'

Patrick Freeman followed Terry Hudson to the front door and watched him walk down the path. Then he wheeled himself back to the kitchen to make a cup of tea. While the kettle was boiling he tore up Hudson's card and threw it in the bin.

Chapter Eighteen

Terry Hudson settled himself into his car seat, but before he put the key in the ignition, he turned on his mobile phone. He had told them at the station that he didn't want interruptions if he was interviewing someone, but the truth was that he hated the way a mobile phone made you so easy to contact and he found being incommunicado for long periods of his working day very convenient.

There was one message, from Todd Woods. He had given Woods his mobile number in case of an emergency at the flat and this was the first time that he had used it. Wondering if he had had a water leak or the electricity had gone off, he returned the call.

'Terry?' said Woods, 'I thought you should know that a man came here today, looking for you. He said it was something about some money you owed.'

'Did he say who he was?'

'He said his name was Garvey.'

'Oh, don't worry. I know what that is about, a bit of a misunderstanding. I'll take care of it. Thanks for letting me know,' said Terry Hudson, sounding more casual than he felt.

He dialled his bookmaker in Scarborough, he knew the number by heart.

Derek Butcher answered the phone himself.

'Derek, this is Terry Hudson. That money I owe you, let's see if we can work this out. I can pay by instalments. There's no need to send people round to my flat.'

'Not my problem anymore, Terry. I sold the debt on.'

'Sold the debt on? Who to?'

'That's part of the deal; I can't tell you.'

'Well, whoever it is has sent a man called Garvey to my flat and scared one of my neighbours shitless.'

'I know you've never taken my advice in the past, Terry, but if I were you I'd take this piece. If that was Ray Garvey, I'd get the money

107

together fast and pay him next time he calls.'

'You're probably right,' said Hudson and closed the phone. This needed some thought. Instead, he found a local pub and sat just outside the back door under the Gazebo cover put there for smokers. He spent the next two hours engrossed in his three favourite pastimes, drinking beer, smoking cigarettes and studying the racing pages of the paper.

After ten minutes, and in the middle of working out the permutations on the card at Aintree, Terry Hudson's phone rang again. He cursed softly and thought about ignoring it, but answered it anyway.

' "Truckin' ",' said Patrick Freeman's voice, 'was infinitely better than "Casey Jones".'

The phone went dead. Terry Hudson shrugged and went back to his paper. Freeman was probably right.

As Hudson was ordering his second pint Daykin had a visitor. Superintendent Wainwright came into the incident room.

'Got time for a briefing, Tom?'

They walked back to Wainwright's office.

'I've had the assistant chief constable on the phone about the staff shortages here. During the conversation, call it an interrogation, I told him about the manpower we put on your case. He was livid, told me to reassign everybody except you and Sergeant Hudson. I think I can avoid that, but I need some ammunition, so what have you got so far?'

'The twelve men fall into three groups, sir. There are the four who are still alive, the six who died over the years and the two who have been murdered.'

'So this is only a two-murder investigation?'

'More importantly, it's an investigation that is urgent because, I believe, whoever killed Van Meer and Miller is out to kill the others.'

'Why?'

'It sounds stupid, but so far it's the only theory we've got. It has something to do with the rape of a girl in Cambridge thirty years ago.'

'Tell me about that.'

'I may have a better picture later; Terry Hudson is speaking to Patrick Freeman, the last one we have to interview. The girl was raped, they all kept silent, the Cambridgeshire Police couldn't prove anything, so they all walked. She was last seen screaming revenge.'

'It's taken her some time.'

'That's one of the unanswered questions.'

'Couldn't Cambridgeshire reopen it as a cold case, re-examine the exhibits with modern technology, DNA, that sort of thing?'

'I've made a couple of calls about that. The exhibits were destroyed about fifteen years ago.' As Daykin spoke, Wainwright was writing in a tiny, neat hand with a gold roller ball pen in a pocket-sized leather-covered notebook.

'Have you any idea where the woman is now?'

'I've got the team working on that, but my guess is that she won't be easy to find.'

'OK, Tom,' said Wainwright, closing the notebook and putting it into his inside jacket pocket. 'I can keep the ACC at bay for a couple of days, but get me something solid to tell him, will you?'

'I'll try, sir.'

'You'd better get back and see what your people have got.'

Terry Hudson would have driven straight back to Scarborough, but he decided to spend the night in Harrogate, in case Garvey returned to the flat or, worse still, was already there.

He took his time driving back to Harrogate and it was well after six in the evening when he arrived at the station. He would drop his diary off in the incident room, ready for the morning. The room was in darkness, except for a bright pool of light from a desk lamp on the right-hand table. Daykin looked up from his papers as Hudson walked in. In the silence Terry Hudson could hear a steady low breathing sound and could just make out the shape of Royston fast asleep in the corner of the room.

'I didn't expect you till the morning,' said Daykin.

'I thought I'd stay overnight in Harrogate to get an early start.'

'I think the Force can stand one more night's accommodation. How was Patrick Freeman?'

'Bitter.'

'Did he tell you anything useful?'

'He says Macdonald, Hastings and Miller raped the girl.'

'Do you believe him?'

'Why not?'

'He's picked three who are dead, so no comebacks.'

'And?'

'If I had to put money on it I'd say Ellington, Cunningham and Freeman.'

'Why those three?'

'Ellington, because he organized the girl and probably had rape in mind from the start. He's totally selfish, antisocial and criminally minded. Cunningham was and is a pompous career-minded man. If he wasn't involved he would have been the first to give up the guilty ones to the police, so there was no risk to his career as a barrister. Instead, he spent a lot of time and energy persuading everyone to keep silent. Freeman, because he lied to you. Macdonald was born without a scrotum. No scrotum, no testicles. He couldn't have raped anyone; he was, effectively, a eunuch.'

'Can you prove it?'

'Right now I don't want to try, it's a distraction. Maybe when this is over. Now, what exactly did Patrick Freeman tell you? Don't leave anything out.'

For over thirty minutes Terry Hudson, his diary opened in front of him on the table, went through the conversation with Freeman. When he had finished, Daykin said, 'Fancy a pint?'

'The best offer I've had all day.'

They found a quiet corner of a pub just down the road. The dog settled himself under the table and Daykin went to the bar and ordered two pints of Tetleys bitter. For a time they talked about Force politics and the pressures of the job. It was Terry Hudson who started the subject of how the long hours can affect a marriage.

'My wife had this idea of a nine to five job with a bit of overtime when we got married. It probably wouldn't have worked anyway, but the calls I used to make from the station, saying that I wouldn't be home for a few more hours, sent it downhill fast. She never understood that you can't just close the book like an accountant and go home, sometimes you have to see something through to the end.

'After nine months of eating meals that had been left in the oven, she stopped doing even that. It was only after she left I realized that when she stopped trying, she stopped caring. Her affair started about then. I'm a copper, I should have seen the signs, made the deductions, but when it is so close to you, you sometimes don't see it, or don't want to.

'After she walked out we only ever met face to face once. We had bought a small house and we had to divide the money from the sale of that and the furniture. We met at her solicitor's office. I couldn't believe how angry she was. She said it was all my fault.'

'It's never just one person's fault.'

'Yeah, but maybe I should have tried harder.'

Terry Hudson took a long drink from his beer, draining the glass, while he thought about what might have been.

'How about you,' he said eventually, 'are you married?'

'I was; she left me.'

'Children?'

'No, I wish we had.'

Daykin didn't seem to want to say anything else, so Terry Hudson got up. 'My round,' he said, picking up his glass. Daykin's was still two-thirds full. When Terry Hudson returned, sat down and put two glasses carefully down on the table, he said, 'Do you have family, Tom?'

'Three sisters, all married, and my mother. My father died twenty odd years ago. You?'

'Both my parents are dead. One older brother, he's also a cop. He had the good sense to get himself transferred to Cornwall, so he has a very quiet life, except for a few weekends in summer when the holidaymakers get too drunk in Padstow or Truro.'

They fell into silence for a few minutes. Terry Hudson examined his pint of beer and Daykin checked on the dog. The beer and the animal were near perfect.

'Any hobbies, Tom, other than rugby?'

'I cook a bit, mainly for myself these days, but we have a family get together every month and I usually make the meal.'

'Meat and two veg?'

'I sometimes stretch to a bit better than that.'

Another silence, while Daykin drained the first pint of beer and started on the second.

'I think the dog's getting bored, so I'm going to head out of here in a few minutes. Have you got accommodation organized for tonight?'

'No, but I'll find somewhere.'

Daykin looked at his watch. 'It's still early, you could be home in about an hour.'

'To be honest, I'm a bit knackered. I'll stay local.'

'Suit yourself. About tomorrow, we've got through the first stage, we know how eight of them died and where the other four are. We've now got to find Kim Nixon. Wainwright's getting pressure from upstairs and he'll start to put it on us if we don't make progress. So, I'll see you at eight-thirty tomorrow. Sleep well.'

Terry Hudson, who thought he was a drinker, was surprised to see Daykin down nearly a pint of beer in one swallow, get up and walk out of the pub with the dog at his heels.

Hudson picked up his pint and strolled to the back door of the building. Just outside the door he put the drink down on a table and lit a cigarette. As he watched the small armada of grey clouds stream past the full moon Ray Garvey was making a phonecall to a former police officer, now a private detective.

'Colin? It's Ray Garvey. I've a bit of work for you.'

'What do you want, Ray?'

'A police sergeant based in Scarborough called Terry Hudson. He seems to have gone out of town for a bit. Call a couple of your old friends on the Force and see if they know where he is, will you?'

'You're not thinking about giving a serving officer a slapping, are you, Ray? If you are that's a bit too hot for me.'

'No, this is only a bit of gentle prodding, nothing more than that. Give me a location by noon tomorrow and its worth fifty quid and there's another fifty if you can get me his car registration number.'

'I'll see what I can do.'

Chapter Nineteen

'OK, people,' said Daykin, the following morning.

Two of three by the coffee machine filled their cups and walked to the table to join the others. Terry Hudson, who looked as if he'd slept in his car, poured coffee into a large mug and went to sit beside Daykin.

'Kim Nixon,' said Daykin, turning over a page on the flipchart. He had written a list on the top half of the page. 'What do we know about her?'

He started to run down the list.

'Female, was in her early twenties thirty years ago, so she's just over fifty. Lived in Cambridge. Was a dancer. Was raped, but the case didn't go anywhere. Anything else?'

'Description?' asked Sarah Fanson.

'I've got that, it was in the papers they sent from Cambridge,' said Daykin, leafing through the fax sheets. 'Yep, here it is. Five feet six inches, medium build, dark-brown hair, worn long, usually in a ponytail but tied up when she danced. Brown eyes and a small birthmark, roughly the shape of Africa, on her left forearm. Not much to go on, but that's it.'

'Did she have a day job?' said Bridget Cooper.

'No information,' said Daykin.

'Did she stay in Cambridge or move on?'

'No information.'

'Did she have any family?'

'No information.'

'Friends?'

'No information.'

'Is she still alive?'

'No information.'

Everyone round the table thought hard about another question, except Martin Brown, who was doodling on the cover of his notebook.

'That's all we know,' said Daykin, 'so now we have to spend the day on the phones, emails and faxes, asking anyone we can think of to give us more information. By six tonight I'd like to know where Kim Nixon is and, at best, to have spoken to her. Let's get moving.'

It was one of those days police officers dread. Hours of phone calls, hours of writing notes but no progress at all. Just blind alleys, indifference and apathy. The day would have been completely wasted but for two calls Daykin received between four and five in the afternoon. The first was in person. Superintendent Wainwright came into the room and sat down wearily with a heavy grunt next to him.

'Hello, Tom,' he said, 'I might have something for you.'

'Sir?'

'After you left yesterday I sent a round robin email to about thirty superintendents I know in various parts of the country, asking about Kim Nixon, your erotic dancer. Bless him, Sam Connors in Merseyside replied about twenty minutes ago. This may not be your girl, but there's a good chance that it is. A local Liverpool villain called Maurice Bateman ran a few strip clubs, some brothels and did a bit of heroin importation about thirty years ago. He took up with one of the dancers and she moved in with him. Maurice or Mo as everyone called him, was not a nice man and, apart from his day job of sex and drugs, he liked a bit of violence. And if he couldn't get enough on the streets of Liverpool, he'd go home and beat the crap out of his girlfriend. After her third visit to the Royal Liverpool Hospital she left him. I guess you know her name.'

'When she left, why Cambridge?'

'At a guess, just a fairly small town at the other end of the country, somewhere, perhaps, Mo wouldn't find her.'

'Perhaps he did. I'm going to have to talk to him. Is he still in Liverpool?'

'He is.'

Daykin opened his diary and wrote a few sentences.

'If anyone is killing the men who may have raped Kim Nixon, Mo Bateman is a much better candidate than she is. It raises one question.'

'I know, why wait thirty years to start? Maybe it took him all that time to find her, but if you're Mo Bateman and you want to find someone, it takes thirty days, not thirty years.'

'So why so long?'

'Four months after Kim Nixon disappeared, Mo was arrested for running guns to the IRA. He was kept in custody until his trial at Liverpool Crown Court where he was convicted of conspiracy to supply weapons to a terrorist organization and he received a thirty-year sentence.'

'Even under the old law he'd have been out ten years ago.'

'He would, except towards the end of his sentence his prison category was reduced "to rehabilitate him into society" is the phrase they use – as if anyone could rehabilitate Mo – and he was moved to a semi-open prison. He had been there for just over a year when, one lunch time, he got into an argument with another prisoner while they were queuing for their lunch. Someone had left a chef's knife on the serving counter, Mo picked it up and stabbed the other man straight through the heart.'

'Who would be stupid enough to leave a knife lying around?'

'That's what the governor thought, so he started asking questions. When the full story came out the man who died, Wyatt, had been running the drugs supply into the prison and Mo decided to take over. He paid for the knife to be left there and he was just unlucky that two prisoner officers came into the dining area at the moment he used it and they saw him kill Wyatt. The judge wasn't impressed and gave him life for murder. He was released two years ago.'

'Where is he now?'

'People like Mo control their businesses even from the inside. Whilst he was away the clubs, brothels and drugs hardly missed a heart beat. When he came out of prison he just took up the reins again, it was like he never left. He operates from an office above his first strip club just down the road from the Grafton in Kensington. He won't be difficult to find, he's not afraid of anything.

'Just one thing, Tom,' said Wainwright, levering himself out of his chair, 'Mo Bateman is a very dangerous man. He has no respect for anyone, especially a police officer. Just be very careful around him. He bites. Fatally.'

When Wainwright left, Daykin went back to making phone calls and between calls, his phone rang.

'Chief Inspector Foster, line one,' said the operator. Daykin pressed the button.

'Bob, what can I do for you?'

'The other way round, Tom, it's what I can do for you.'

'How so?'

'We had no joy finding Kim Nixon, but it struck me that a dancer, even a stripper, might have an agent. It took a while, but I found him.'

'Where?'

'He retired to one of those homes for show-business people. This one is just outside Bournemouth. I've got the number, his name is Harry Shapiro.'

'I'll give him a call.'

'He must be nearly ninety by now, I can't guarantee he'll be compos mentis.'

'Even if he's not, it's more than I had five minutes ago.'

'Best of luck, Tom.'

'If it means I have to come back to Cambridge, I'm buying.'

'Sounds good to me. See you, Tom.'

When he put the phone down Daykin looked at his watch. Quarter to five – as good a time as any to try to talk to a very old man. He dialled the number, called Terry Hudson over and put the phone on speaker. While they waited for it to be answered he quickly explained to Hudson who Harry Shapiro was.

The phone was answered by a female who didn't give her name, but said she would see if Mr Shapiro was awake. Daykin and Hudson looked at each other, it did not sound good. After three or four minutes, there was the sound of carpet slippers shuffling towards the phone. There was another sound, a regular clicking sound every three seconds, followed by the squeaking of plastic pressing on metal. Hudson frowned at the noise.

'Zimmer frame,' whispered Daykin.

The noises stopped and the phone handset was picked up very slowly. Someone was breathing into the mouthpiece, a heavy, rasping breath as if the journey had exhausted him.

'Harry Shapiro,' said a voice. It was a voice full of confidence and warmth, like an easy listening disc jockey.

'Mr Shapiro, my name is Tom Daykin, I'm a policeman from North Yorkshire.'

'Police? So you've finally rumbled the great Drury Lane scam?' He chuckled to show he was joking.

'No, I need to ask you a few questions about a dancer you had on your books many years ago, a girl called Kim Nixon.'

'Kim? Why, what's she done?'

'So you remember her?'

'I had literally thousands of acts pass through my books over the years, Mr Daykin, and I wouldn't pretend to remember all of them, although I probably could tell you something about most of them. One time maybe all of them, but that's the thing about getting old, you stop using your brain and so my memory isn't what it was.'

'Kim Nixon?'

'That's another thing you forget. In here time doesn't matter, no one is going anywhere. I know you have things to do so you're in a hurry.'

'No problem, Mr Shapiro, take your time.'

There was a long pause, so long they were both beginning to think that he had wandered off, physically or mentally. But Harry Shapiro was either putting his thoughts in order, or taking a slow trip down Memory Lane.

'Kim came to me,' he said suddenly, 'about thirty years ago. She wanted to be a dancer. She was a pretty girl, well put together with a dancer's body. I auditioned her and, I'll tell you, she couldn't dance to save her life. There was something else, a sadness about her and when I told her I couldn't use her she almost burst into tears. We talked for a bit, I was on the point of telling her to get a job as a receptionist somewhere, a hotel or a dentist's, when she said she did a bit of erotic dancing. It wasn't the sort of work I was interested in, but she seemed desperate and she certainly needed the money. I knew a couple of strip-club owners in Cambridge who would give her regular work and I wasn't going to turn my nose up at the commission, so I took her on. That's why I remember her, she was the only erotic dancer I ever had on my books.'

'Do you know where she is now?' asked Daykin.

'That's something I can't tell you. I remember her coming to see me one day. She used to confide in me, so she told me the whole sad story about doing her act for some group of drunken students in a room above a pub, getting raped and the police giving her a hard time.' His voice changed. 'Why do you policemen do that to young girls?'

'It's very different now,' said Daykin.

'Good job, if you ask me, well that was it for her. She asked me to release her from her contract, which I did gladly, she said goodbye and I haven't seen or heard from her since that day.'

'Have you any idea where she went when she left you?'

'No. She walked out of the door and for all I know she walked off the edge of the earth.'

'Well, thank you for your time Mr Shapiro, you've been very helpful.'

'Don't lie, Mr Daykin. I haven't told you anything you didn't already know. However, I've got a big finish for you.'

'Big finish?'

'Show business talk. Her name wasn't Kim Nixon, it was Raisa Dunyasha.'

'Now that is interesting, Mr Shapiro. Thank you.'

'Happy to help, Inspector. If you find Kim remember me to her, will you?'

'Glad to. Goodbye.'

'She sounds Polish,' said Terry Hudson, as Daykin switched the phone off.

'Russian.'

'How do you know?'

'Dunyasha is a minor character in *The Cherry Orchard*.'

'So?'

'It's a play by Chekhov.'

'And Chekhov was Russian?'

'Easy to see how you passed the sergeants' exams. One more call,' Daykin said.

He picked up the phone and dialled Bob Foster's number.

'Bob, can someone find out if there is a Russian club in Cambridge?'

'I'll do better than that,' said Foster, 'I'll tell you where it is. I dealt with the renewal of their drinks and dancing licence two years ago.'

He gave Daykin the address and phone number.

'Early start for you tomorrow,' said Daykin to Terry Hudson.

'Where now?'

'Cambridge, The Russian Club.'

'I've just done Manchester, why me? Why not one of the others? Or you?'

'I have someone to visit tomorrow.'

'Who?'

'Nothing to do with the case, just something I have to do.'

'What, if I'm going to Cambridge, am I looking for at The Russian Club?'

'Kim Nixon was Russian. A foreigner in a strange city will gravitate to the club of her home country. Maybe she didn't, but if she did, they may know where she is now.'

'Does it have to be me?'

'You're the one I trust, Terry.'

'Bollocks.'

Chapter Twenty

Daykin got up late and took his time driving to the Dales. Part of him desperately wanted to go, some of him dreaded it. Anyway, there was no time set for the visit, the woman he was visiting didn't care about time.

Once he got out of Harrogate he took the A1, driving at 60 m.p.h. in the inside lane to Bedale where he turned on to the country road passed Leyburn and Middleham into the heart of the Dales.

In Shapford he drove straight to the address and parked the car at the kerb by the front gate. He got out of the vehicle and put the dog on a short lead. They walked up the dirt path and round the side of the building. Ten yards from the back door Daykin stopped. He stood there, silent and motionless, for a long time, staring down at his wife's grave.

It was a neat and simple grave, well tended and without weeds, its boundaries picked out by straight narrow rows of white pebbles. For three minutes he stared at the headstone, black marble, the best he could afford, inscribed with gold lettering now faded by the weather 'Jennifer Claire Daykin, beloved wife of Thomas' it stated in the centre of the stone.

'Well, Jennifer Daykin,' he said eventually, 'it's three years today since you left me, so I've come to tell you all the things I should have said to you before you went away.'

For the next twenty minutes he stood, tears streaming down his face, talking to the headstone. He talked about love and loyalty and how proud he was of her. Then he talked about loss and pain and loneliness.

The dog, who had heard it all before, pulled against the lead, testing Daykin's grip and, when it didn't give, lay down on the grass and put its head on its front paws.

Jenny Templeman had been one of the best looking girls in the Dales and appeared not to know it. She was kind and witty and popular with men and women. Her parents' friends told them that she would marry well, the son of one of the landed gentry, and live in a fine house and never have to worry about money.

If she had given all that up for looks, some handsome, well-dressed young man, heads would shake but no one would blame her. But it was a mystery why she took up with the untidy, overweight, bespectacled local policeman.

She and Daykin knew why. They were best friends, lovers and soul mates. Their marriage was a team game, the two of them against the rest of the world. Their only disappointment was they didn't have children. They went for tests at the hospital and found that it wasn't one or other of them, it was both of them. By now they were just past the age of adopting, so they made do with spoiling their nephews and nieces. There were days when Daykin thought about his marriage and how, children apart, he could not have been happier. It was a day like that, a Tuesday he always remembered, when he came home to find that Jenny had laid the table with the best crockery and glassware. Two candles burnt in the silver candlesticks. She had cooked his favourite meal.

Over the meal she told him she had not been feeling well, had been to the doctor and he had sent her to the hospital. She had been told that morning that she had cancer, it had spread to her liver and there was nothing they could do. They gave her six months, but the cancer took her in three.

When Daykin had talked and cried himself dry, his gaze shifted from the grave to the dog.

'Come on, Royston, let's see if Mr Scanlon at the butcher's shop has a bone for you, then we'll go to the Malt Shovel.'

Mr Scanlon found a marrow bone and the dog followed Daykin through the front doors of the Malt Shovel, the bone clenched firmly between its teeth. It was a narrow doorway, the ancient terrazzo floor laid out in the name of a small brewery which had been taken over by the conglomerate which now owed the public house.

Through the inner door, kept closed by a spring to keep out the draughts, Daykin saw that it was quiet in the lounge bar, only two locals, Fred Knight and Paul Croft, both retired, making halves of mild ale last most of the afternoon. Daykin nodded a greeting to them both as he walked to the bar. They both nodded back, but nobody spoke.

In the other bar, to his right, the log fire, which would not be lit until the evening, was laid in the grate but the bar was empty.

'Hello, Tom,' said John Wolmersley, the landlord. 'I thought you were in Harrogate.'

'I am. Day off.'

'Pint?' asked Wolmersley, his hand reaching upwards towards the rack of silver tankards above the bar.

'Sounds good,' said Daykin.

John Wolmersley pulled the pint, put it on a beer mat in front of Daykin and folded his arms on the bar top.

'How's Harrogate?' he said.

'It's all right, John, but Jarvis conned me, there's no way I'm going to be there for only a couple of months.' Daykin stared at his pint morosely. 'And the beer's not as good,' he said.

'I suppose you've come home for Jenny,' said Wolmersley. 'Are the family coming round?'

'Yep, at six o'clock. Mum, my sisters and their husbands.'

'You cooking Jenny's favourite meal?'

'I've been to Scanlon's and got the fillet steak. Lobster bisque, Beef Wellington and crème brûlée.'

'Hadn't you better make a start?'

'One pint, John, and I will.'

Daykin was settling into his pint of beer as Terry Hudson drove into Cambridge city centre to find the small side street that housed The Russian Club.

It was an unremarkable building, distinguished from the others in the terrace only by a small brass sign on the door, announcing The Russian Club in small red letters, the word repeated in Cyrillic script.

The barman, who was drying glasses with a linen cloth, looked suspiciously at Terry Hudson as he entered the club. Hudson put his warrant card down on the bar top.

'I'm looking for Raisa Dunyasha.'

The barman looked down at the warrant card, then up at Hudson.

'I can't help you,' he said in a thick accent. 'I've worked here over fifteen years and I've never heard of her.'

'Is that *never heard of her*, never heard of her, or *never heard of her*, I don't want to tell you?'

'I've never heard of her, that's the truth.'

'Is there anybody here,' said Hudson, looking at the small groups of men sitting round the circular tables, 'whose memory goes back thirty years?'

The barman looked round the room.

'Dimitri,' he said finally. 'The club opened in the 1950s and Dimitri, as he will tell you, was a founding member. Hey, Dimitri!' he shouted. 'There's someone here wants to talk to you.'

An old, bald-headed man, one of a group of three at a table at the far end of the room, turned his head towards the bar, said something to the other two men, then got slowly to his feet and, just as slowly, shuffled across the room. He was a small man, neatly but cheaply dressed and, by the way he moved, he was not just old, he'd had a few to drink.

'I'm Sergeant Hudson,' said Terry Hudson, taking the warrant card off the bar and holding it up to the old man's face. 'I'm looking for Raisa Dunyasha.'

'Raisa?' said the old man, his eyes glazed over with either distant memory or alcohol. 'Yes, she used to work here,'

'She worked here?' said Hudson.

'Yes, I think there's a photograph of her.'

Dimitri began walking slowly round the edges of the room, staring at the photographs that hung on the walls.

'Here she is,' he said, pointing to a photo not far from where he had been sitting.

The barman, deciding to take charge, marched across the room and took the photograph from the wall, dusting the top of the frame as he held it out to Dimitri.

'We closed the club for refurbishment about thirty years ago,' said Dimitri. 'This is the photograph that was taken on our grand reopening night, the staff and some of the customers, there's me.' He pointed to a younger man with more hair and a moustache who was wearing what Terry Hudson later swore was the same suit.

'Which one is Raisa Dunyasha?' he asked.

'There she is,' said Dimitri, pointing at a young woman, her dark hair tied in a ponytail, who was standing, smiling, behind what Hudson now saw was the bar of the club.

'Where is she now?' he asked.

'Nobody knows,' said Dimitri. 'Something happened to her shortly after this photo was taken, and she didn't come back to the club. I heard some rumour that she had gone into nursing, but we haven't seen her since.'

'Do you have a photocopier?' asked Hudson.

'In the office,' said the barman.

'Can I have a copy of this photograph?'

'I don't see why not.'

With the photocopy of the photograph in his diary, Hudson said to Dimitri, 'thank you very much, you've been very helpful.'

'If you want to know anything about this club ask me, I'm a founder member.'

'I heard,' said Terry Hudson and walked out to his car to start the journey home. He would spend one more night in Harrogate and maybe go back to Scarborough tomorrow.

As Daykin opened the front door of his house, the familiar sights and sounds came to greet him at the door. And the smell of the place was the same, but never quite the same as when Jenny was there. There was always the background smell of her perfume. She was only woman he ever knew who wore that brand and every Christmas he bought her a bottle especially ordered by Mr Parsons at the chemist's. He stood by the door, remembering the other smells. Her bath salts when she decided to have a good long soak instead of a shower. The times when she had the day off and he would come home to the smell of freshly baked bread. She baked loaves in two terracotta flower pots and locally churned butter melting on to bread fresh from the oven was one of the simple luxuries of life.

He put the groceries he had bought on the draining board in the kitchen and spent twenty minutes looking round the house, reliving the memories. Then he started to cook the meal.

Chapter Twenty-one

Terry Hudson would be late for work, although he was out of bed in good time and ate his usual breakfast at the B & B, two fried eggs, bacon, sausage, baked beans and toast, washed down with two cups of tea. It was when he got to his car that there was a problem.

He saw it from forty yards away. Someone had poured acid all over the paintwork and it had bubbled like a leper's skin. Then he saw the splinter lines that ran in every direction across the windscreen and the smashed headlights. As he got closer to the vehicle, he could see that all the side windows were now piles of tiny pieces of glass, lying on the floor carpets, carpets that were now a pattern of dark and light where the bleach had been poured. The car stood on its wheel rims as all four tyres had been slashed. The seats had also been slashed, so that the foam was pushing through the leather like so many gaping wounds. Fabric hung down from the roof lining, cut in a giant cross from corner to corner. The dashboard had been smashed with great force with something heavy and all the dials had been forced from their mountings and lay in the driver's foot well.

In the middle of the steering wheel, the only undamaged item in the car, was a small computer-generated written note: 'This time it's just your car. Soon this could be you. Pay what you owe.'

Terry Hudson had bought the car, a twenty-year old Aston Martin, with the only big win he had ever had at a casino. In the divorce settlement he had fought hard to keep it and had had to give up a lot of other possessions to his wife. It was the only thing in life that he really loved. As he left it he was in tears.

'You're late,' said Daykin, as Hudson walked into the incident room at nearly nine o'clock. It was a statement, not an accusation.

'Sorry, Tom, kids have vandalized my car.'

'Badly?'

'It's a write-off.'

'We'll deal with that later. You and I are going to Liverpool.'

'Mo Bateman?'

'Yes. I guess there's no choice about which car we take.'

Terry Hudson grimaced.

'We're not taking the dog, are we?'

'He's always wanted to see Liverpool.'

Daykin looked at the other officers, working at the tables.

'While I get the car started, brief Bridget, everything you know about Raisa Dunyasha. While we're gone she'll see if she can turn anything up on her. You can tell me about her in the car.'

By the time they reached the M62 Daykin knew as much about Raisa Dunyasha as Terry Hudson did.

'Give Bridget a call will you, tell her to try Equity to see if Raisa Dunyasha is working in show business. Tell her to call any Russian clubs in other cities, there maybe a federation that will give her all the names and addresses, try the Russian Embassy to see if they have any records of her renewing her passport, the registry of births, deaths and marriages, the Inland Revenue, the National Health Service and the Home Office: she may have applied for British Citizenship. Can you think of anything else?'

Terry Hudson's pen caught up with Daykin and he shook his head.

After Hudson had finished his phone call to Bridget Cooper they drove in silence for fifteen minutes.

'Tell me about your car,' said Daykin, as they started the long descent from Yorkshire into Lancashire and passed the dark stone monolith mounted with a large red rose that marked the border.

'As I said, kids vandalized it.'

'Kids smash the side window to steal a mobile phone or a laptop computer. If they really don't like you, they might slash a couple of tyres. Kids don't total a car, so what happened?'

'I don't know. I thought it was kids.'

'You're a good copper, Terry, the reason I send you out to interview people is because I know you'll come back with the goods. I need you on this case. I will do all I can to protect you from whoever damaged your car, but I won't do a damn thing if you lie to me. So, crunch time, what's this about?'

Terry Hudson reached for a cigarette, then thought better of it. He started to bite his lower lip, a habit he had had since childhood when he had an important decision to make.

'I owe some money,' he said eventually.

'Who to?'

'It was my bookmaker, but he's sold the debt on.'

'How much?'

'About fifteen thousand.'

'Bloody hell, Terry. So you've no chance of raising it anytime soon?'

'Maybe in about six months, but these people won't wait that long.'

'Who are they?

'I don't know and my bookmaker won't tell me. All I know is that the debt collector is a man called Garvey.'

'Do you have any other names for him, or a description?'

'No name, but one of my neighbours has met him, so I can get a description.'

'Do you have a mobile number for him?'

Terry Hudson nodded.

'Call him now. If he's watching you, which he probably is, I'd like to be able to put a face to the name.'

'What then?'

'If they're as short-handed as they claim in Harrogate, they must have some spare CID cars. I'll arrange with Wainwright to allocate one to you. If this man Garvey found your car, it's a fair bet he knew where you were staying last night. I'm moving into a flat this evening, you'd better stay with me. Do you sleep all right on a sofa?'

Daykin parked his car just off Boaler Street and they walked until they found a doorway with a sign above it showing the silhouettes of two girls pole dancing and, in a semicircle on gold letters over that, the words Starlight Lap Dancing Club. The men who came through the entrance came only to watch naked girls, so nobody had wasted money making the doorway expensive or even appealing. The doors had been painted a dull matt black years ago and, in spite of the scratches, dents and scuff marks, they had not been repainted. The sign above the door, when floodlit at night, appeared glamorous and inviting but now, in the daylight, it just looked drab.

There was no one guarding the door so Daykin and Hudson went into the club. The first things Daykin noticed was the way the floor sloped down towards the stage and the ornate plastic mouldings on the walls and ceilings. It must have been a cinema in a former life. Now the rows of seats in the auditorium had been replaced by small tables, surrounded by chairs, all leaning at an angle. The black ceiling, from which the spotlights shone at show time, was now lit by fifteen 100 watt bulbs, casting harsh light and shadows on to the floor.

In the centre of the auditorium, chewing frantically on some gum, was a pitbull of a man with a round, snub-nosed face and a short, thick neck that seem to grow out of his muscular shoulders. He was glowering quiet fierce intimidation towards three young women on the stage. They largely ignored him, standing talking to each other, their body language screaming boredom. Two of them had one arm across their midriffs, holding the elbow of the other arm, their forearms pointing straight up, the fingers holding cigarettes. Occasionally, almost in unison, they put the cigarettes to their mouths and blew the smoke away from each other at the third girl, flicking the ash on to the stage.

'Let's get this fucking show on the road!' roared the man. The women all looked at him, more in disinterest than fear.

'Before you do that,' said Daykin, 'can we have a word?'

The pitbull turned to face them.

'Who the fuck are you?' he shouted.

Daykin showed him his warrant card.

'I'd like to see Mo Bateman.'

'He's not in.'

'There's a brand new Bentley parked outside in a street of Ford Escorts. Tell me that's not his.'

'It is, but he went out.'

'One last chance, do I see Mo Bateman?'

The man stopped chewing for a moment. 'Go stuff yourself.'

Daykin looked at the three women on the stage. 'You see the girl on the left? She's under sixteen.'

The man turned round to look at the stage.

'She ain't.'

'I'm so sure that she is that I can get a warrant to raid this club.'

'You wouldn't dare.'

'And,' continued Daykin evenly, 'with the way the courts look after children these days, I can turn up here with two dozen very large coppers in full uniform. I won't come at this time of the day, I'll come right in the middle of your show and those coppers will start asking your customers some very searching questions. And when Mr Bateman wants to know why his club has been raided, I'll tell him it was your fault. Do I see him, or do you want me to go and get my warrant?'

The man started chewing again, more frantically than before.

'Wait there,' he said and walked towards a door in the far wall. 'You three,' he shouted at the girls on the stage. 'Take five!'

The girls ignored him and carried on smoking and talking.

Just before he went through the door, as a parting shot, the man pointed to the girl on the left of the group.

'And you! I want to see a birth certificate!'

When the door the pitbull had gone through opened five minutes later it was filled by a man much larger in every way. He was about six feet three, his head and shoulders touching the door frame. He had a crew cut of black hair and a pair of mutton chop sideboards. He was dressed in a maroon suit and, under it, a black sweatshirt. He scowled at them.

'Mr Bateman says he'll see you,' growled the man in the doorway in a low guttural voice that exactly matched his appearance.

'You lead on when your ready,' said Daykin pleasantly.

The man's scowl deepened, he wasn't used to polite conversation. He grunted and turned to walk up the flight of stairs to his right. At the top of the chairs, at what looked to Daykin like a steel door, the man knocked. A voice inside the room shouted something and the man opened the door and stepped aside to let them in. As he did so the big man scowled at them again, but he may have been just practising his scowl.

They walked in to find a man standing in the centre of the room, facing them. If anything, he was larger than the man in the maroon suit. He wore a pair of jeans and a T-shirt, both very tight to show off the muscles that bulged in every direction, a testament to hours on a weight bench and steroids.

Just visible at his neck was a thick chain, his wrist watch was large and diamond encrusted, he wore four rings, a black onyx signet ring, a tri-coloured wedding ring, a sovereign ring and a large diamond ring. On his right wrist was a heavy bracelet. His hair, pure white, was combed straight back, the white hair contrasting with the even suntan that came from a recent exotic holiday, not a sun bed.

'Inspector Daykin,' he said, smiling an even smile and offering his hand. 'You don't need to threaten my club manager to see me, I'm always happy to help the police.'

As he said this, the man in the maroon suit followed them into the room, closed the door and stood with his back to it. Nobody was leaving unless Mo said so.

Sitting on a sofa to their right was another man. He leaned back in the sofa, one leg crossed casually over the other, texting someone on his mobile phone. He appeared uninterested in them, but Daykin could tell that he was watching them carefully. Daykin shook hands.

'We're looking for a woman named Kim Nixon,' he said.

'Kim Nixon?' the man frowned. 'Can't say I've ever heard of her.

Why are you asking me?'

'We believe she worked for you about thirty years ago.'

'Thirty years? Before I did my last stretch? Nah, I can't remember every girl in my clubs from so long ago, sorry I can't help you.'

'She lived with you.'

'I don't think so. I'd remember her if she lived with me, and I haven't a clue what you're talking about.'

'She worked for you, she lived with you, then something made her leave suddenly. She went to Cambridge where she continued working. She was gang-raped by a group of students. Now they're being killed and we think you may have some answers we need,' said Daykin.

The man held his hands out in an expression of regret. The movement put the T-shirt in danger of ripping at the seams.

'Sorry, Inspector. Can't help you.'

The man on the sofa put down the mobile phone and stood up.

'Cambridge she went to, was it?' he said. He looked at the man in the T shirt and jeans. 'OK, Lenny, I'll have a word with them.'

He turned back to Daykin and Terry Hudson.

'I'm Mo Bateman,' he said. 'I just wanted to see how much you knew.'

For the first time Daykin took a good look at him.

Mo Bateman wasn't as large or as flashy as Lenny, and he had more class. Not muscular, but he was in good physical shape and his expensive clothes hung well on his lean frame. The wrist watch was gold but with a thin, black leather strap and the shoes, black lizard skin, looked handmade. He was about sixty years old but his full head of hair hadn't any grey in it.

If it wasn't for his eyes, he would be just another well-dressed, wealthy man. The eyes, pale blue, seemed bluer against the surrounding whites and they had a fierce barely hidden fire in them. They were the eyes of a man who was used to having his own way.

'Have you found her?' asked Mo Bateman, walking to one of the windows in his office and looking out on to the street.

'Not yet; that's why we're here, we thought you may be able to help,' said Daykin.

Bateman turned round.

'That little tart took five thousand of my money with her when she left. Do you think that if I knew where she was I wouldn't have gone to have a chat with her?'

Nobody in the room doubted what Mo Bateman's chat would involve.

'There's another reason we're here,' said Daykin. 'Some of the men involved in Miss Nixon's rape have been killed.'

'What, you think I'd lift one finger to help that little slut? You must be off your head.'

'What was your relationship with Kim Nixon?'

Mo Bateman now moved to sit at his desk, but turned his chair so he was still staring out of the window and he was half hidden from Daykin by the large leather back of the chair.

'She was just a scrubber on the make,' came the voice from behind the chair back. 'She latched on to me because I was the boss. I gave her a good time, but when she could see it wasn't going to go any further, she pissed off with five grand of my money. That's it. Apart from the money I never want to see her again.'

'Can you tell us,' said Terry Hudson, 'where you were on 19 October and 2 December?'

'What is this, an interrogation?' Bateman reached for the phone on his desk. 'Do I need a lawyer?'

'If you just answer the question you don't.'

Mo Bateman put the phone back in its cradle.

'To be honest,' he said, 'I can't be bothered trying to remember. You've overstayed your welcome. Get out.'

He nodded to the man in the maroon suit, who opened the door.

'I'm running a quiet little business,' he shouted. 'We invest in people.'

As he went down the stairs Daykin could hear the man in the T-shirt laughing.

They went back through the club. One of the girls who had been on the stage was gyrating round a vertical brass pole. Everyone, including her, looked bored to death.

Chapter Twenty-two

They were half a mile from the motorway when Daykin's mobile phone rang. He scrambled in his pockets for it while trying to drive. He looked at the number as he opened it. It was the incident room.

'Daykin,' he said.

'It's Sarah Fanson, sir. You're not going to like this.'

'Try me.'

'Darius Moore, sir. He's dead.'

Daykin took a long, deep breath. 'Where, when, how and how do you know?'

'In his office, yesterday afternoon. There's no doubt about whether he was murdered or not, he got a carving knife through his neck. Berkshire Police were looking through the records and saw you'd visited him recently, so they phoned us.'

Daykin glanced at his watch.

'I'll be back in two hours. I want everyone in a meeting in the incident room at three. In the meantime get on to Berkshire, will you, find out who is in charge and see if you can persuade him to fax me a summary of what he's got so far.'

'Anything else?'

'Contact Freeman, Ellington and Cunningham. Make sure none of them has slipped off the coil. And tell them about Moore, offer them protection. That's it for now. I'll call you if anything else strikes me.'

He shut the phone and was about to put it back in his pocket when it rang again.

'Tom, Trevor Wainwright. Have you heard about Darius Moore?'

'Yes, sir, I've just been told.'

'God, Tom, this is a mess. The Press will have a field day if they get wind of it, we're supposed to be protecting these people.'

'We've offered to give them protection, they all refused.'

'Let's not discuss this on the phone. Are you on your way back to the station?'

'I'll be back in about two hours, sir.'

'Come straight to my office as soon as you get back, Tom. We need to decide the best way forward.'

On the journey from Liverpool to Harrogate, Daykin and Hudson talked about Moore's death and about Mo Bateman. When they arrived at the station Terry Hudson went to check if any faxes had arrived from Berkshire and to dig up some background on Moore. Daykin went to Superintendent Wainwright's office door and knocked.

'Sit down, Tom,' said Wainwright, after he had ushered Daykin in, 'and tell me what you know about this new death.'

'You probably know as much as I do, sir. Darius Moore was the bishop of a fringe church called the Church of Enlightened Reality. There is a compound near Reading, in it are the church, a school and some other buildings. It is surrounded by a high wall and the only entrance is guarded by a security officer. Yesterday morning Moore was stabbed and killed.'

Superintendent Wainwright took out his small leather-bound notebook.

'You met him, what was he like?'

'A bit patronizing, vain, arrogant and a snob.'

'You liked him, then?'

'For all that, he was all right. He didn't deserve a carving knife shoved through his neck.'

'Any suspects?'

'We're still trying to trace Kim Nixon and we've just come back from Liverpool. One of her ex boyfriends, a local villain called Mo Bateman is more than capable of doing that to Darius Moore.'

'While you're here, give me a general update.'

For the next twenty minutes Daykin told his superintendent everything about the case from the time he had been given Van Meer's file to the meeting with Mo Bateman.

'I think we had better tackle the Press head on,' said Wainwright, when he had finished. 'I'll organize a Press conference.'

The meeting in the superintendent's office made Daykin late for his own meeting in the incident room and by the time he got there he could hear the sound of several informal conversations before he opened the door. In the room the six people were sitting around one of the tables. There were several empty coffee cups and bottles of water on it.

'Change of direction,' said Daykin as he walked to the front of the room. 'Darius Moore's death means we are now sure that we are dealing with a serial killer. That adds urgency both to tracing him or her and to protecting the three who are left.

'Bob, I'm assigning you to Clive Ellington. Go to see him, see if you can persuade him to have protection. That may be easier now. If he won't co-operate, make the arrangements anyway. He's a serving prisoner so we can make decisions for him. Martin, you've got Cunningham; the same applies. Sarah, you take Freeman. Bridget, find out everything you can about Mo Bateman, particularly where he was on 19 October and 2 December. I want to know everything about him from his kindergarden teacher's name to his inside leg measurement. Did you find anything on Raisa Dunyasha?'

'No, sir. She a mystery.'

'Frazer,' continued Daykin, 'you get to stay here to input everything into the computer. Terry, anything from Berkshire?'

'Not yet, Tom. I can tell you the officer in charge of the case is Inspector Barker, stationed at Reading.'

'Frazer, chase that up. I want to see anything as soon as it comes through. Terry, you and I will have to find Kim Nixon.'

'Try to find her,' said Terry Hudson.

'No, we will find her and within forty-eight hours. OK,' he said, turning to the others in the room, 'let's get on with it before one of the last three gets himself killed.'

Daykin and Hudson spent the next three hours making phone calls. They telephoned the Department of Work and Pensions, the Russian Embassy, credit card companies, the DVLA, the Inland Revenue, Somerset House, the Home Office and more local councils than they could count. Nobody had heard of Raisa Dunyasha and there was no record of her anywhere. Daykin sat back in his chair, took off his glasses and polished the lenses, gazing absently at the desktop. After five minutes he put the glasses back on and got up.

'Where are you going?' asked Terry Hudson.

'To take the dog for a walk.'

Royston had the run of The Stray. He bounced unthreateningly round small children, played tag with the other dogs and wandered off on his own, always keeping Daykin in sight. Daykin sat on a park bench and stared into the far distance, deep in thought.

When he came back to the station 40 minutes later Daykin sat down with a sigh in a plastic chair in the incident room.

'Deed poll,' he said.

'What poll?' asked Terry Hudson.

'Deed poll. She changed her named by deed poll. She wanted to cut all ties with the past and the rape so she changed her name. That's why we can't find her.'

'Great. So now all we have to do is to find the solicitor who drafted the deed poll and ask him what her new name is.'

'Maybe not. It's not who drafted the deed poll, it's what she did with it. She must have used it to change documents, like her driving licence and passport. Call the Russian Embassy again and ask if their records show passports being issued in a changed name. Didn't the old man at the Russian Club say something about nursing? I'll ask the Royal College of Nursing about deed polls and changes of name.'

When Terry Hudson put his phone down nearly half an hour later he smiled triumphantly at Daykin.

'Got her!' he said.

'Katrina Voitskaya,' said Daykin impassively.

'How did you know?'

'The college didn't have a Raisa Dunyasha, but when I mentioned a change of name their records department said that they had a piece of software that traces the name backwards through any changes. They need it because so many nurses get married and change their surnames.'

'Very bloody clever,' said Hudson. 'I'm going to make a cup of tea.'

When he came back with two mugs of tea Daykin said, 'Once you've stopped sulking, do you want to tell me about the Russian Embassy?'

'Pretty much the same story. She applied for a new ten-year passport, then two years later sent it back with a copy of the deed poll and asked them to change the name to Katrina Voitskaya.'

He took a drink from his mug and swore loudly when it burnt his tongue. 'What now?' he said, gently feeling his tongue with his forefinger and thumb.

'She's a pretty nurse with a new identity. She used her charms to get Mo Bateman, what would you do if you were her?'

'I'd set my sights on a consultant surgeon.'

'The Royal College of Nursing say that the last trace they had of her was at Nottingham General Hospital twenty-six years ago. Perhaps that's where she caught her surgeon.'

Twenty-six years is a long time in the life of a hospital and after Daykin called them he was taken on a carousel of departments and people until he spoke to a semi-retired consultant who had been a registrar when Staff Nurse Katrina Voitskaya married the hospital's up-and-coming bone specialist, Dr Charles Appleyard, fifteen years her senior.

'Is he still alive?' asked Daykin.

'Retired to improve his golf handicap two years ago.'

'Do you know where he lives?'

'I should do, my wife and I were there for dinner last Saturday.'

'We know where she is,' said Daykin, as he put the phone down.

'We're not setting off now?' asked Terry Hudson, looking at the clock on the wall above the door.

'She's been there over twenty years, one more day won't make any difference. Besides,' he said, watching Fritz Schmidt walk towards him with an armful of fax paper, 'I think you and I have some homework to do.'

'Present from Inspector Barker, sir,' said Schmidt, as he dumped the papers on to the table, 'he says he's sent most of the paperwork because he'd value a second opinion.'

'He can have my boot up his backside for a second opinion,' muttered Terry Hudson.

'The sooner we get started—' said Daykin, as he pulled some of the papers towards him.

'Yeah, I know, the sooner we get finished.'

Terry Hudson moved his chair to sit opposite Daykin and they began sifting through the crime reports, storm logs, photographs, witness statements, CSI data, pathologist report, house-to-house enquiries, a forensic dossier and intelligence documents. The light outside faded to black, the other officers went home and the station changed shifts, but by 10.30 they were finished.

'Let's see if you agree with what I have,' said Daykin, leaning back in his chair and stretching his arms high above his head.

'As the staff were always at the church on Sundays, most of them took Thursdays off, so there weren't many people around. Bishop Moore wrote his sermon on Thursday morning and, if he wanted peace and quiet, he often locked the door of his office. There was nothing unusual about the day. The security guard logged a delivery lorry in at nine-twenty, the usual driver delivering groceries, and the postman came with some letters and one package about fifteen minutes later. A routine security patrol of the grounds didn't show any break-ins or anyone having scaled the perimeter walls.

'About twelve, Bishop Moore left in his four x four, saying that he was going into town to get a new battery for his watch. He returned about half an hour later. He went, as far as anyone knows, straight back to his office where he locked the door. We know that because Mrs Francis, his secretary, had left some papers in the office and she tried the door at about one o'clock.

'Mrs Francis always made the Bishop a cup of tea at 3.30 and she knocked on the door when she took it to his office. She stood there for two or three minutes and when he didn't answer her knocking she went back to her room and called his telephone extension. He didn't pick up the phone so she called security. They tried the windows to his office, but they were locked and the curtains were closed. Eventually, someone had the courage to get a fire extinguisher and batter the door open.

'Darius Moore was sitting at his desk, palms flat on the desk top, eyes wide open, staring at the door as they came through it. Then they noticed the carving knife sticking straight through his neck. It had gone in just below his left ear and the point had come out nicking the lobe of his right ear. The pathologist thinks it was an underarm blow struck by someone standing to his left. That person was probably between five feet two and five feet seven inches tall. The key to the office wasn't found, so whoever killed him had locked the door on their way out and took it with them.

'There are no forensics to speak of, no eye-witnesses and no suspects. Have I missed anything?'

'There was a broom closet next to the bishop's office, traces of his blood were found in that closet, apart from that, that seems to be about the size of it, Tom,' said Terry Hudson, getting up and putting on his jacket. 'Are we done for tonight?'

'Not quite. We need a theory to fit the facts. Whoever killed Darius Moore wasn't seen entering or leaving the compound or anywhere inside it. Suggestions?'

'He wasn't noticed because he was one of the staff who were always there.'

'Possibly, but most of them have no motive or opportunity. And they have alibis, they were nearly all working with someone else at the time he was killed.'

'So you're saying that someone got into the compound without being seen, killed Bishop Moore and then left, again without anyone noticing them? It sounds like a 1930s detective story to me. Where's Hercule Poirot when you need him?'

'See if this makes any sense. Someone came into the compound to kill Darius Moore. The only way they could get past the guard was by hiding in a vehicle and the only vehicles to enter the compound were the delivery lorry and Bishop Moore's four x four. The delivery driver would have seen her, she could only have been in the cab, or where he carried the groceries. She must have come past the security guard in Moore's car, so he must have known she was in there.

'He couldn't get to Reading, have his watch battery changed and get back in thirty minutes. He met her, she hid in his car – it was a good car to hide in as it is high off the ground and high waisted – and he smuggled her into his office.'

'You keep saying "she", why?'

'Look at the size of the person who killed him. He was heterosexual, so if he was smuggling someone into the compound for sexual reasons, it had to be a woman. Thursdays were quiet days, ideal for an afternoon of passion in the office with the curtains drawn and the door locked.'

'How did she get out?'

'She killed Moore, walked out of the office, locking the door behind her, then hid in the broom closet until the security guard was in Moore's office, then she simply walked out of the compound.'

'Raisa Dunyasha or Katrina Voitskaya or whatever she calls herself?'

'She now calls herself Katrina Appleyard at a guess. Maybe her, maybe not. It seems too neat a package if it is her.'

Terry Hudson looked at his watch. 'Do we have time for a pint?'

'I'm going to rustle something up to eat, I've got a bottle of wine in the fridge.'

'I'd prefer beer.'

'Lager? I have a couple of cans.'

'That will do.'

Daykin collected Royston from the kennels and the three of them walked to Daykin's car. As they got in Terry Hudson picked up an unread newspaper and a soft drinks can from the passenger foot well and tossed them on to the back seat. The dog, who was sitting on the seat, looked at the paper and the can and then at Hudson, turned its back on him and lay down.

The flat Daykin had rented was on the third floor of a modern block to the east of the town. The public areas were freshly painted and the oatmeal carpet showed no signs of wear or staining. By the entrance door was an oriental table with a white orchid on it. Hudson stroked one of the petals as he went past. It was imitation, but a nice touch.

They took the lift and Daykin unlocked the door to a neatly furnished flat with an open kitchen, two doors to the right leading to the bathroom and bedroom and full-length windows, through which Terry Hudson could just see a small balcony overlooking, he guessed, open fields. He put his battered holdall on the sofa.

137

'Help yourself to a beer, they're in the fridge,' said Daykin, walking to the kitchen, 'and pour me a wine, will you?'

He took a white porcelain bowl and a small whisk from one of the eye-level cupboards.

'It's late. I don't want anything too heavy, do you like Eggs Benedict?'

'Fine,' said Hudson, pouring the beer. He had no idea what Eggs Benedict were.

Daykin cracked an egg into the palm of his left hand and let the white drip through his fingers into the sink. He put the egg yolk in the bowl and separated two more eggs. Then he put some butter in a pan over a low heat and let it melt while he beat the egg yolks with the whisk. After he had put four split muffins under the grill he added Tabasco sauce, paprika and lemon juice to the egg yolks then, whisking vigorously, he slowly added the melted butter. He set the bowl over a pot of hot water and replaced the muffins under the grill with four slices of ham. While the ham was heating he poached four eggs, then put two muffin halves on plates, topped each with the ham, a poached egg and hollandaise sauce. He put the two plates on the kitchen table.

'Ready?' he said to Terry Hudson.

'Sure, do you mind if I grab another beer?'

'You know where they are.'

They sat down and ate the meal in silence. Terry Hudson hadn't realized how hungry he was. When he had finished, he wiped his mouth on the napkin Daykin had laid on the table.

'In some ways you're a strange man, Tom,' he said.

Daykin took a sip of his wine.

'How so?'

'I have a mate who transferred to Scarborough from Shapford. When I started working with you I rang him to see what he knew about you. No offence, I just like to know who I'm working with.'

'And what did he tell you?' asked Daykin, stacking the plates.

'That you were a very good rugby player. You played for Yorkshire and everyone knew it was only a matter of time before you got the call from England. Then you broke your leg and it ended your career.'

'Not so,' said Daykin, taking the plates to the sink and starting the water running.

'No?' said Terry Hudson.

'Ankle. It was my ankle that was broken.'

'But the rest is true?'

'Just about. I do a bit of coaching now.'

'And Cambridge, you had a scholarship to go to Cambridge, but you didn't go.'

'Yes.'

'What happened?'

'My father died.'

'So?'

'I had a widowed mother and three sisters to look after. How could I go off and abandon them? So I joined the police force instead.'

'Hell of a sacrifice, Tom.'

Daykin shrugged. 'Family,' he said.

'There's only one good thing,' said Hudson.

'What's that?'

'If you'd gone to Cambridge, you might have joined The Greenrush Club.'

'I don't think so.'

Terry Hudson looked round the kitchen. 'Have you got an ashtray?'

'No, that's because no one smokes in here.'

'I'll go outside then.'

'Do you want coffee?'

'Sure.'

While Terry Hudson went out on to the balcony Daykin scooped coffee into a large cafetiére and poured hot water on to it. He set the oven timer for seven minutes and washed up. When Hudson came back into the flat the timer on the oven was sounding and the cups and saucers had been placed beside the cafetiére on the kitchen table.

'When you're not gambling, what do you do off duty?' asked Daykin, as Terry Hudson sat down opposite him.

'I watch a bit of football. I used to play.'

'Were you any good?'

'I think maybe I was. I got signed as an apprentice by Rochdale when I was sixteen years old and two years later I had just broken into the first team. Then the manager called me in and said that Everton had had a look at me and were interested in signing me.'

'So you should be retiring now as a premiership footballer, but you're a detective sergeant in Scarborough. What went wrong?'

'The medical at Everton. They found a hole in the heart. Who wants a midfield dynamo with a dicky heart? Everton didn't want me and neither did any of the other big clubs. About six weeks later, the manager phoned me – he couldn't even do it face to face. He said they'd spoken to their insurance company and would have to let me go, they couldn't risk me keeling over in the centre circle during a match.

'These days I'd have had an agent who would have redrawn my contract to give me a pension, compensation if I was injured or medically unfit, and a thousand other benefits. The only person who looked at my contract was my dad and he was a fireman.

'When Rochdale let me go no professional club wanted anything to do with me, so I played a bit of semi-pro soccer for clubs that didn't have any money, so they didn't care if I died on them. By the time I went down to the amateur game, I decided I needed a full-time job. I applied to the police, and here's the final irony, I passed the medical A1. It turns out the Everton doctor got it wrong, there was no hole in my heart. By that time it was too late for a football career, so here I am.'

'Did the gambling go with the football?'

'Yeah, it's a lad culture. We'd go down to the training ground at ten and be finished by one. That left the rest of the afternoon free and some of the senior professionals at Rochdale went to the bookies. I started joining them, a couple of afternoons a week at first. By the time I left Rochdale it was every training day and I'd be the first into the betting shop and the last to leave.'

Daykin drank his coffee and put his mug in the sink. He went into the bedroom and came back to the living room with a duvet and a pillow.

'I hope the sofa is comfortable. Get some sleep, we've an early start in the morning.'

'How early?' asked Terry Hudson suspiciously.

'We need to be on the road by six.'

Chapter Twenty-three

Terry Hudson hated early mornings. He liked to get up when the day was light and he wasn't so tired he felt sick. He never ate breakfast and now he sat in the passenger seat of Daykin's car, his stomach growling, half listening to a current affairs programme on the radio, smelling the dog's wet fur and badly needing a cigarette.

'There's a café just before we get on to the M1,' said Daykin, turning the radio off, 'they serve passable coffee. We're making good time so we'll stop there for fifteen minutes.'

Faced with the imminent twin rushes of café and nicotine, Terry Hudson cheered up.

'This Russian bint,' he said, as he walked into the café, breathing cigarette odour, sat down and wrapped his hands round a large mug of coffee, 'do you think she did it?'

'And as soon as we knock on the door, she collapses on to her hall carpet and confesses everything? No, its never that simple, is it?'

'Mo Bateman?'

'With the choice of him or the wife of a consultant bone specialist, my money would be on him.'

Hudson took a long gulp of coffee.

'You think there's something else, don't you?'

'All we can do is follow the leads we've got. I wouldn't be surprised if we get taken off in another direction.'

Daykin took the dog for a short walk while Terry Hudson refuelled his nicotine tank, then they set off towards the motorway junction.

If Daykin had bothered to think about the house the Appleyards lived in, the reality would have matched his imagination. It stood on a wide street of detached suburban houses, the boundaries of its land marked by solid brick walls. Looking through the wrought-iron gates, they could see a long straight gravel drive leading to the front door of the house. Either side of the drive were twin lawns, rolling down from the house through two large tiers. At the centre of each was a hexagonal rose bed, divided by patterns of bricks laid at angles into the soil. The roses had been pruned hard back at the end of the summer, but by next spring would be a giant splash of colour in the middle of each lawn.

The house itself was the best imitation Tudor that modern builders could manage. Steeply pitched roofs, ornate chimneys and black beams against white stucco.

To the right of the house, Daykin could see a small greenhouse, the windows misted with condensation from an internal heater and just beyond the greenhouse, the wooden frames of two compost heaps, their tops covered by tarpaulin weighted down with old tyres.

The front door, half hidden in the shadows of a deep porch, was painted white, the woodwork shiny and spotless. Pinned to the door by a drawing pin was a piece of cardboard that read 'Delivery men, please ring bell and wait.' Daykin pressed the bell. He was about to press it again when the door was opened slowly with a lot of effort by a stooped middle-aged woman. As she looked up at Daykin there was no mistaking the face of Katrina Voitskaya, the young woman in the photograph at The Russian Club. Her long hair was no longer dark brown, it had faded to several shades of grey and it was cut in the shorter, more sophisticated style of a middle-aged woman. Her figure, once lithe, was much fuller and her face was now wrinkled, not with deep creases but with the fine lines of a woman who takes care of her skin. If the years had changed her appearance, they had not altered the look in her large brown eyes, or the set of her full-lipped mouth.

Daykin gently kicked Terry Hudson's foot to stop him staring at the other thing that was obvious about Katrina Appleyard. One hand held the door open, the other was on the handle of a small trolley. Resting on the trolley was an oxygen cylinder from the top of which two narrow plastic tubes were draped over her right shoulder, ending in a clip which held them to her nostrils.

'Mrs Appleyard?' asked Daykin, politely.

She nodded, as if a verbal answer would take too much energy.

Daykin held out his warrant card.

'I'm Inspector Daykin, this is Sergeant Hudson, we'd like to talk to you.'

She took three full breaths of oxygen through her nose before she answered.

'I'm not used to having the police call at my house, Inspector. I'm sure you have a good reason.'

She spoke in a very detached upper-middle-class way, the sentences clipped and the vowels rounded. All trace of her Russian accent had almost, but not quite, disappeared.

'We'd like to talk to you about a room above a pub in Cambridge thirty years ago and some young men called The Greenrush Club.'

Her breathing, already laboured, grew worse.

'How dare you' – she paused for breath – 'come to my door raising long dead ghosts! I won't speak to you!'

She started to shut the door but Daykin put his foot in the way.

'At least three of the men in the room that night have been murdered. We need to find out who is killing them and why.'

'They are getting what they deserve.'

'If three of them raped you, then nine were innocent. You wouldn't want them killed, would you?'

'I am indifferent.'

'Mrs Appleyard,' said Daykin, 'this isn't going to go away. If you don't talk to us now other officers will come back, perhaps with a search warrant.'

He let the words sink in.

'You'd better come in,' she said eventually and grudgingly.

While Terry Hudson closed the front door Daykin followed the oxygen cylinder through the entrance hall. At the far end was a sideboard with two vases of flowers and, on the wall behind it, a long mirror. Mrs Appleyard would have used it in the days before her illness limited journeys out of the house, to check her appearance just before she went out. Now she didn't even glance at it. She led them into a spacious living room with a black baby grand piano by the window, covered with silver-framed family photographs. She sat down on a Regency sofa and waved an almost regal hand to them to sit in the chairs opposite her.

Daykin watched, fascinated, as she bent down, turned off the oxygen supply, unclipped the pipes from her nose and laid them across the top of the tank. Then she reached into her handbag beside her on the sofa, took out a packet of cigarettes, put one in her mouth and lit it with a small gold lighter. She inhaled deeply and blew out the smoke.

'Don't worry, Inspector,' she said softly, 'I can't do myself any more harm. You will have guessed that I have emphysema. My husband, as you would expect, has a wide circle of friends in medicine and I have seen the best specialists. It is only a matter of time before my lungs fill with fluid and it will all be over.

'So,' she said, studying the cigarette, 'these little rascals caused it and I hope will now speed my end.'

Terry Hudson was searching for his own cigarettes. Daykin saw him and shook his head firmly.

'Tell us about Cambridge,' he said, as she gently tapped the end of the cigarette on the edge of a porcelain ashtray.

'I can't give you long,' she began, 'my husband will be home soon and I would prefer it if you were gone by then.'

Daykin didn't say anything, he just sat and watched her.

'We have a good marriage and we've brought up three children we can be proud of. But my husband doesn't know anything about Cambridge, except that I arrived there from Russia and got a job in a couple of pubs – he doesn't even know their names – while I finished my nursing studies. Then I moved around a few hospitals before I met and married him.'

'Does your husband know anything about Mo Bateman?'

For the second time she seemed lost for words.

'Where on earth does he come into all this?' she asked eventually.

'We were hoping you might tell us,' said Terry Hudson.

She looked at him for a long time before speaking, as if trying to decide whether to tell some terrible secret.

'Mo Bateman,' she began, 'I heard somewhere he was in prison.'

'He was released about two years ago,' said Hudson.

'Yes,' she said after taking another long draw on the cigarette, 'I suppose he would be by now. If you have any dealings with him, Inspector' – she turned back to look at Daykin – 'be very careful, he is a dangerous, dangerous man.'

'What makes you say that?'

'He thrives on violence.'

'He's a sadist?' said Hudson.

'No, he doesn't get any sexual pleasure out of hurting people, he just enjoys violence.'

'Did he ever hit you?' asked Daykin.

She stubbed the cigarette out and watched the last wisps of smoke die away in the ashtray.

'Not at first. But then it started, as I suppose I always knew it would. When it got too bad I left him.'

'Taking some of his money with you?' asked Hudson.

She turned her head with surprising speed to look at him.

'Is that what he told you? No, I didn't steal any of his money. That would have made him come after me and I didn't want anything else to do with him.'

'Do you know how he made his money?' asked Daykin.

She smiled for the first time since she had opened the door.

'He used to say who needs a university degree when you can sell girls, gambling and guns? I knew that's how he could afford his lifestyle, but did I know anything about how he operated? No, this wasn't a small family business where the girlfriend is invited to sit on the board of directors. I was there to warm his bed and look good on his arm, nothing else.'

'Is he a killer?' asked Terry Hudson.

This time she did not even bother to look at him. She busied herself reconnecting the tubes to her face and taking deep breaths of oxygen.

'Mo Bateman came from the back streets of Liverpool, he carved a little crime empire for himself in Kensington. If people crossed him, or tried to muscle in on his turf, they got hurt. There were rumours of people disappearing. Knowing Mo, knowing what he did for a living, I'd be surprised if he hadn't killed a few people over the years.'

'Did he know you'd been raped?' asked Daykin.

'I don't know, I've not had any contact with him since I left him.'

'How would he take it if he knew?'

'After a few drinks one night he once said people didn't take liberties with him or anyone close to him, that he'd settle any scores.'

There was silence in the room.

'I know this may bring back painful memories, but we have to know. Tell us about the night you were raped, in as much detail as you can remember,' said Daykin.

'Must I?'

'And then we'll go,' promised Daykin.

She looked at her handbag, as if deciding whether to have another cigarette. Instead she toyed nervously with the string of pearls round her neck.

'When I came to England, I settled in Liverpool and I was very short of money,' she began. 'In those days work permits were nearly impossible for someone from the Eastern bloc, so I worked for cash in hand in pubs and clubs while I tried to get a student visa to study nursing. The bar work didn't pay much and Liverpool can be expensive. One of the other barmaids worked as a dancer. It wasn't until she took me to the club that I found out what sort of dancer she was. I worked at the club and occasional rugby-club stag evenings. When I left Mo I moved to Cambridge. I was still trying to get a student visa to study nursing, so I went back to working in bars and dancing. I even got an agent. One night my agent got me a job at a private function over a pub. I didn't like the sound of it, but he told me, they're students from respectable families, there's a pub full of people on the floor below and the club said they'd send a bouncer with me. When I got there the bouncer didn't turn up. I know I shouldn't have taken the risk, but I was really short of money that week, so I gambled and lost.'

'You went straight to the police,' said Daykin.

'And a lot of good they were. Now I'd be taken to a special unit, they would take care of me and a doctor would take forensic samples. Back then I had two fat detectives breathing beer and tobacco over me and telling me I was a whore and asking for all I got. Then they told me the students they had arrested all refused to talk to them, so they didn't have a case.'

'You left the room swearing vengeance. Have you done anything about it?'

She took the tubes off and reached for another cigarette.

'At first I would have killed every single one of them. Time, as they say, is a great healer and my life moved on. I put it all behind me. I qualified as a nurse, moved away from Cambridge, got married and had children. I had no desire to see any of those men ever again, let alone kill them.'

'Do you know anyone who would?' asked Terry Hudson.

'Apart from Bateman?' She looked at her watch and turned to Daykin. 'I'm sorry, Inspector, my husband will be back soon, I think I've given you enough time.'

At the door Daykin said, 'Harry Shapiro asks to be remembered to you.'

She smiled a sad smile. 'I'm glad he's still around.'

As they drove along the wide street a BMW 7 series was driving slowly towards them.

'What odds will you give me that this is Mr Appleyard?' asked Terry Hudson as it passed them.

Daykin said nothing, but watched in his rear view mirror as the car turned into the driveway they had just left.

Chapter Twenty-four

Daykin didn't like driving in traffic and he said little, concentrating on the road. Terry Hudson wrote up his notes of the conversation with Katrina Appleyard. When they reached the motorway Hudson tossed the book into the back seat, waking up the dog, and said, 'So the Russian stripper is out of the frame?'

'Unless you can persuade a jury she smuggled herself into the Church of Enlightened Reality, put a knife through Bishop Moore's throat and then sneaked out, all the time dragging an oxygen cylinder behind her.'

Daykin tapped the fuel gauge and frowned at it.

'Do you believe she stole the money from Bateman?' he said.

'I can't think of any reason for Bateman to lie about it.'

'I can.'

'What?' asked Hudson.

'To distance himself from her. Pretend that he hates her, so nobody thinks that he would kill for her.'

'Is that likely?'

'Who knows? Probably not, but we ought to take a long look at Bateman, of all the leads we have, he's the only one who's likely.'

They drove in silence for a long time, the only sounds in the car were the regular deep breathing of the dog, asleep on the back seat, and the worrying knocking sound from the driver's front wheel arch. Daykin patted his pockets.

'Have you got your mobile phone on you?' he said.

'Yep,' said Terry Hudson, taking it out of his shirt pocket, 'where's yours?'

'I think I left it plugged into the charger at the flat. Call the incident room, will you?'

Terry Hudson dialled the number and when it started ringing he passed the phone to Daykin. Sarah Fanson answered it.

'Anything new?' asked Daykin.

'Two things, sir. You're not going to like either of them.'

'Go ahead.'

'Superintendent Wainwright says that he's organized that Press conference and he wants you to give him another update when you get back.'

'And?'

'They've gone to ground.'

'Freeman, Ellington and Cunningham?'

'All of them. This morning. Cunningham told his chambers he wasn't feeling well, to cancel his conferences and give his pending briefs to other barristers. He left chambers and all we know is that he hasn't gone home.'

'Freeman?'

'He's got a car that is adapted for an invalid. He packed a bag and drove away from his house at about ten o'clock and hasn't been seen since. He didn't leave any way of contacting him.'

'Ellington can't have escaped.'

'He was in an open prison. He walked up to the gatehouse, saying that the governor had given him permission to go to the local town. He'd forged some sort of docket. The stupid sods let him go. It was over an hour before someone asked where he was.'

'Mobile phones?'

'All switched off.'

'Relatives?'

'We've contacted as many as we can, nobody has heard from any of them.'

'I'm on my way back. Get as much information as you can on all of them, places they may hide, where they once lived, friends who might take them in, that sort of thing. I'll see you as soon as I can.'

'There's something else you should know, sir. Mo Bateman wasn't in Liverpool on the 19 October or 2 December.'

Five minutes after Daykin closed the phone and handed it back to Terry Hudson it rang again. Hudson answered it.

'Terry,' said a very nervous voice, 'it's Todd. That guy was back again first thing this morning.'

'What did he want?'

'Some money. He's getting worse, Terry.'

'Calm down, Todd, and tell me what happened.'

'I was on my way to work. I came down the stairs and opened the front door. He must have been waiting. He barged straight into me, then pinned me against the wall and told me to show him which was your flat. I had no choice. I took him up to the flat and he just let go of me and kicked the door in. He had a good look round, threw a few things on the floor. He had a baseball bat with him and he smashed your stereo. Then he left. He told me to say to you that if he doesn't get his money by this time tomorrow he'll come back and torch the place.'

'I'll take care of it, Todd.'

'You can do what you want, Terry. I'm going to stay with my parents until this blows over.'

'Trouble?' said Daykin, as Terry Hudson put the phone back in his pocket.

'Garvey's been to my place again.'

'Did he say he'd be back?'

'First thing tomorrow morning.'

'Then I'll have to solve it by then.'

Chapter Twenty-five

'Tell me what's happened since yesterday,' said Superintendent Wainwright.

'We found Katrina Voitskaya. She's married to a surgeon, three grown up children and she can't be our killer.'

'Why not?'

'She has to cart an oxygen tank everywhere with her, she's in the last stages of emphysema.'

'Where does that leave us?'

'Mo Bateman.'

'The Liverpool villain?'

'He's a former boyfriend of Katrina's. He runs strip joints and he's probably into drugs and gambling. He's just come out from serving a long stretch for gun-running then, while he was in for murder.'

'Doesn't sound like the sort of man you would ask to take your granny down to the shops.'

'He says that when the girl left him she stole some money, so he's got no love for her, but I don't know if I believe him.'

'You want to take a look at him?'

'I'd like forty-eight hours to follow him around, see what he's up to.'

'No, Tom. I can't have you and Hudson going all over the country, leaving a team of mainly inexperienced constables in charge of a case this size.'

'What if I go on my own?'

Wainwright thought for a few seconds.

'I know a Chief Superintendent in Liverpool and he's told me some horror stories about the city over the years. You go somewhere like that and you don't know the streets, you don't know the people, if Bateman gets wind of you, you will just disappear, into the Mersey more than likely. I'll speak to Sam Connors. If he can spare someone to ride shotgun for you, you can go. If not, leave it to the Liverpool police to deal with Bateman.'

He pulled out a large linen handkerchief with a blue 'W' embroidered on the corner and blew his nose.

'What,' he said, putting the handkerchief away, 'about the three survivors? I hope I can tell the Press that you've got them somewhere safe.'

'They've disappeared.'

Wainwright looked hard at him and a half smile came to his lips. 'Tell me you're kidding, Tom,' he said gently.

'This morning, sir. They'd been talking, because they all went AWOL at the same time.'

'But, Ellington. He's in prison. What's he doing, hiding in the library?'

'Open prison, sir. He walked out.'

Wainwright picked up a pen and started tapping it on the desk.

'Inspector Lumsden is organising the Press conference, I can get him to delay it by a couple of days. If you're going to Liverpool, Tom, I need that wrapping up in less than forty-eight hours. In the meantime, the whole of your squad, and I mean all of them, will devote their energies to finding Cunningham, Freeman and Ellington. Understood?

'Right, you'd better go and talk to them. Tell them no leave and no days off until these three are found. I'll try to get hold of Connors Lumsden.'

Daykin walked in to the incident room. 'Any news of the missing three?' he asked, as he came through the door.

'Silus Cunningham has a cottage in the New Forest,' said Bob Foster.

'Too obvious. He wants to lose himself and he'll have worked out that if you can find that place in a couple of hours, so can the person who's trying to kill him.'

'Freeman has a share of a fishing lodge in Ayrshire.'

'Same applies. Think, people, put yourselves in their shoes. You want to disappear so no one can find you, what do you do?'

'Book yourself into a small hotel under an assumed name.'

'Good. But Ellington can't do that, he's got no money and no credit cards. That makes him the easiest to find. He has to go to friends or family. Start checking both. Terry,' he said to Hudson, 'you and I will concentrate on the other two. Get me the files on them, will you?'

They sat side by side at one of the tables, the open diaries in front of them. Daykin took off his glasses and spent a long time looking short-sightedly at the ceiling.

'Money,' said Daykin, after five minutes.

'What's money got to do with it?'

'Cunningham has oodles of money, but he's only got limited ways of getting it.'

'You mean going to his bank?'

'He won't do that. So either he gets the bank to wire the money somewhere else, or he has to use an ATM. We find out where his money is going to, or which ATM he's using.'

'It's not the same for Ellington.'

'No, it's the lack of money for him. Where would you hide if you had no money?'

'A monastery?'

'More likely a relative. That leaves Freeman. It's not the money with him, its his handicap, it limits where he can go.'

Daykin stretched. 'Right,' he said, 'let's get details of their bank accounts and get court applications ready to make the banks tell us where money is drawn from those accounts. Apart from that, we'll concentrate on friends and relatives, anyone who would take them in. The further from their homes and the more distant the relative the better. Lets make a start. I'll take the banks, you take the relatives.'

They worked for the rest of the afternoon, interrupted only once.

'Tom,' said Superintendent Wainwright, 'can I have a word?'

They went out into the corridor.

'I've spoken to Sam Connors, he's assigned a detective sergeant to you. You can meet him tomorrow morning, seven-thirty at Len's Transport Café on the A5047.'

'Why not the station?'

'He's an undercover officer. He doesn't like to spend any more time than necessary in the police station.'

'How will I recognize him?'

'He'll find you.'

By 6.30 they had made all the phone calls they could and had the evening meeting.

'Early night, Terry, I have to be on the road again at six in the morning.'

'How does that affect me, Tom?'

'I thought you'd want a lift to the station.'

'That's OK, you leave me on the sofa, I'll catch a bus in.'

Daykin, who had stood up, sat back down again.

'I have to be away for forty-eight hours, maybe less. I need to know that you are here cracking the whip.'

'Trust me, Tom.'

As they walked through the reception area on their way out of the station they passed Superintendent Wainwright, talking a uniformed chief inspector.

'I'm glad I've seen you, Tom,' he said, 'Lumsden has set the Press conference for nine-thirty in the morning, the day after tomorrow.'

'See you in your office at eight, sir?'

Wainwright nodded and went back to his conversation.

As Daykin and Hudson drove out of the police station, from fifty yards away, Ray Garvey watched them through the windscreen of his car. Garvey recognized Terry Hudson, he had seen a photograph on Hudson's breakfast bar which showed him at Wembley Stadium. He started up the car and, waiting for three cars to pass him, set off to follow Daykin's Renault. The Renault began to drive east out of the town, then headed north and seemed to circle round the town centre. After twenty minutes Terry Hudson said, 'I know its been a long day, Tom, and you may be tired, but aren't we going the wrong way?

'Did your friend tell you what car Garvey drives?'

'No, why?'

'A grey Volvo has been following us since we left the police station.'

Terry Hudson pulled down the visor and pretended to look at his face in the mirror.

'The one three cars back?'

'That's the one. I left my phone in the office, can you dial the station on yours?'

Daykin pulled his car into the side of the road. The Volvo indicated left and parked twenty yards behind them. Terry Hudson dialled Harrogate Police Station and passed the phone to Daykin.

'This is Inspector Daykin. I'm on Victoria Avenue, just past the roundabout. About twenty yards behind me is a X-registered grey Volvo. He seemed to be swerving in the road as he drove, then he had difficulty parking, I think he hit one of the other cars. Send someone to check him, will you?'

They waited for three minutes, then Daykin saw in his rear-view mirror a police car pull alongside the Volvo, blocking it into its parking space. The blue flashing beacons were turned on. An officer got out of the car and motioned the driver of the Volvo to wind his windscreen down. Daykin started the Renault's engine and pulled out into the traffic.

'I will be back sometime in the next two days,' he said. 'I'll ask Wainwright to organise that CID car for you tomorrow. Any time you come into the station, park it in a quiet side street at least half a mile away and walk. Going out, get someone to drive you and keep your head down, lie down on the back seat if you have to.'

'What shall I tell them?'

'You'll think of something.'

Chapter Twenty-six

Len's Transport Café looked like it had been built by a jobbing builder with the odd materials he had left in his yard. Nothing matched. The roof tiles were three different colours. The bricks were either red or grey, the window frames brown or white and the walls brick, plaster or clapboard.

Daykin drove his car on to the piece of spare land that served as the car park. It was not tarmacked, just compacted earth that must be a sea of mud after heavy rain. He parked between two heavy lorries and in front of a council refuse truck. He decided to leave the dog in the car.

Just inside the door was a serving hatch. He asked for a mug of tea and a bacon sandwich.

'Do you want butter, dripping or margarine on the sandwich?' asked the man behind the counter. He had greasy hair and a greasier apron.

'Dripping,' said Daykin. He might as well send his cholesterol off the scale.

He walked to a table at the far end of the room, stopping by a small rack on the wall that held three tabloid newspapers. There was not much call for the *Financial Times* at Len's Transport Café. The tea arrived in a pint mug and the sandwich lay, oozing with melting dripping, on a cracked plate.

He had gone through the stories of the government minister and the secret slush fund, the lottery winner who still couldn't resist stolen goods, and the vicar who eloped with the choir-master's wife and was on which footballer's wife had thrown his clothes on to the front lawn because of his serial adultery, when someone slid into the bench on the opposite side of the table.

'Are you Daykin?'

Daykin closed and folded the paper and laid it on the chipped Formica table top. He looked into a pair of eyes so dark brown that the pupils and the irises blended into each other. Two black circles stared back at him.

'And you are?' said Daykin.

'Padraic Carroll, people call me Paddy.'

'Irish?'

'Scouse born and bred. So was my father. Both grandfathers came over on the boat.'

He took off a pair of fingerless woollen gloves, but didn't offer to shake hands. He looked round the room. One of the lorry drivers had gone, the other was lost in a plate of fried eggs, baked beans and sausages. Three of the refuse collectors were listening to the fourth tell a joke. Paddy Carroll leaned forward.

'What is it you want to know about that scumbag Mo Bateman?'

'I think he may have killed three men, maybe others.'

'Everyone who knows Mo, except his mother, would think you are right.'

'I need to follow him for a couple of days and I need some local knowledge.'

'It's not really my field, but my chief says I have to give you all the help you need.'

Daykin took a swig at the last of his tea. It was cold, but he wanted to take a good look at Paddy Carroll. He was just what an undercover cop should be, a mix of a man without any distinguishing features and someone you wouldn't want to meet in a dark alley. He was medium height and build, he had three days' growth of dark stubble and Daykin guessed he had black hair under the navy-blue ski hat pulled down low over his ears so only the small gold ear-rings in each lobe showed below it. He wore a leather jacket that, if it had not been distressed when he bought it, it was now. Under it he wore a black crew-neck sweater.

Ignoring the no smoking sign, Carroll pulled a tin from his pocket, took out a hand-rolled cigarette and lit it. The man behind the counter looked over at him, but nobody objected.

'Mo's a night owl. He won't be up and about for another ninety minutes. Then he'll leave his home in Formby at about 10.30 and take a tour round his strip clubs. He'll be in either a black Mercedes or a Porsche Cayenne. He never drives, he always sits in the back. Both cars have tinted windows. He knows that the regional crime squad have him down as a target criminal, so every now and then, just for a laugh, both cars come out of the gate of his house at the same time and drive off in opposite directions.'

'He's got a sense of humour, then?'

'If he has, it's the only good thing about him. Just so you know who you're dealing with, rumour has it that two drug dealers tried to muscle in on his territory about a year ago. He had them tied up, then cut them into pieces with a chain saw like beef carcasses. The bits were dumped under a new motorway spur road.'

'Nice man.'

'Just don't get too close, you'll get burnt, maybe fatally.'

'How far is Formby?'

'Plenty of time, besides I've got a mug of tea coming.'

Daykin's phone rang. On the way to the transport café he had called at the police station to pick it up. He patted his pockets until he found it. Paddy Carroll leaned even further forward and whispered, 'If that is police business, take it outside. I don't want anyone in here knowing you're a copper!'

Daykin slid out of the bench and opened his phone.

'Just a minute,' he said into it and walked outside.

'Tom? It's Trevor Wainwright. I just wanted to give you some news. We've got a forensic psychologist.'

'A what?'

'A girl who analyzes the evidence and comes up with a profile of the killer. I say "girl", she's got a university degree from St Andrews in Scotland and a post graduate Ph.D. She must be nearly thirty. Very bright. She's called Ilona Mancini.'

'Strange name.'

'Italian father, German mother.'

'How did you get her?'

'She phoned me. She heard about the case through some contacts; she thought she might be able to help. She sent her CV and a couple of letters of recommendation. Very impressive. And' – he paused as if, unsure whether to tell Daykin – 'she's a friend of the Chief Constable's daughter.'

'Let's just hope she comes up with Mo Bateman's profile.'

'She's looking through the files now. She's says three or four days and she'll be finished. Keep in touch, Tom.'

'Yes, sir,' said Daykin. He closed the phone and went back into the café.

Paddy Carroll's tea had arrived and he was reading the paper Daykin had left on the table.

'It's about forty minutes through traffic to Formby. I'll finish this tea and we'll get going.'

He didn't offer to give the paper back.

Finishing his tea, Paddy Carroll got up from the table, picking up a small canvas bag he had slid under the bench as he sat down. They left the café and in the car-park Carroll said, 'We'll take your car.'

Daykin looked round the car park. There wasn't another car to take. He didn't ask how Carroll had got there. He unlocked the car and noticed, before he got into it, Paddy Carroll's eyes scan round the car-park and into the nearby buildings.

'Big dog,' said Carroll, as he got into the car.

'You don't seem surprised.'

'I checked your car before I came into the café.'

The only conversation on the way to Formby was Paddy Carroll giving directions and showing Daykin shortcuts through the morning traffic. Eventually they came to a T-junction.

'Stop here,' said Carroll. He got out of the car and, being careful not to show more of himself than his face, looked round the corner up the road to his left. Then he got back into the passenger seat.

'Sometimes he puts a man at the gate, but this morning he's just relying on the cameras. There's a space about ten cars up the road on the left. Drive round the corner and pull into it.'

When they were tucked into the parking space Paddy Carroll unzipped the holdall and took out a pair of compact binoculars.

'The house with the fancy brickwork columns and the high gates,' he said.

Daykin pointed the binoculars at the gateway and adjusted the focus.

'You see the cameras, one at the top of each column, facing up and down the street? Well they have telephoto lenses and can turn and zoom, so don't keep the binoculars up to your face for too long.'

As Daykin handed the binoculars back to him Paddy Carroll looked at his watch and said, 'If he's on time this morning we've got about forty-five minutes to wait, so we might as well be as comfortable as possible.'

He took a large flask and two plastic cups out of the holdall and poured coffee into the cups.

'Just to give us maximum warning, I'll switch this gizmo on,' he said, taking a small black box from the holdall. Daykin looked at it quizzically.

'About two months ago Mo's Mercedes had to go into the dealer's for a service. The regional crime squad got a court order to fit a covert listening device in his car. We can hear and record everything that's said in the vehicle.'

He flipped a small switch but the box was silent.

They sat in the car, drinking bad coffee, for nearly thirty minutes. It was the box that told them it was time to go to work. The tiny loudspeaker came to life with a car door opening and closing, the grunt of a man as he adjusted his position in the driver's seat and the sound of an engine starting up.

'It's a cold morning; the driver's running the engine to heat the car before Mo gets in,' said Carroll as a radio in the car was turned on and tuned to a popular music station. After five minutes there was the sound of two other doors opening and closing, then a voice Daykin recognized as Mo Bateman's saying impatiently, 'OK, let's go.'

As the engine note changed the large gates swung apart silently and a black Mercedes drove slowly through them and turned down the road away from Daykin's car.

'There's a man in the front passenger seat,' said Paddy Carroll, 'who's job is just to look out for anything that might be trouble. Try to keep a couple of cars between you and him. If the car stops suddenly just drive by, we'll try to pick him up again when he starts moving.'

For the rest of the day they followed Mo Bateman, playing hide and seek in the traffic and spending long, boring hours sitting in the car and looking through the binoculars at whichever club Mo had stopped to inspect. Daykin rang the incident room five times during the day, but nothing much had changed. He took the dog for three short walks in the streets away from the nightclubs. Night fell and the lights in Mo's club came to life.

'What time does he normally pack it in?' asked Daykin.

'Depends. On a quiet night about eleven, sometimes as late as two in the morning.'

'We've been here for four hours, so do you want to call it a day and start again tomorrow?'

'Suits me,' said Carroll, and started to put the binoculars back in the holdall. Then the black box broadcast three doors opening and closing on the Mercedes.

'He doesn't normally do this,' said Carroll.

They set off to follow the Mercedes. Now that it was dark, hiding was easier, but seeking more difficult. The journey wasn't long. After ten minutes the Mercedes turned into Mission Street.

'Stop on the main road. Don't follow him, it's a dead end,' said Carroll.

Daykin pulled the Renault into the side of the road. They listened to the black box and heard the Mercedes pull to a halt, wait with its engine running for ninety seconds, pull forward a short distance, then the engine was turned off.

'When are they due?' asked Mo Bateman's voice.

'About ten minutes.'

'What the fuck are we doing sitting here for ten minutes?'

'We have to be here when the driver arrives. He needs paying and he ain't going to hang around. If we're not here he will just dump the goods and go.'

'There's a couple of derelict buildings on Mission Street,' said Carroll, 'let's see if we can get into one of them and take a look at what Bateman's doing.'

If Mo Bateman didn't want anyone watching him he had chosen Mission Street well. It had never been a major road, just one of the arteries that carried light traffic from one side of the district to the other. As the area went downhill, so did the street. Then a business consortium, with a government grant in their pocket, negotiated with the council to build a new factory in Kensington. The council, seeing hundreds of new jobs, bent over backwards for them. Part of the factory was built across Mission Street, dividing it into two cul-de-sacs. With no passing trade, two local shops and a petrol filling station withered and died. Then the factory closed. Now it was an empty shell, used only by vagrants and young men with spray cans who practiced their graffiti on the walls.

Paddy Carroll took the pair of binoculars from the holdall and slipped them into his jacket pocket. He also took out a small jemmy which he slipped up his right sleeve as he got out of the car. Daykin followed him along the main road, past the junction of Mission Street and into a small park. They walked through, Carroll constantly looking at the backs of the houses that bordered it and faced on to Mission Street. Not far from the factory wall he suddenly changed direction and walked to the back door of a house. Turning to watch the park, he let the jemmy slip down his sleeve into his right hand and put the end of it into the door jamb. He gave a sharp pull, there was a soft crack and he pushed the door open.

Inside the house was darkness. There was the smell of damp and decay. A soft cool breeze blew through some of the windows that had been smashed and it was so quiet they could hear the traffic on the main road. Daykin followed Carroll through the open door, across the bare floorboards of the living room and up a flight of stairs, trying not to brush against the wallpaper that someone had tried to tear off the walls and which now hung in uneven strips across the staircase. In the first-floor bedroom facing on to Mission Street they looked down through a broken window, standing well back and away from the light.

The large canopy of the filling station was still there, although the pumps had long gone and the grass and plants grew through the gaps between the large concrete rectangles of the fuelling area. A high wire fence had been put round the filling station and hung on it were signs for a local security company. There was a gate in the fence, it stood open. Under the canopy the black Mercedes was parked facing the gate. At the back of the car Mo Bateman, his long grey overcoat buttoned up against the cold night wind, stood with his hands in his pockets, talking to the large man who was still wearing the maroon suit.

As Daykin and Carroll watched, three old mini buses drove down Mission Street, through the open gate and parked in a line next to the Mercedes. The three drivers got out, exchanged nods with Bateman, then stood in a small group. One of them produced a packet of cigarettes and handed them round.

'What the hell are they waiting for?' whispered Carroll.

'A container lorry,' said Daykin. 'Bateman said he was an investor in people.'

'You're going to have to explain that one to me.'

'He's people smuggling. That's why they need the minibuses, not Transits. You'd better phone the station. We need as many officers as they can give us, two armed response units and enough meat wagons to transport about thirty people.'

'I need to borrow your phone.'

'Haven't you got one?' asked Daykin, desperately patting his pockets. He found the phone and handed it to Paddy Carroll.

'Too dangerous. If I get it taken off me they'd know exactly who I've been phoning. Public phone boxes are safer.'

He took the phone and walked to the back of the room where he whispered into it urgently. He didn't need to whisper, no one was listening, it was just habit.

'How long before they're here?' asked Daykin, as Carroll handed the phone back to him.

'About ten minutes.'

'Great, I think the merchandise has just arrived.'

A pantechnicon lorry turned into Mission Street and drove slowly towards the filling station. All the men inside the wire turned to watch it. The driver drove past the site then stopped and reversed, turning the cab at an acute angle so the trailer curved gracefully across the road and through the gate. There was no more than a couple of inches between the two sides of the vehicle and the gate posts, but it didn't pause until, with a gentle sigh of the air brakes, it came to a stop, the cab just inside the gateway. The driver opened the door and jumped down. Bateman waved him towards the Mercedes and handed him a large manila envelope. The driver opened it, looked inside, nodded and walked to the back of his vehicle.

'If it only takes them five minutes to unload, we're in trouble,' said Carroll.

'Then we'll have to go down and delay them until the cavalry arrive.'

'What's this "we" business?'

Daykin looked at him in surprise. 'Because two of us have twice the chance of holding them up.'

'Look, I don't know what you've been told about what I do, but I've spent the last four years making people believe I'm a drug wholesaler. If I go down there with you it's obvious I'm a copper and I've blown four years' work in twenty seconds. Mo Bateman is a heavyweight, but he's not worth that.'

'You'd let them get away?'

'In a heartbeat. No contest.'

Daykin looked at the pantechnicon, the back doors were being swung open.

'Me it is then,' he said, and walked towards the stairs. He retraced his steps, walking quickly through the park, back to the main road, then followed the route of the pantechnicon down Mission Street. At the gates of the filling station he stopped, quietly climbed up to the cab, took out the ignition key and threw it across the road. If all else failed, everyone inside the compound was now trapped by the vehicle.

As he stood at the gates, in the silence he heard Mo Bateman say, 'Who's that by the cab? Go take a look, tell him to get lost.'

The man in maroon started to walk towards Daykin. In the darkness he seemed even larger than he had the day before yesterday. Ten yards from Daykin he stopped and turned his head to one side, his face changing into an expression of recognition. Then he said over his shoulder, 'What do you want me to do, boss, it's—'

His last word was drowned by the sound of sirens coming up Mission Street at speed.

'Thank, Christ,' said Daykin softly.

Chapter Twenty-seven

By the time Mo Bateman, five of his employees, a lorry driver and twenty-five illegal immigrants had been booked into custody it was the early hours of the morning. Daykin found an office at the station with a folding bed. He took the dog for another walk, then slept until nine.

After a morning of writing a statement and listening to the covert tapes from Bateman's car, he set off back to Harrogate. The tapes had told him that whatever Bateman had been up to for the past few months it didn't involve murdering members of The Greenrush Club.

He drove back across the Pennines to Yorkshire. On his way he phoned Terry Hudson and arranged to meet him at the station.

They went to the cafeteria for a coffee. Hudson told him they were making slow progress in tracing the missing men and Daykin explained about Mo Bateman. Terry Hudson wanted a cigarette, so they went and stood by the back door. Daykin, who was tired of stuffy rooms and cars, was happy to stand in the fresh air.

'This Garvey guy,' he said, 'is causing a distraction. I'd like to get him out of the way.'

'How are you going to do that?'

'I've been thinking on the way back. He's a Rottweiller, he wants your throat and he's not going to stop. I have to get his master to call him off. What's the name of the bookie who sold the debt?'

Terry Hudson was unsure. He shuffled from foot to foot.

'I have a good relationship with my bookmaker,' he said lamely.

'You had. He's not going to give you credit again. Name?'

'Derek Butcher.'

'Phone number?'

Hudson gave it to him.

'Anything about him that I can use?'

Hudson thought for a moment. 'About a year ago there were a lot of rumours about him putting some money into match-fixing.'

'You get back to the incident room, I'll give him a call.'

Daykin went to his office and dialled the number.

'Butcher's Bookmakers,' said a voice.

'Can I speak to Mr Butcher?'

'He's with a customer, he'll be a couple of minutes.'

Daykin waited patiently until a voice said, 'Derek Butcher.'

'Mr Butcher, my name is Tom Daykin. I'm a police inspector with the North Yorkshire Force. You recently sold on the debt of my sergeant, Terry Hudson. I want to know who you sold it to.'

'I don't care who the hell you are, my business arrangements are private.'

'I'm asking politely, Mr Butcher.'

'Meaning?'

'Your licence must be up for renewal soon. I could persuade the local licensing officer to object to it.'

'This is beginning to sound like harassment, Inspector.'

'If you make me talk to him, I will.'

'You've nothing to tell him,' said Butcher, the first echoes of doubt in his voice.

'Match-fixing. Last year?'

'Just a minute.'

There was no sound from the phone while Derek Butcher thought about the alternatives. Then Daykin could hear his footsteps and the sound of a door closing. He guessed Butcher had gone to his office.

'Dennis Bradley. He's got a garage just outside Middlesbrough,' said Butcher eventually, 'and you didn't hear that from me.'

The phone went dead.

Daykin spent the next half-hour on the phone to the Middlesbrough District Headquarters of Cleveland Police. By the time he put the phone down he knew a lot about Dennis Bradley, a man who had left school at fifteen and started selling second hand cars. Within five years he had two car lots and twenty employees. He fell foul of the local trading standards department a few times, but nothing that landed him in court. That had to wait for an argument with another dealer at a car auction. The fight outside ended with the dealer going to hospital and Bradley being charged with causing grievous bodily harm. In the next few months every eye-witness had an attack of amnesia and forgot what they'd seen. The iron bar that was mentioned by them was never found and then the complainant suddenly left the area and hadn't been seen since.

After that Dennis Bradley led a charmed life. There were rumours of a large-scale vehicle fraud and secret warehouses to change the identity of thirty or forty vehicles at a time, but no one was talking. Bradley became wealthy. He bought a large house and twenty acres of land near Saltburn, rental properties in Middlesbrough, Thornaby and Wolviston and two years before he had gone into semi-retirement. He sold all his garages except one and although the local police knew he was still ringing cars and did some debt collecting, knowing and proving, Daykin was told, are very different.

Daykin took off his glasses and polished the lenses on his tie, then he looked at the dog in the corner of the room. 'Come on, Royston, I think I need to think.'

They left the station and turned right along North Park Road towards The Stray.

An hour later, Daykin was back in his office. He searched in his briefcase for an old battered cloth-covered address book and, when he found it, dialled a number.

'Peter? It's Tom Daykin. I need a favour.'

'Your favours usually spell trouble, Tom. What is it this time?'

Peter Davies and Tom Daykin had played rugby against each other many times before they were both picked for Yorkshire. Peter was a journalist with the *Leeds Evening Post* and gradually drifted into investigative journalism. He was a man who took offence easily and, just like on the rugby field, was a little too quick to use his fists. He had got himself into several scrapes with the law, most of which Daykin had got him out of. Like Dennis Bradley, he was now semi-retired.

'I need some information on a man called Dennis Bradley.'

'Have you tried Google?'

'It's the sort of information he wouldn't want to get out. Car ringing, debt collecting, that sort of thing.'

'There's nothing wrong with a bit of debt collecting.'

'Not the way he does it.'

'How soon and how thorough?'

'Yesterday and some photos would be nice.'

'No promises, Tom. I'll see what I can do.'

When he put the phone down Daykin went to the incident room and asked Terry Hudson what leads there were on tracing the three missing men. He was told that the officers were all working hard but wherever these men were hiding they had chosen well because there was no real news.

'I've been thinking,' said Daykin.

'I know, I saw you take the dog for a walk.'

'Are you taking the piss, Sergeant?'

165

'No, sir. The guy who gave me some background on you said you often walked the dog when you wanted to think.'

Daykin shrugged. 'Cunningham,' he said, 'what car does he drive?'

'Sarah!' shouted Hudson across the room. 'Cunningham, what car has he got?'

'A Bentley Continental, Sarg.'

'If you had a car like that, wouldn't you have a tracker fitted to it?'

'Probably.'

'Find out where he bought it, call them and see if he had one fitted. Get the name of the company and, if you can, their phone number. I'd like to know where that car is now.'

Daykin went over to where Bridget Cooper was sitting. 'Bridget, how far have you got with Patrick Freeman?'

'We've eliminated friends, he hasn't got the money for a hotel, and he couldn't sleep rough with a wheelchair, so he has to be staying with family.'

'How many of those have you contacted?'

'Four, except a maiden aunt who nobody has heard from for years.'

'Mother's side or father's?'

Cooper looked through her notes. 'Father's.'

'So she is a Freeman too. I think I read that Patrick came from County Durham so, if she hasn't moved, we're looking for a middle aged woman called Freeman in County Durham.'

'Not easy, sir.'

'Go back to the family, see what you can find out about her. Job, hobbies, close friends. Anything to narrow the field of search.'

Bridget Cooper leaned across the table. 'What about Ellington, sir?'

'He's as bright as the others, but he's also street smart. We won't find him in a hurry. We have to gamble on finding Cunningham and hoping he keeps in touch with the others.'

For the rest of the day all of them made phone calls. At six they had their now usual meeting to discuss the day, then started to make their way home.

On his way out, Daykin's mobile phone rang.

'Don't forget the Press conference tomorrow, Tom. In my office at eight-thirty?'

'Yes, sir.'

'And don't bring that dog with you, the cleaners are beginning to complain.'

'Understood.'

On the way to the car park. Daykin said, 'We'll take your car.'

'But yours is just here, mine is parked on the other side of town.'

'You're a betting man. What odds would you give me that Ray Garvey is watching us right now? He knows my car, he's probably changed his. We'll leave the Renault and walk to your car and take a good look round us before we get into it.'

Chapter Twenty-eight

'I've brought coffees in,' said Wainwright, as Daykin sat down in his office. There were two cardboard cups on the desktop.

'Latte, double shot of espresso. I think we're going to need the caffeine.'

They both carefully took the plastic tops off the cups and watched the steam rise.

'Have you done many Press conferences, Tom?'

'A few.'

'Thank God for that. So you know what's coming.'

Daykin stopped watching the steam and looked at Wainwright. 'You're not nervous are you, sir?'

'Well,' said Wainwright, shifting uncomfortably in his chair, 'it's a bit like being in the witness box. You get a load of questions fired at you and the best you can hope for is to bat most of them back without looking too stupid.'

'Then what are we putting ourselves through this for?'

'I thought that an injection of publicity might give you some leads. Now I'm not so sure. Still,' he said, picking up his coffee cup, 'too late to cancel it now.'

He took a sip of his coffee and almost managed to hide the slight tremble in his hand. This was the first time Daykin had seen him display any nerves.

'Now,' said Wainwright, putting the cup back down carefully, 'I think it best if we divide the questions between us. I'll take the direction of the investigation, you take the day-to-day running of it. Agreed?'

'Makes sense, sir. What about Miss Mancini?'

'What about her?'

'Isn't she going to be there?'

'I asked her, but she said that she had too much work to get through.'

'When you mention her, aren't the Press going to want to fire a few questions at her.'

'I said the same thing to her. She got very defensive. She insisted that I don't even mention that she's here. She doesn't want her name in the papers.'

'Why not?'

'Search me. Shy? Anyway, let's talk about where we are in this case, so we're both ready for the questions.'

For the next forty-five minutes they talked their way through every detail of the case until finally Wainwright looked at his watch.

'Five minutes to go,' he said, getting up, 'let's not antagonize them by keeping them waiting.'

There was a room on the first floor of the station that was known as the conference room, although no-one could remember any conferences ever being held there. It was a large room, fifty feet long, by thirty wide, with tall windows along one wall, overlooking the car-park. At the far end a trestle table had been set up with two chairs behind it. The table was draped with a white cloth to the front of which was pinned a large embroidered North Yorkshire Police badge.

Facing the table were five rows of chairs, separated by a central aisle. It was a good turn out for a wet weekday morning in Harrogate, the chairs were nearly all taken. As they entered the room it suddenly filled with harsh white lights as three television lights were switched on. Daykin, caught by surprise and dazzled by the glare, groped his way towards the nearest chair at the table.

If Trevor Wainwright was still nervous, he wasn't showing it. He sat down and looked slowly and confidently around the room.

'Good morning, ladies and gentlemen,' he said, 'thank you for coming. I am going to read a short statement and then we'll take questions.'

He leaned forward towards the microphone and his voice boomed round the room. He read from the typewritten page in front of him.

'A few days ago the body of Christopher Van Meer was discovered at his home. He had been poisoned. In his youth he had studied at Cambridge University where he became a member of an organization called The Greenrush Club. Shortly before Mr Van Meer's death another member of the club, Robert Miller, had also been murdered.

'Enquiries showed that there had been twelve members of the club. Of the other ten, one had committed suicide, one had been killed in an incident not connected to this case, one had died on active service and two were killed by accident. One is missing, presumed dead, and four were still alive.

'Unfortunately, during our investigation, another member of the club has been murdered. We believe that these are serial killings, connected in some way to The Greenrush Club and that the killer will strike again.

'The three survivors have gone into hiding and our first job is to ask them to come forward so that we can offer them the proper protection.

'Sitting beside me is Detective Inspector Daykin who is in charge of the investigation. If you have any questions we will try to answer them.

'Questions, please.'

'Have you any suspects?' said a voice from the darkness.

'We're working on a number of lines of inquiry and it's early days yet,' said Daykin, hoping that would satisfy the journalists. It didn't.

'So after several days you've not arrested anyone and you've lost one of your club members?'

'That's correct. He was offered protection, but unfortunately refused.'

'How many officers are on the case?' said another voice.

'Seven experienced detectives working under Inspector Daykin,' said Wainwright.

'What was The Greenrush Club?'

'Just a student club. They seemed to have spent most of their time together eating, drinking and enjoying themselves.'

'So why does someone want to see them all dead?'

'That's what we're trying to find out.'

'Let's understand this,' said a reporter in the front row. 'You're investigating three murders and you only have eight detectives working on the case?'

Wainwright was lost for words for a second.

'And a forensic psychologist,' he said.

'Who is that?'

Again Wainwright paused.

'Ilona Mancini.'

Daykin looked at him. Wainwright avoided his gaze.

'If you don't have a suspect, do you have a motive?'

'Revenge,' said Wainwright.

'Possibly,' said Daykin.

The questions continued, but after twenty minutes petered out. Wainwright wound up the conference, the television lights went out, the reporters put away their notebooks and dictaphones and left

Wainwright and Daykin sitting alone at the cloth-covered table in a large empty room.

'That seemed to go quite well,' said Wainwright.

'It could have been a lot worse.'

'What was that you said about the motive, you don't think it was revenge?'

'I never was sure about it, now I'm certain it wasn't.'

'Then what was it?'

'I don't know yet, sir. Sex, love, hate, money. Take your pick.'

'Well,' said Wainwright, getting up, 'I suppose you'd better get back to work. For God's sake, Tom, at the least find us a suspect or the Press will tear us to pieces.'

Daykin returned to the incident room.

'Any news on Cunningham's car, Terry?'

'Just came in from the tracker company, it's parked in a lock-up garage in Henley.'

'What connection does Cunningham have with Henley?'

'We're working on it. We're trying family, friends and contacts at the Bar.'

Daykin sat down and took his glasses off. He held them up to the light then polished both lenses.

'If you were a successful barrister and didn't want to be found, who would you go to?'

'Money no object?'

'Sure.'

'I'd book into a small hotel or, better still, I'd rent a flat, maybe in someone else's name.'

'He wouldn't want to walk far from the car to where he's staying. Get on to Buckinghamshire Police and see if they can tell you about any hotels or flats within two hundred yards of the lock up. See if you can find out who owns the lock up and ask what Cunningham said to them. Talk to his immediate family, see if he told them where he was going. Enough to be going on with?'

Terry Hudson who was writing in his diary, nodded without looking up. Daykin strolled over to talk to the other officers.

No more than eight hundred yards away from them, Ray Garvey had been busy. As he had followed their car he had made a note of Daykin's registration number. The DVLA had confirmed the car was registered to Thomas Charles Daykin at an address in Shapford, a small Dales town. From a public phone box he had telephoned Harrogate Police Station and said that he was Chief Inspector Porter of the Metropolitan Police. Could he speak to Mr Daykin. She asked if he meant Inspector Daykin? He did. While she tried to put the call through he hung up. Then he dialled Colin Williams.

'Colin? It's Ray Garvey. I need another piece of information.'

'As long as its not about a police sergeant this time, Ray.'

'No, it's an inspector.'

'I had enough trouble last time, Ray. Police officers stick together, you know? It's too difficult and too risky.'

'A hundred quid.'

Williams whistled softly through his teeth. Ray Garvey smiled. Colin always did that before he agreed to do something difficult.

'All right,' he said, 'but I'm not doing it again, OK?'

'I need the address of Inspector Tom Daykin, North Yorkshire Police. He's living somewhere in Harrogate. And top priority, Colin, I need to know as soon as.'

'You don't ask much for your hundred quid, do you?'

'Stop moaning and start dialling.'

Chapter Twenty-nine

They had finished the day without moving any further forward. Two-dozen phone calls had been made to everyone they knew who had any contact with Silus Cunningham, but nobody could help them with an address in Henley. After the evening meeting broke up they had made their separate ways home. Daykin and Hudson had walked to where Hudson had parked the Ford Mondeo the department had lent him and they had driven to Daykin's flat, stopping briefly at a supermarket on the way. Daykin had cooked tenderloin of pork with a mushroom sauce. They sat at the kitchen table and ate it with oven roast baby new potatoes and asparagus spears. Then they finished the bottle of wine Terry Hudson had insisted on buying.

'Tell me about your wife,' said Hudson, as he poured the last of the wine.

'Jenny? Bright, beautiful. When she walked into a room you could feel the mood change. Women loved her and men adored her. She used to laugh a lot. She had one of those really infectious laughs. And she used to sing, always out of tune, totally tone deaf, but that didn't stop her. Well dressed, sophisticated. God knows what she saw in me. We had a great marriage. Only two things stopped it being perfect, one was that we couldn't have children. We both went for tests and the doctors said it was both of us. Children would have been nice.' The last few words drifted away and he stared morosely into his wine glass.

'Two,' prompted Terry Hudson, 'you said there were two things.'

'About three years ago,' said Daykin, still looking into the glass, 'I came home from work. Jenny hadn't been working that day. She had made me my favourite meal, the dining table was set and she lit candles, we didn't usually go to that kind of trouble during the week. She talked all the way through the meal and when we finished we sat down on the sofa in front of the fire and she brought me a glass of brandy and told me that she had had the results of some tests. She hadn't told me she was going for tests, I didn't know anything was wrong. She had terminal cancer and had six months to live.'

He took a drink of the wine.

'I didn't believe anyone could fight so hard to hang on to life, but she just wasted away. We didn't get our last six months together, she was gone in under three.'

He stood up and said sadly, 'And now, if you don't mind, I'm going to bed.'

Terry Hudson slept fitfully that night and was yawning as they drove towards the station.

'This fifteen thousand you owe,' said Daykin, 'how much can you raise?'

'What, right now?'

'Yes.'

'There's the money I'll get from the insurance company for the car and I put a bit aside for emergencies from my last good win. I'd say about five grand.'

'Get it for me today, in cash.'

'You didn't say cash, I can't raise five grand in cash.'

'Phone your bank manager, explain about the car, see if he will give you cash while you wait for the insurance company to pay up. It's important, Terry. I'm trying to get you out of a boatload of trouble and cash is always a sweetener.'

Terry Hudson parked the car in a quiet avenue off Montpellier Street and they walked to the station.

'Inspector Daykin,' called the receptionist, as they passed her desk, 'Superintendent Wainwright wants to see you as soon as you get in.'

'This is becoming a habit,' said Daykin to Terry Hudson. 'Get the team cracking in the incident room, I'll be there as soon as I can.'

'Oh, and Terry,' he said as Hudson started to walk away, 'five thousand by the end of the today.'

'I know, in cash.'

'Are you in any sort of trouble, Tom?' asked Wainwright, as Daykin sat down in his office.

'Trouble, sir?'

'One of my senior officers approached me yesterday and said that he'd been asked by Colin Williams for your address.'

'Who is Colin Williams?'

'That's the reason I ask if there is any problem. Williams was an officer with this Force. He left about six years ago under a bit of a cloud. Nothing was proved and he got a full pension, but there was talk of some money going missing. He resigned before anyone started talking about a disciplinary hearing. Now he works as a private enquiry agent, tracing missing wives, that sort of thing.'

'Why would he want my address?'

'With all due respect to you, Tom,' said Wainwright, looking at Daykin's untidy hair, his outdated glasses and scruffy clothes, 'I don't think anyone's wife has run away to share a life of passion with you. Colin Williams has the reputation for supplying information, the sort that he can only get through his police contacts, to some very unsavoury people.'

Daykin busied himself examining a small stain on his lapel. Eventually, he said, 'Sergeant Hudson has a gambling debt he can't pay. The debt has been sold to a villain in Middlesbrough. He's sent one of his people to put the frighteners on Terry Hudson. He's done some damage at Terry's flat in Scarborough, so I said he could stay with me for a few days, until I can solve the problem.'

'And can you? Solve the problem?'

'I believe so, sir. With a bit of luck, sometime tomorrow.'

'All right, Tom, but you don't need distractions right now. If this thing is not solved, or it gets out of hand, I want to hear about it. Understood?'

'If this thing gets out of hand, sir,' said Daykin, getting up, 'I may not be able to tell you about it.'

As Daykin walked into the incident room his detectives were waiting for him.

'No work to do?' asked Daykin.

'We were just talking about what to do next, sir,' said Fritz Schmidt. 'We've found Silus Cunningham,'

'Dead or alive?'

'Alive, we believe.'

'How did you find him?'

'Martin went back to Cunningham's chambers. One of their barristers has been away on a case in Birmingham for nearly three months. He was back today. He owns a flat in Henley. There isn't a garage so he rents a lock up round the corner.'

'Address?' said Daykin, reaching for his diary.

'Twenty-five Chamberlain Mews.'

'Phone number?'

Schmidt handed him a piece of paper.

Daykin picked up the phone and dialled the number. It rang five times, then an answering machine clicked in. Daykin waited for the recorded message to end. 'Mr Cunningham, this is Inspector Tom

Daykin, we spoke a few days ago, it didn't take long to find you, which means if anyone wants to kill you, they can find you just as easily. I'd like you to come into protective custody. If you agree, please pick up the phone, just in case you're out, I'm at Harrogate Police Station, you can call me there.'

He waited, but nobody picked the phone up. He was just about to give up when a tired, resigned voice said, 'It appears that I'm not as good as hiding myself as I thought I was.'

'It's never easy, Mr Cunningham.'

'I'd better take you up on your offer.'

'I'll send two constables round from the local station. Before they arrive I will telephone you again. Do not pick up the phone. I will leave a message giving you their names and collar numbers. Do not answer the door to anyone else. Everything clear?'

'Yes, Inspector.'

'One last question, are you still in touch with Patrick Freeman and Clive Ellington?'

'I phoned them to tell them about Darius's murder. We agreed it would be safer if we all went into hiding and each of us didn't know where the others were.'

Daykin phoned Henley Police Station and arranged for two officers to pick up Silus Cunningham from Chamberlain Mews. He phoned the flat and left their details on the answering machine.

'Terry,' he said, 'can we have a word outside?'

'Sounds serious, Tom,' said Hudson, when they were outside in the corridor.

'Wainwright spoke to me this morning. From what he told me I believe that Ray Garvey may have my address.'

'You're not going to move, are you?'

'No, you are. Find a hotel for tonight, I'll deal with Garvey if he comes to the flat.'

The door to the incident room opened and Bob Davies stuck his head round it.

'There's a phone call for you, sir, some professor. He said it was very important.'

Daykin walked back into the room and picked up the phone.

'Inspector Daykin, this is Professor Weir at St Andrews University. I read about your Press conference yesterday. Is Ilona Mancini still working with you on the case?'

'Yes, Professor. Why, do you know her?'

'Where is she now?'

'As far as I know, she's in an office we gave her here at the station.'

'She was a student of mine, a very bright girl. She graduated with first class honours and showed all the signs of being one of the top forensic psychologists in the country. She was killed in a car crash two years ago.'

It took three seconds for the information to crystallize in Daykin's mind.

'So you're saying whoever we have looking through all our files isn't Ilona Mancini?'

'CVs are very easy to forge and it seems highly unlikely that there are two women called Ilona Mancini in a field as small as forensic psychology, so I'd say it's a fair bet.'

'I want to thank you for the call, Professor and I don't want to sound ungrateful, but I have somewhere to go, so do you mind if I cut this conversation short?'

'I quite understand. Good luck.'

Daykin slammed the phone down and said to Terry Hudson, 'The forensic psychologist, the Mancini woman, which office is she using?'

'Inspector Sullivan's office, first floor, room 116,' said Martin Brown.

Daykin moved quickly to the door and threw it open. Terry Hudson followed him, he thought he'd better. By the time Hudson had got through the door Daykin was halfway down the corridor. In the way the overweight, middle-aged man ran, Hudson saw the ghost of how he must have been in his rugby-playing youth – fast, powerful and determined. Daykin ran down the stairs two at a time with surprising agility and by the time Terry Hudson caught up with him he had opened the door and was standing in the middle of the office. Hudson looked at the untidy piles of files, the empty coffee cups and the chair pushed back from the desk and lying on its side on the floor. The woman who called herself Ilona Mancini had left in a hurry. Daykin shoved his hands deep into his pockets in a gesture of frustration. He walked round the room, looking at everything she had left, but touching nothing.

'Seal this room,' he said, as he strode out. 'Nobody in except CSI. Tell them we want fingerprints, DNA and handwriting. When they're finished you and I will go through it. When you've organized that I'll be in the incident room.'

Daykin didn't go straight there, he went down the stairs to reception. He didn't run this time, he took the stairs gently, one at a time. Whoever the woman who said she was Ilona Mancini was, she had gone by now.

'The forensic psychologist, Ilona Mancini,' he said to the receptionist, 'have you seen her?'

'Not today,' said the receptionist, without looking up from her computer screen.

'Can you describe her?'

This time the woman did look up. She frowned and wrinkled her nose to show she was thinking. 'You wouldn't pick her out in a crowd,' she began.

'I'm not going to ask her out on a date, I just want to know what she looks like.'

'Well, sort of medium.'

'Height?'

'Medium.'

'Weight?'

'Medium.'

'Hair?'

'Brown.'

'Light brown?'

'No, sort of medium. Could have been a wig.'

'Clothes?'

'Now, there she was unusual. Wore the same clothes every day. I'm surprised she didn't smell.'

'What did she wear?'

'A loose-fitting floral dress, black patent shoes and black tights.'

Daykin thanked her and climbed the stairs to the third floor.

'We need to look at what we've got,' said Daykin, to the officers in the room. 'Let's start with Ilona Mancini. Why don't you all pull up chairs?'

When they were all sitting round the table Daykin said, 'Has anyone seen her?'

'I have, sir,' said Bob Davies, 'but not for long. She seemed anxious to get away.'

'Me, too,' said Fritz Schmidt, 'but, yeah, she told me what she wanted, then left.'

'What do you mean, "told me what she wanted"?'

'She said her job would be a lot easier if she could tap into our computer.'

'Could you do that for her?'

'Oh yeah, all we needed was a back door trojan horse, so everything on the computer, including what we were doing right then, could go on to her remote screen.'

'On her remote screen?'

'She had a laptop in Inspector Sullivan's office.'

'Just when was the information about Silus Cunningham put into the computer?'

'First thing this morning.'

'So she would have seen it?'

'If she was looking at her laptop, yes.'

'Sarah,' said Daykin, 'get on to Henley, tell them to pick Cunningham up now. Get a patrol car outside his house within five minutes and tell them to use their beacons and sirens.'

'Description?' he said, turning back to Schmidt.

'Five four, about nine stone, although she could have been heavier because she wore a loose fitting dress, brown straight hair, long, down to her shoulder blades, black tights, black shoes, large glasses with fancy purple frames.'

Terry Hudson came into the room. 'The office is sealed, CSI are on their way.'

Daykin nodded to a chair and Hudson sat down.

'So far, people, we've got this wrong. A few days ago we had four possible victims, a motive and a suspect or two. Now we're down to three victims, no motive and no suspect. On top of that someone knows every detail of this investigation, including where one of the potential victims is right now. Let's have a briefing and let's start with motive. We thought it was revenge, it's not. So, suggestions?'

'Hate?' said Bridget Cooper.

'These aren't hate crimes. The bodies would have been mutilated, we'd have found evidence of threats, and there would have been an obvious suspect if they were.'

'Love?' said Schmidt.

'Love can't be a motive for murder,' snorted Martin Brown.

'If you want to marry someone's wife badly enough, you might kill the husband.'

'Or if you wanted to marry someone and your wife wouldn't divorce you, you might kill her,' said Daykin. 'But there would only be one murder, we have three.'

'Supposing two of the murders were just to cover up for the third, so we didn't suspect that the motive was, say, love?' asked Bob Davies.

'Good point, keep it in mind, but I think there's only one motive we should be looking at.'

'Money,' said Terry Hudson.

'If it's none of the others, it's always money.'

179

'You want us to go over all twelve of them again, looking for a money motive?'

'No, we haven't time. Forget the ones who are still alive. Concentrate on the murdered men, Moore, Van Meer and Miller. Look for a money motive, there are six of you, including Sergeant Hudson, take as many as you can each.'

'What about you, sir?'

'You're looking for the obvious; I'm going to see if I can find the less obvious.'

He started towards the door.

'Where are you going, Tom?' asked Terry Hudson.

'I'm going to take the dog for a walk.' He patted his trouser and jacket pockets before finding his phone in the breast pocket of his shirt. 'If you need me, I've got my mobile.'

Daykin drove out of Harrogate and took the A1 to the edge of the North Yorkshire Moors. He got out of the car and began to walk, letting the dog off the lead after fifty yards. There was a strong easterly wind blowing across the moors from the sea but, apart from turning up the collar of his jacket, Daykin didn't seem to notice. The dog, with unlimited freedom, ran in all directions until, tiring at last, it settled itself into padding silently at Daykin's heels. After thirty minutes it started to spot with rain, a drizzle that turned quickly into a steady downpour. Daykin occasionally absent-mindedly took his glasses off and, without looking at them, wiped the lenses with a large blue handkerchief.

Two hours after they had left the car, they returned to it, both soaking wet. Daykin took an old towel from the boot and laid it across the back seat. The dog shook itself vigorously, sending fine sprays of water in arcs like a garden water sprinkler, before jumping into the car. It sat on the back seat, panting gently, its pink tongue hanging out, a large happy grey and white ball of wet hair.

On the way back down the A1 the rain got heavier and the temperature started to fall. Daykin turned his heater on, it didn't work. He banged the switch five times with his fist before a slow trickle of warm air came through the vents in the dashboard. At the station, he left Royston on the towel in the corner of his office and went to the Incident Room.

'Can we gather round?' he asked.

They drew chairs round the table in a semi-circle, trying to ignore his wet hair and clothes.

'Let's take the victims in order. Darius Moore?'

'If the church was a business, it would be called successful. They were making a lot of money. If some of it got into Darius Moore's pockets he hid it well. He had a good salary and the church paid for his car and gave him a clothing and grooming allowance. On top of that, any money he made from writing he kept. He took exotic holidays three times a year and lived in a six-bedroomed house. He made a lot more than your average parish priest, but not enough for someone to kill him.'

'Jerry Merchanto?'

'What you see is what you get. A man who ran up massive debts and when the vultures began to circle he threw himself from a tall building, no money, no motive.'

'Dominic Lucas?'

'If money is the motive, he has to be your prime target. Very, very wealthy and getting richer by the year. If you want to know what a player he was, someone told me he didn't just predict moves in the market, he controlled them. I looked very closely at his death. It had to be nothing to do with any serial killer, just a burglar desperate not to be caught who whacks a householder harder than he meant to.'

'Who gets his money?'

'Mainly his wife. There was some left to his college and some more to a foundation, but why would his wife kill him? Everyone said she was devastated when he died. Besides, why kill the goose while it's still laying golden eggs? She could have divorced him and walked away with about ninety million.'

'Francis Sheppard.'

'A man who spent what little he earned on his hobby. Climbing mountains can be expensive. He was in so much debt he might just have followed Merchanto's lead and thrown himself off the side of the Eiger.'

'Christopher Van Meer?'

'Wealthy, but just like Lucas, no obvious candidate who would bump him off to get at his money.'

'Robert Miller?'

'He made several million, but he spent a lot of it. The bank warned him that the recording studio idea might not work and they wouldn't advance him any money, so he funded it himself. It wasn't a success and was haemorrhaging money. No one person benefited under his will by enough to want to murder him.'

'Joshua Swanson?'

'An accident, pure and simple. Enough evidence of that for the insurance company to pay out.'

'Did they pay much?'

'He was only insured for £25,000.'

'Peter McDonald?'

'You don't get rich on a soldier's salary and that's all he had. He'd decided to stay in the army and round about now would be retiring on a service pension. No money worth killing him for.'

'Finally, John Hastings?'

'He'd lost one fortune and was trying to build another, but he'd hardly started. His properties were heavily financed and when he died he probably owed more than he was worth.'

'That give you any ideas, Tom?' asked Terry Hudson.

'Only this: the key has to be Lucas. You and I need to take another long look at his life. In the meantime I don't want to lose any of the three who are still breathing. Get on to Henley, will you? Tell them I want Cunningham here, where I can keep an eye on him. They can transport him in one of those vans they use for category A prisoners, the ones with an internal cage and no windows. They'd better send three armed officers with him. Ask them to give us an arrival time and we'll meet the van here.

'The rest of you, now look at the remaining three, Cunningham, Ellington and Freeman. I want to know if they could have a motive and, more importantly, where Ellington and Freeman are now.'

'When you've made the call, Terry, meet me in Inspector Sullivan's room.'

When Daykin got there, the CSI team had finished and were re-sealing the room.

'OK to go in?' he asked.

'Yes, sir,' said Sergeant Tennant, 'we're taking some things away for forensics, but my guess is that she left nothing that would give us any clues about her.'

The three CSI officers walked off down the corridor, Daykin tore back the broad adhesive strips that sealed the door and opened it. He turned on the light and stood in the doorway, looking round the room. It was just an ordinary office. The desk in the middle was old, but not yet falling apart, the three chairs were standard police issue and didn't match, there were four pictures on the walls, Inspector Sullivan at his passing-out parade, receiving some award and two with his family. The desk was clear and the wastepaper basket was empty. CSI must have cleared the desk and emptied the basket. There was no trace of the woman who had occupied this room for days. Except one thing. It would have meant very little to anybody else in this station, but it meant a lot to Tom Daykin. Every Valentine's Day and Christmas he bought his wife a perfume. It was an unusual scent. He didn't know where Jenny had first been introduced to it, but it was made by a small independent perfume company in Grasse. Mr Parsons at the family chemist's in Shapford always kept a couple of bottles in stock and it was the only place Daykin had ever seen it. In all the years of his marriage he never smelt it on another woman, only Jenny. But he smelt it in this room and a wave of sadness came over him.

'Penny for your thoughts, Tom,' said Terry Hudson's voice behind him.

'Just holding a seance,' said Daykin, and he closed the door softly.

Terry Hudson didn't ask him what he meant.

Daykin hated computers. But he knew they were a necessary evil. He sat in front of the screen Fritz Schmidt used and typed in Darius Moore's name. A photograph of Moore came up on the screen, telling him Dr Darius Moore had a Ph.D. in theology and was Bishop of the Church of Enlightened Reality. He opened his diary and began to note down anything unusual about Bishop Moore.

It was late afternoon and he was halfway through the information on Clive Ellington when he received a message that the van bringing Silus Cunningham would arrive at eight that evening. He let the others go at six and worked on his own in the incident room until 7.30. He took Royston for a walk round Harrogate town centre and was back at the station just before eight. At five past the hour a white Nissan van drove slowly into the car-park and reversed up to the main entrance. The back doors opened and two officers dressed in black baseball caps, black flack jackets and trousers tucked into combat boots, got out. Each had a machine pistol hanging across his chest. They looked around the car park and up at the surrounding building. One of them gave a nod to someone inside the van and Silus Cunningham got slowly and stiffly out of the vehicle.

'I'm Tom Daykin,' said Daykin, offering his hand.

Silus Cunningham didn't take it, he seemed nervous.

'Yes,' he said, 'we've spoken on the phone.' He looked down at Royston who was sitting by Daykin's leg and staring back at him impassively. 'Dogs,' said Cunningham. 'I don't like dogs, nasty, vicious things.'

'Inside, Royston,' said Daykin. The dog took a final, long look at Silus Cunningham, then turned and padded moodily into the building.

'Follow me, Mr Cunningham,' said Daykin.

183

They went along the corridor and upstairs to Daykin's office. Standing by the window were two men.

'I have organized a safe house for you. These gentlemen will stay with you to make sure you don't come to any harm. Before you go with them I need to talk to you.'

Silus Cunningham sat down in a chair by Daykin's desk and looked round the office.

'I can imagine,' he said, 'what you want to talk about.'

'I need you to tell me where Ellington and Freeman are?'

'I don't know.'

'All three of you disappeared at the same time, almost to the minute. Coincidence?'

'Perhaps.'

'You are the one who keeps in touch with everyone. You called them and told them about Darius Moore. It was a joint decision to go to ground and it was timed that way.'

'So?'

'So you know where they are, or at least how to contact them.'

'You're speculating,' said Cunningham, examining his fingernails. He held both hands at arm's length with the fingers facing away from him. Satisfied that the nails were flawless he crossed his arms, but still didn't look at Daykin.

'Are you saying you haven't contacted them?'

Cunningham focused his best cross-examination stare at Daykin.

'Two people I know have been murdered. You have been in charge of the investigation for some time. You have no idea of who killed them or why they were killed. In the meantime you have stood by whilst another man has been murdered. Give me one good reason why I should trust you, or anyone from the chief constable down, with sensitive information.'

'Because it may save their lives.'

'Like Darius Moore?'

'He refused police protection.'

Silus Cunningham looked across the room at the two men standing by the window.

'Are you gentlemen ready to take me to what Inspector Daykin assures me is a safe house?' He got to his feet and turned his back on Daykin.

'Just before you go,' said Daykin, 'in case of emergencies, can you give me your mobile phone number?'

Silus Cunningham recited the number over his shoulder while the two men by the window, at a nod from Daykin, walked towards the office door.

Daykin strolled to the window and watched the three men get into a car parked in front of the building. As it drove out of the main gates he took his mobile phone from his pocket and dialled Terry Hudson's number.

'Terry? When you went to see Patrick Freeman he called you, was that using his mobile?'

'I think so, why?'

'Go into your recent calls menu, will you? See if the number comes up.'

There was a pause while Hudson scrolled through his menus.

'Yes, here it is.'

'Thanks, Terry, see you in the morning.'

Daykin closed the phone and put it in his pocket, then went to find Royston. He drove them back to his flat. As he got out of the car, a man in the car parked across the main road was watching him through night vision binoculars. Ray Garvey was a careful man. They had seen the grey Volvo, so he had parked it in the station car-park and rented a dark-blue Vauxhall, a car that blended into the background. The inspector and the dog got out of the car, but not Terry Hudson. Someone must have heard that Colin Williams had been asking questions. Williams was too careless. When he had finished in Harrogate, Garvey would have to pay him a visit and give him a gentle slapping to remind him to be more careful. And Hudson? Garvey had hired the car for forty-eight hours, two days should be enough to finish this job off. If it took any longer it wasn't worth the money he would get. If, by this time tomorrow, he hadn't found Hudson the inspector would tell him where he was. He felt under the driver's seat to check that the electric cattle prod was still there. A few blows from that and people were usually only too anxious to talk.

Chapter Thirty

Terry Hudson was late. It was the sort of bright, sunny but crisp day that Daykin loved. If he had been in the Dales he would have found the excuse to take the dog for a walk over the tops of the hills, just to get the cold clean air deep into his lungs. Instead, he walked down to the main door of the station and let the dog off the leash in the car-park.

At 9.30 Hudson sauntered through the main gate, drawing on the last of the cigarette.

'Hello, Tom,' he said cheerfully, 'walking the dog?'

'Waiting for you, you're late.'

'Because I got this,' said Hudson, taking a thick white envelope from his pocket and handing it to Daykin.

Tom Daykin had never seen £5000 in an envelope and he thought it would be a larger bundle than it was. It seemed very ordinary as he held it in the palm of his hand.

'It wasn't easy,' said Terry Hudson, lighting another cigarette, 'I don't have a great relationship with my bank manager, but when I signed over the payment I will get for the car and he saw that I still had some of my salary left this month, he agreed to loan me the money.'

'Does he know what it's for?'

'Are you kidding? He thinks it's for another car and he doesn't know that I've drawn it in cash.'

Daykin whistled for the dog.

'When you finish that cigarette, we'll get off,' he said.

'Get off? Where?'

'Ravenscar.'

'What the hell are we going to Ravenscar for?'

'Patrick Freeman, it's where he's hiding.'

'How do you know?'

'I'll tell you in the car.'

They were leaving Harrogate before Terry Hudson said, 'You were going to tell me about Ravenscar.'

'Silus Cunningham gave me his mobile number, you gave me Freeman's. First thing this morning I got the hi-tech unit at Northallerton to check which phone company Cunningham used. I called them and they faxed me a copy of the calls he has made and received in the last ten days.

'On the morning they all disappeared Silus Cunningham called Patrick Freeman just before nine. Late afternoon, Freeman called Cunningham. When you call from a mobile phone the signal is sent to the nearest transmission mast. There is technology to tell you which transmission mast received the signal, so you can tell which area a person was in when he made the call. I've seen the path of a drug dealer traced this way as he drove down the M1, using his mobile phone. I got the hi-tech unit to give me the co-ordinates on the transmission masts that received Freeman's signal. The conversation lasted just over ten minutes, for the first four the signal was at a mast on the moors, for the last six it transferred to the mast in Ravenscar. That's where he is.'

'But you don't know where he's staying.'

'Ravenscar isn't exactly a metropolis, is it? Freeman is handicapped, so he'll have to park his car somewhere near where he is living. We'll drive round until we see the car, then we must be somewhere near him.'

Terry Hudson recognized the car, a Vauxhall Astra with a sticker of the National Trust in the back window and handicap controls on the steering wheel. It was parked in a road of terraced houses each with a small front garden. All the gardens were carefully tended, as if their owners were in a competition with each other. Daykin looked at the house nearest to where the car was parked. He nodded at the two steps leading to the front door. Someone had laid a wide piece of plywood over them.

'You should know Ravenscar,' he said to Terry Hudson, 'is there a police station?'

'No, it's policed from Whitby.'

'If you know anyone there, give them a call and see if they can tell you about 23 Jasmine Street, will you?'

Terry Hudson made the phone call. When he had finished he snapped the phone shut.

'My mate Don Lister at Whitby says the house is owned by Gloria Freeman, she's lived here for years.'

'Cousin?'

'Probably a maiden aunt; she's about seventy years old.'

'Let's pay Miss Freeman a visit.'

Patrick Freeman had chosen the person to guard him well. She was aggressive in her fierce protection.

'Yes?' she demanded, as she answered the door.

'We'd like to speak to Patrick Freeman,' said Daykin quietly.

'I don't know who you are talking about.'

'The man whose car is parked outside,' said Daykin, showing his warrant card.

'There must be some mistake, Inspector,' she said calmly. 'As I said, I don't know who you are talking about.'

'Your nephew may be in a lot of danger, Miss Freeman, we're only trying to help him.'

'Go away and help someone else.'

Daykin and Miss Freeman faced each other in the doorway. Daykin didn't know how long they would have stood there in silence, because Terry Hudson interrupted.

'I'm fed up with this, luv,' he said to Gloria Freeman, 'we're only trying to stop the poor sod getting his throat cut.'

He leaned forward so that he was looking over her shoulder.

'Paddy, you pillock! If you won't talk to us we're off, but don't expect us to pick up the bloody remains of what's left of you!'

'How dare you!' said Gloria Freeman.

'It's all right, Aunt Gloria,' said a resigned voice from behind her.

Patrick Freeman appeared from the kitchen at the far end of the hallway and wheeled himself towards them.

'How did you find me?' he asked Terry Hudson.

'My governor found you,' said Hudson, nodding towards Daykin. 'And although he's very good, if we're here, the person who wants to kill you can't be far behind us.'

Patrick Freeman shrugged. 'What do you want to do?'

'Take you into protective custody, Mr Freeman,' said Daykin.

'Where?'

'Whitby Police Station tonight, then to a safe house in Harrogate.'

'And if I refuse?'

'Darius Moore refused.'

Patrick Freeman rubbed his palms nervously across the tops of the wheels on his chair.

'I'm sorry, Aunt Gloria,' he said eventually.

'That's all right, Patrick, it was nice to see you again.' She smiled down at him.

'I'll go and pack,' he said and turned the wheelchair around.

With a bad grace, she invited them into the hall, but no further. Terry Hudson called Whitby Police Station and arranged for officers to come in a van to collect Patrick Freeman, then he and Daykin left.

'Back to Harrogate?' asked Hudson, as he fastened his seat belt.

'No, Middlesbrough.'

'You're not going to see the piece of trash who's trying to have me worked over?'

'You'd prefer Garvey to come at you with a baseball bat?'

'You could be right.'

They stopped near Danby for a cup of tea and were walking towards the car when Daykin's phone rang.

'Tom? It's Trevor Wainwright. Clive Ellington is nicely tucked up again.'

'What happened, sir?'

'I sometimes wonder about these men who are supposed to be so intelligent. I don't know about you, but if I was trying to get to Europe and I had a dodgy passport I'd hop on Eurostar or a cross channel ferry where the security isn't so tight. Our hero tries to get on a plane for Spain at Birmingham Airport. I don't know how much he paid for the passport, but the airline people spotted it straight away and called Customs.'

'Why Spain?'

'He has some friends or relatives in Marbella. I guess a con man like him could make a good living on the Costa del Crime.'

'Where is he now?'

'Somewhere with a little less sun. I called in a favour with a police officer in the Met. They've given him a comfortable cell at Paddington Green until I get him back to a category B prison.'

It took some time to find the garage and when they did, Daykin didn't like what he saw. It was a modern two storey building on a large piece of land, near the end of a cul-de-sac. There were four closed circuit television cameras pointing at the entrance and the forecourt and the steel security gates looked like they could be closed quickly to keep people in as well as keep them out. If his talk with Bradley went wrong, it looked to him like one giant trap.

'Turn your horses for home.'

'Sorry, Tom?'

'Turn the car round, so it's facing away from the garage and keep the engine running,' said Daykin, as he got out of the car.

'Keep the engine running? You could be half an hour.'

'Sometimes, more often than not, it doesn't start first time. If I come running out of there with two gorillas chasing me, I don't want you to be sitting here swearing at the ignition.'

Daykin opened the back door, reached in and took out a large white envelope. Terry Hudson hadn't noticed, the dog was sitting on it.

'What's that?' he asked.

'Your get-out-of-jail card,' said Daykin as he started to walk towards the front door of the garage.

The package had been waiting for Daykin when he arrived at the station, it had been delivered by a courier. When he opened it he saw what a thorough job Peter Davies had done in a short space of time. There were paper trails showing stolen luxury cars passing through the garage and coming out with new identities, then put on transporters to Hull docks where they were shipped abroad. There were copy invoices for spare parts, transport delivery notes and shipment manifestos. And there were photographs. Taken with, Daykin guessed, a telephoto lens, they showed men driving cars into the forecourt, mechanics working on the cars and transporters picking up the same vehicles with their new identities. Daykin tucked it under his arm as he walked through the open garage doors. A mechanic was leaning into the engine compartment of a Mercedes. He stood up and faced Daykin as he walked in.

'Is Dennis Bradley in?' asked Daykin.

'He's busy.'

'I didn't ask for an appointment, I asked if he was in,' said Daykin, showing his warrant card.

The mechanic nodded to the office at the top of the metal steps. He didn't need to warn Bradley, who was looking down at them, arms folded and chewing on the end of a cigar, from the office window.

Daykin climbed the stairs to the office doors. Dennis Bradley opened it.

'Copper?' he said.

'Tom Daykin, North Yorkshire.'

Bradley smiled from behind the cigar. It was not a warm smile, the eyes remained cold.

'Come in and sit down,' he said, opening the door wider to let Daykin walk in. 'No offence, but can I see your warrant card? I like to know who I'm talking to,' said Bradley as they sat down. Daykin passed the card across the desk.

'Inspector?' Bradley said, as he looked at the card. 'Why would North Yorkshire Police send an inspector out to my back-street garage?' He smiled again, but the eyes were still cold.

'It's about the cars you've been ringing and exporting.'

Daykin knew that Dennis Bradley had too much experience for an outburst of injured innocence.

'You want to watch what you say, Inspector, there are slander laws. Besides, the local plod have crawled all over this place and haven't found anything to worry them.'

'That's because you were tipped off, you knew they were coming. It's all in here.'

Daykin laid the large envelope down on the desk and patted it gently.

'And what would that be?' asked Bradley. He leaned back and put his thumbs behind the Union Jack braces and moved them up and down a few times in a nervous gesture. The smile was not quite as wide and a trace of concern ran through the coldness in his eyes.

'Have a look,' said Daykin, pushing the envelope across the desk. 'Keep it if you like, I can make lots of copies.'

Dennis Bradley held the envelope up to shoulder height and poured the contents on to the desk. Papers and photographs landed and spread across the surface like lava.

'Excuse me,' as he turned papers and photographs over and examined them.

'Take your time,' said Daykin. He got up and walked to the window that overlooked the work area. One of the three cars that had been worked on when he came in was gone.

'So what?' said Bradley eventually.

Daykin turned from the window.

'So those documents prove you are dealing in stolen luxury vehicles.'

'They don't.'

'If I put those documents in front of a Crown Prosecution solicitor he'd tell me to charge you.'

The smile returned to Bradley's face. This time it was genuine.

'You haven't, have you?'

'Not yet.'

'Why not?'

'Because you and I need to talk about something else.'

Dennis Bradley got up and walked round the desk.

'That means either you think I've got my hands dirty somewhere else, or you want a pay off. Which is it?'

'Neither. I want you to call the dogs off my sergeant!'

Bradley knew immediately who Daykin was talking about.

'That guy from Scarborough who can't pay his gambling debts, he's your sergeant? Get rid of him, he's bad news.'

'You sent a debt collector after him.'

'I need to recoup my losses.'

'I have a solution so nobody loses.'

'So have I. I paid good money for the debt, so your Sergeant Hudson pays me in full. Today.'

'If that's what you want, I take copies of these documents to the Crown Prosecution Service.'

'And you think that's a threat? What am I going to get at Court, a slap on the wrist, maybe a fine? Well, the fifteen thousand Hudson owes me can go towards that.'

'It's not the court room you should be worried about. You've built a nice lifestyle for yourself. When your case gets into the papers and on local television, the members at the golf club won't be impressed. You won't get invites to the Lord Mayor's dinner any more, the local rugby club won't want you on the board and the invitations your wife gets to charity lunches will dry up. Your social life is going to change, dramatically and for good. If that's not enough, your bank manager won't be so understanding and your legitimate contacts will start sending their business elsewhere.'

Bradley looked at him calmly, but the thumbs went back behind the braces again.

'I don't think so,' he said eventually. 'This is going to cost me too much to write off.'

'Maybe not.'

The thumbs, which had been moving quickly up and down behind the braces, stopped.

'Meaning what?'

'The debt is fifteen thousand but you won't have paid that for it. Terry Hudson is a detective sergeant, that means collecting from him has its own problems. I'd bet you only paid about three thousand to the bookie. I can give you five. That's three for the debt, a thousand for Garvey and a thousand profit.'

'Not enough'.

'It's in cash,'

Daykin put the envelope on the desk.

Dennis Bradley looked at the envelope and licked his lips thoughtfully.

'If I agree to this,' he said slowly, his eyes not leaving the envelope, 'you'll have to give me the disc of these photographs.'

'That's not part of the deal. I won't report what I know, but in twelve months' time I will call the local station. If you're still ringing cars, this information goes to the Crown Prosecution Service. I want you to stop now.'

'What makes you think you're in a position to start shouting the odds?'

'You do what you want, I'm just telling you what I will do.'

Bradley rubbed his face with his hands.

'I'll tell you what I will do, Inspector Daykin. I'll take your money and I'll call Garvey off. Debt paid. No promises about my business.'

'Your choice,' said Daykin, pushing the envelope with the money across the desk. He got up. They had come to a deal, but neither of them offered to shake hands.

Chapter Thirty-one

Terry Hudson, who was more nervous than he looked, had spent his time watching the rear-view mirror and saw Daykin walking towards the car, not being chased by anyone. He got out of the driver's seat and walked round the vehicle to the passenger side.

'You can relax,' said Daykin as he got into the car, 'he's taken the five thousand.'

'How did you make him do that?' asked Terry Hudson, as he fastened his seat belt.

'I gave him some options – he liked the easiest one.'

They drove out of Middlesbrough and headed south. Just before Thirsk, Daykin said, 'Do you fancy a pint?'

'You mean as a celebration?'

'If it is, you're buying. We need to take a detour.'

Instead of heading towards the A1 he turned left on the A roads that turned into B roads as they headed into the heart of the Dales. The further they drove along the winding, narrow roads, bordered on both sides by high dry-stone walls, the more relaxed Daykin appeared. The more relaxed he became, the more agitated Royston was, sitting up, his head moving from side to side as he recognized familiar landmarks. After what seemed to Hudson to be half an hour of slow driving they crossed a humped-back bridge and, as the light began to fade, he had his first view of Shapford.

It was more a large village than a town and, in a backwater in the middle of the country, it was a place that had stopped in time fifty years ago. It was too small and too isolated for the supermarket chains to have any interest in it. So the local shops, the butcher, the greengrocer and the general store, survived and even thrived. There was a row of these friendly, family-run stores along both sides of the High Street. The sort of shops where the staff knew the customers' names. Some of the shopkeepers were winding in the awnings as they drove past. Daykin waved to most of them.

The High Street ended at the town square, an oversized village green, surrounded on three sides by buildings and on the other by open farm land. The only other road out of the square was to the left of the High Street, running at right angles to it, towards the magistrates court, police station, the branch offices of firms of solicitors and accountants and a vet's practice. The buildings in the square were larger, but there was nothing modern. No smoked glass and concrete towers, just Dales grey-stone buildings that had stood here since the grass was laid for the square and long before the children's roundabout and swings at its centre. There was a small branch of a bank, a doctor's surgery and a restaurant and wine bar, the trendy distressed pine and stainless steel spoilt by the gingham table cloths and plastic cruets.

Standing alone, opposite the bus shelter, at the narrow end of the square was the Malt Shovel Public House. It was an oblong building, the wide side taking up most of the side of the square, with the public rooms on the ground floor and above them the private living quarters. Daykin parked his car directly outside the pub. He got out, opened the back door and Royston jumped to the ground, then trotted to the door of the pub where he sat down and waited for Daykin to follow him.

Daykin and Hudson walked through the main door, set off centre in the front of the building and protected by a pitched roof porch. Inside the door a bar twenty feet long was directly in front of them and standing in the space between the bar and the optics on the mirrored back wall was the landlord, John Wolmersley. Like Daykin, Wolmersley had been a rugby player in his youth, but he had played rugby league. A large second row forward for Wakefield Trinity all his career, he had taken this pub on his retirement and had been here for over twenty years. He kept a neat and orderly house; he didn't like rowdy behaviour. Nobody could remember the last time someone had the nerve to be rowdy. He watched them come into his pub, his large hands placed flat on the bar top. He was dressed in a shirt with the sleeves rolled up, a tie and waistcoat. When he saw Daykin he smiled and reached for a pewter tankard hanging from one of the tow of pegs above his head.

'Pint, Tom?'

'Please, John. This is Terry Hudson. You'll like him, he's paying.'

John Wolmersley nodded to Terry Hudson.

'Handle or schooner?'

'Handle, it's been a long day, I might drop a schooner.'

'No trouble from you, Royston,' said John Wolmersley, looking at the dog.

The dog gave him a withering look from behind the veil of hair and padded to lie down by a table near the window. When they had their beer, Daykin and Hudson went to sit at the same table.

Three old men at the next table, all wearing cloth caps, looked up from their game of dominoes. They nodded to Daykin and one of them said, 'Tom.'

Daykin nodded back and the three men went back to their game with the intensity of chess grand masters.

'I spent a lot of time thinking when I was walking the dog yesterday,' said Daykin to Terry Hudson. 'Have you noticed how many women crop up in this investigation?'

'You mean Katrina Voitskaya, or whatever she calls herself,' said Terry Hudson, picking up his glass of beer.

'Yes, and the woman impersonating Ilona Mancini. Darius Moore was killed by a woman. And the woman who was asking Silus Cunningham about Dominic Lucas.'

'What's she got to do with it?' said Hudson, lifting the glass to his lips.

'I'm not sure, its just a feeling I've got. Like the nagging feeling that there can't be so many women standing in the shadows. Supposing they're all the same woman.'

'You mean,' said Terry Hudson, putting the glass back down on the table untouched, 'that a woman serial killer has the nerve to spend several days in the middle of the police station investigating her? The chances of that are what, fifty per cent worse than a lottery win?'

'She's a serial killer – what do you know about serial killers?'

'I don't know what it's like here in the Dales, Tom, but serial killing isn't exactly popular in Scarborough.'

'There's something else.'

'What's that?'

'One of the twelve is an odd man out.'

Terry Hudson, who had always hated guessing games, gave up straight away.

'Which one?'

'Francis Sheppard.'

'Why?'

'We know if all the others are dead or alive. We don't know for sure if he's gone, or is still with us.'

'And that's important?'

'I've got a feeling we should think he's dead when he's actually alive.'

'You get a lot of these feelings, do you?'

'Yes, and I wouldn't pay any attention to them, but they usually turn out to be right.'

Daykin's phone rang. He dug into his inside jacket pocket, pulled it out and answered it.

'Tom, it's Trevor Wainwright. I had the chief constable on the phone, he's been given a bit of a mauling by the editor of one of the national dailies and he needs to call him back to tell him we're making progress. So, he kicks my backside, I kick yours and you kick Sergeant Hudson's and so it goes on down the line. To avoid this being more than just an arse kicking contest, have you got anything new I can tell the chief constable?'

'We believe that money is the motive and we're taking a much closer look at Lucas and Sheppard,' said Daykin lamely.

'I've just been to the incident room to look for you, where are you?'

'On my way back from Middlesbrough.'

'The last time I heard, you were in Ravenscar. What has Middlesbrough got to do with this case?'

'Nothing. I had someone to see on my way back.'

'Good God, Tom! This is a multiple murder investigation and you go off for a social visit!'

'It wasn't a social visit, sir. Just nothing to do with this case.'

Wainwright didn't say anything. Daykin couldn't work out if he was thinking or just speechless with anger.

'I can hear background noises, you're not in a pub, are you? Never mind, I've got a meeting of the court liaison committee first thing in the morning, so I won't need to phone the chief constable until after eleven. See if you can give me something to tell him, will you?'

Chapter Thirty-two

Evangelium

Tom Daykin was in early the following morning and, as he walked into the incident room, he saw that someone was already there.

Sitting at the far table, concentrating on his computer screen, was Fritz Schmidt. He didn't look up until Daykin was standing almost directly over him.

'What are you doing here so early?' said Daykin.

'You wanted Dominic Lucas's finances looking into. I'm used to following paper trails of money, so I set the computer up. It's very detailed, but I think I now understand most of it.'

'Have you got much?'

'Loads, sir.'

'Then let's grab a cup of coffee and sit down, so you can tell me all about Mr Lucas and his money.'

When they sat down at a table with a mug of coffee in front of each of them, Daykin opened his diary and said, 'In your own time, in any order you like, tell me what you can about Mr Lucas's millions.'

'Do you know a lot about high finance, sir?'

'You go ahead, I'll let you know if you lose me.'

'The business is structured through a network of holding companies and trusts. The holding companies were mainly registered in Liechtenstein, Jersey and Panama. They feed money through the trusts in bank accounts, often set up in London for ease of access, but he had accounts in New York and Hong Kong, so he was near the main financial markets and could move money electronically between them.

'He bought and sold futures, usually in copper and tin, but occasionally he dealt in precious metals, platinum, gold and silver. If he saw the opportunity for a good and quick profit, on rare occasions he went into wheat, coffee or oil.

'His real strength was the way he could influence markets. About five or six times over the last thirty years he would start buying futures in large amounts through maybe thirty intermediaries. The more he bought, the more the price went up and pretty soon others were buying on a rising market. Then, just before the price peaked, he would tell the intermediaries to dump all the futures he had purchased on to the market. The price went down like a lead balloon and he took his profit, but he had also sold futures he didn't have and, as the price he had to buy them for was less than the price he had agreed to sell, he made a second profit. Every time he did that he never made less than forty million pounds.

'I've taken a look at the bank accounts he held. They fall into four groups. Holding company accounts, trust accounts, trading accounts and property accounts. Almost as a sideline, he bought property, held on to it for a few years while the local market went up, then sold it. Of all the accounts I looked at there were only three that didn't fit the mould.

'There are two held in Jersey. Money was fairly regularly paid into them over a number of years, then it stopped. Since then nothing has gone in and nothing has gone out, the money just sits there, earning interest. The two accounts between them now have about 20 million pounds in them. I think that these were an emergency pension. If he lost his touch, or made a few disastrous investments and it all came crashing down around his ears, then he would retire on his twenty million.

'The other account is a mystery. It is in a bank in Venezuela and is simply called T54. Money did come in and out of that account, but always in increasing amounts as far as I can tell. There was no pattern to the movement of money, just every few months a large amount would go out and a few days later a much larger, sometimes five times larger, amount would go back in again. I can trace monies in the account up to about fifteen years ago, then they improved the security on the account and my computer software can't get into it.

'It is odd, because it looks like a trading account, but it must be a trust. The account is in Venezuela but it is operated by a firm of solicitors in the City called Rosenthals. They specialize in administering trusts and they operated four charitable trusts for Dominic Lucas. He had a nephew, Paul Chapman, who he hoped would follow him into his business. Paul died of leukaemia in his early twenties and Lucas set up trusts for hospices and research into leukaemia and bone cancer.

'That's about all I can tell you.'

'This firm, Rosenthals, they won't tell you anything about the account?'

'They just stone-walled me when I asked, said it was privileged information and they didn't have their client's permission to say anything to me.'

'Thanks, Fritz. I don't know what it means, but it is interesting.'

Daykin refilled his coffee mug then sat down at the other table and started to make a list of people to contact about Francis Sheppard. His phone rang.

'Tom? Trevor Wainwright. I'm about to go into my meeting but, in case I miss you before I have to call the chief constable, any news?'

'Fritz Schmidt has done some digging into Lucas's finances. There's an account in Venezuela operated by some city solicitors as administrators for Lucas and I'd like to see what the account is for, but I would need a court order.'

'There's a barrister in Leeds, a Queen's Counsel called Jeremy Allenbrook, who has done a number of similar applications for me over the years. Try calling his clerk in Queen's Square, he'll tell you if Jeremy is available.'

The clerk said that Mr Allenbrook might be available, but he was out of chambers. Would Daykin like his mobile number? In the meantime, just in case, the clerk negotiated a fee for Allenbrook. Daykin called the number.

'Allenbrook,' said a rich, deep, public-school educated voice.

Daykin explained the problem. 'Look, Inspector,' said Allenbrook. 'I don't want to drag you all the way over to my chambers in Leeds. I'm working at home at the moment, I live just outside Harrogate. Why don't we meet up at the Old Swan in, say, an hour?'

The detectives drifted into the incident room over the next thirty minutes and Daykin set them all work to do. The last one in, smelling of the cigarette he had just stubbed out, was Terry Hudson.

'Terry,' said Daykin, 'I have a meeting to go to. While I'm there I want you to concentrate on Francis Sheppard's disappearance. Find out where he was staying, where he was going, when he left, if he was with anyone and anything else you can think of. Get Fritz to help you, the computer might short circuit a few things.'

'Where are you going?'

'Only into the town centre.'

'How long will you be?'

'I'm meeting a barrister. They're never people to hurry.'

The Old Swan is a hotel so old that the road it stands on is named after it. Daykin walked from the police station to the centre of town, along Swan Road and up the drive to the main entrance. He went through a revolving glass and mahogany door, protected by a large white portico, the front wall of the building above it covered in ivy.

Standing in front of the grandfather clock by the reception desk was a man who could only be Jeremy Allenbrook. Dressed in court dress, pin-striped trousers and black barathea jacket and waistcoat with a white stiff-collared shirt and a pale-grey tie, he was tall and elegantly slim. His hair, now thinning on top, was brushed straight back, the short sideboards pure white and grown long so that they could be swept back over his years. He was standing, hands in pockets, rocking gently on his heels so the gold charm hanging from the watch chain on the front of his waistcoat swayed in small arcs, like a hypnotist's pendulum.

'Inspector Daykin?' Jeremy Allenbrook stopped rocking and smiled over the top of his half-moon gold-framed glasses. He didn't offer to shake hands, barristers often don't.

'Shall we go through to the lounge? I've ordered coffee,' he continued, turning to walk across the Persian rug towards the lounge. Daykin followed him, he hadn't been given a choice.

They sat down in the lounge, a large room flooded with light from the skylight that ran across nearly the whole of the ceiling. Coffee arrived in a silver coffee pot with matching hot milk jug and a sugar bowl filled with a mound of large brown crystals. Set in front of each of them was a china cup and saucer. Laid carefully on the table they were, like the room, quaintly old-fashioned and timeless.

'I thought this hotel was an appropriate place to meet,' said Allenbrook, 'you being a detective. When it was the Hydra in 1926 and Agatha Christie went missing for ten days, she was found here, claiming loss of memory after a car crash.

'Anyway, tell me about this bank account you want the High Court to open up,' he continued, as he leaned forward and poured the coffee.

'Do you know anything about my case?'

'Not a thing, Inspector, I am a blank canvas.'

Allenbrook added milk to both cups without asking Daykin. Then he eyed the sugar bowl for several seconds, but overcame the temptation.

'There was a student club in Cambridge about thirty years ago. It was called The Greenrush Club and it had twelve numbers, all male. Over the years some of the men have died either naturally or by accident, but lately three have been murdered. We believe that the motive is money, although I can't give you any details, yet. One of the group, Dominic Lucas, was a financial genius and had accounts all over the place. This bank account is in Venezuela and is operated by Lucas's London solicitors, Rosenthals. I think that the reason why that account exists may be very important to the investigation.'

'That's not much, Inspector.'

'I know, but it's all I have.'

Jeremy Allenbrook took a sip of his coffee, carefully put the cup down in the saucer and leaned back in his chair.

'High Court judges, for good reason, don't like police officers trawling through people's private bank accounts. They will only allow it on the strongest grounds and they don't want any fishing expeditions, just to see what's there. Still, let's see what we can give them. This chap Lucas, was he one of the ones who was murdered?'

'No.'

'Pity.'

He took an envelope from his inside pocket and wrote a few notes on the back of it with a gold pen.

'Well, Inspector, if I'm going to make any sort of fist of this you'd better tell me all you know about The Greenrush Club, the murders, and Dominic Lucas.'

When Daykin got back to the incident room Hudson and Schmidt were sat side by side, staring at the computer screen like a pair of teenagers watching a porn film.

'What have you got?' asked Daykin, pulling up a chair so he could look at the screen over their shoulders.

'By this time twenty-three years ago,' said Schmidt, 'Francis Sheppard had been climbing for about six years. He'd been to the Alps a number of times, starting with the smaller mountains like Petite Fourche and Monte Rosa. He moved on to Mont Blanc which he first climbed in a team, then on his own. Mont Blanc, they say, isn't that tough, but having done that he set his sights on the Eiger. Again in a team, he climbed it, although one of the team fell and was badly injured. He decided he was good enough to take on the Eiger on his own.

'When he went back to the Alps the following year he told them that he was going to climb solo and they all said he was mad. Early one morning he set off from the Belvedere Hotel in Grindelwald and never came back. At that time of year there are foehns, a dry, almost warm wind that melts the snow and causes avalanches. After the wind stops there's usually a sharp frost that glazes the wall of the mountain with verglas, a sheet of ice too thin to hold an ice axe and slippery as a piece of glass.

'We know he got some of the way. It's an easy walk up to Kleine Scheidegg, a small hamlet of about four buildings in the shadow of the mountain. The mountain rescue people saw him there. He was wearing a bright orange anorak and, through a telescope, they watched him start to climb the Nordwand. He reached an overhanging slab called Rotefluh and got over that. Then he started the Hinterstoisser Traverse, a hundred and forty yard end run round a series of unclimbable overhangs. That's when the foehnsturm started and, as he was midway across the traverse, they lost him as an avalanche came down from about two hundred feet above him. When the snow settled he wasn't on the traverse any more.

'Over the next three days two teams of mountain rescue went up the mountain. They found his ice axe and one boot, but no sign of Sheppard. We checked the records of the local morgues, but nobody of Francis Sheppard's description had been brought in.'

'What if he survived?' asked Daykin.

'The mountain rescue would know about it. They have no records of bringing a climber down anywhere near that time.'

'Have you checked the hospitals?'

'Why?' asked Terry Hudson, 'my bet is that he's at the bottom of a crevasse somewhere and they'll never find him. If he's alive, where's he been for the last twenty years?'

'Fair point, but check the hospitals anyway. What's the nearest large town to Grindelwald? Start there, get a map and identify all the towns nearby. Then get on to the Swiss medical authorities and find out the names and telephone numbers of all the hospitals in those towns.'

The phone on the other table rang.

'Superintendent Wainwright for you, sir,' said Bob Davies. Daykin took the handset.

'Tom, two things. I'm out of my meeting, so I can't put off calling the chief constable any longer; he seems to have a sixth sense if you're avoiding him. Anything new?'

'I've spoken to Jeremy Allenbrook. We're working on Francis Sheppard now.'

'I know about Allenbrook. His clerk called me five minutes ago. There's a High Court Judge sitting in Leeds this week, so they've set up a hearing at Leeds Crown Court at nine-thirty tomorrow morning. You'd better be there. Jeremy Allenbrook doesn't hold out much hope.

They've had to notify Rosenthals and they're sending some high flying Queen's Counsel, Sir Christopher Benson, to oppose the application. What's this about Sheppard?'

'If the bank account is what I think it is and Sheppard's still alive, we're nearly there.'

'I won't ask. The Chief will only want details I can't give him. I'll tell him you're making steady progress, that usually satisfies him. Wish me luck.'

As Daykin put the phone down one of the other telephones rang.

'Mr Allenbrook's clerk, sir,' said Martin Brown, holding up the handset.

'Mr Daykin? It's Paul from Queen's Square, can you give Mr Allenbrook some more details?'

Daykin spent the next ninety minutes on the phone, answering questions on every detail of the case. Then he took the dog for a walk, had a late lunch and worried about Leeds Crown Court in the morning.

Chapter Thirty-three

Daykin found number one court at Leeds Crown Court and sat down behind Jeremy Allenbrook who was assembling a folding lectern on the table in front of him. The door at the side of the court opened and Sir Christopher Benson glided in with the slow solemnity of a funeral march.

If Jeremy Allenbrook was impressive in his wig and gown, Benson beat him by a short head. Taller and broader he had a craggy face that must have been handsome when he was young. He stopped at the table he would share with Allenbrook. He looked with distrust at Jeremy Allenbrook and distaste at Daykin.

Like two Samurai warriors before they get down to the serious business of combat, they were formally polite to each other.

'Jeremy,' said Benson, as he put files and law books on to the table, 'do North Yorkshire Constabulary really want to go on this fishing trip? If they do, I'm afraid we're going to ask for extortionate costs.'

'We've got some points, Christopher,' said Allenbrook, who knew him well enough to call him by his first name, without the title, 'and we will make them. We may just get our order. Stranger things have happened.'

Daykin sensed that, through the courtesy, they really didn't like each other.

'If you withdraw now, and I see,' Sir Christopher said, looking down at Daykin, 'you have an officer with you who can give instructions to do so, my clients will cap their claim for costs at five thousand.'

Sir Christopher had the air of a man who was so important that someone would pay him ten thousand pounds to travel to Leeds for an hour's work. They had.

'What I will do for you, Christopher,' said Jeremy Allenbrook, turning away from the table, 'is have a talk to Inspector Daykin over a cup of coffee, but no promises.'

'Are you going to throw in the towel?' asked Daykin, as they walked along the corridor.

'Good God, no. Chris is so arrogant he thinks I will, but we'll go back into court two minutes before the judge comes in and won't give him time to reorganize his thoughts.'

After a cup of coffee they went back to court, Allenbrook told Sir Christopher Benson in a voice just above a whisper that they had decided to proceed and then Mr Justice Hall came into court.

'I have read the written skeleton arguments submitted by both counsel,' he said, 'it seems to me, Mr Allenbrook, that you have an uphill task.'

'That may seem so at first sight, My Lord, but I hope to persuade you otherwise,' said Allenbrook smoothly.

For an hour Daykin sat and watched the legal arguments sway back and forth until, with one eye on the clock, knowing he had a murder trial to start at ten thirty, the judge said, 'I'll go this far for you, Mr Allenbrook. I will make an order, but on a limited basis. I will order that the Respondent firm of solicitors tell a representative of North Yorkshire Police when this account was opened, the identity of the trustees, the purpose of the account and the current balance. If the applicants want any further information as a result of that disclosure, they must apply again to this court.'

'Costs, My Lord?' asked Benson

'Each side to pay its own, Sir Christopher,' said the judge. He didn't appear to like Benson much either.

'Give the court half an hour to fax the order to Rosenthals,' said Jeremy Allenbrook outside the courtroom, 'then you can call them.'

Daykin decided to leave the phone call until he was back at the station. The traffic was light, the sun had started to shine through a bank of high cirrus clouds and, by the time he pulled into the car-park, fifty minutes after leaving Leeds, he was whistling softly to himself.

In the incident room he asked Fritz Schmidt to turn the phone on to speaker.

'You'd better all listen to this,' he said.

He dialled the number that Christopher Benson had given to Jeremy Allenbrook and asked the receptionist to be put through to the senior partner.

'David Rosen.'

'Mr Rosen, my name is Thomas Daykin, I'm an inspector of police in North Yorkshire. Have you received an order by fax from the High Court at Leeds today?'

'I have, Inspector and although I don't like it, I'm not going to disobey a High Court order, so here's the information you want. Account T54 was opened by Mr Lucas exactly thirty years ago, initially at his local bank in Cambridge. Then, for tax reasons, the account funds were transferred to Venezuela fourteen years ago. It is an interest bearing trust fund account. Initially, Mr Lucas was the sole trustee, but ten years ago he appointed me as joint trustee, with power to appoint another trustee in the event of his death, to take the trust to its maturity. It is a tontine trust and, at today's rate of exchange, the account holds five million, two hundred and forty-two pounds and five pence.

'Have I fully complied with the High Court order?'

'You have, Mr Rosen, thank you. I don't think we'll be troubling you again.'

Daykin switched the phone off. There was silence in the incident room.

'What's a tontine trust?' asked Terry Hudson eventually.

'An arrangement where a number of people put money into a kitty and the last one alive scoops the pot.'

'Who's money is it?'

'You remember Ellington said that Lucas asked them all to put five hundred into an account? That was six thousand. Over the years when he saw a sure-fire money-making investment, he invested his own money and drew most of the money out of the account and invested that too. When he took his profit he replaced the money, plus any profit, back into the trust account. Over the years until he died, with interest, it has grown to over five million. If money is the motive that's a hell of a motive.

'Now,' he said, looking round the table. 'Finding Francis Sheppard has become a priority. Terry, any news from Switzerland?'

'We now know,' said Hudson, looking at the notes in his diary, 'that he came off the mountain alive. He had fallen two hundred to three hundred feet and was badly injured. If he had lain there for a few hours he would have died of hypothermia.

'There were no records from mountain rescue because they didn't find him. He was found by a Russian mountaineering team who were descending from the summit. They were catching a plane from Innsbruck to St Petersburg later that day, so they didn't stay to file reports or make statements. They brought him down and got him to the local hospital in Grindelwald. We know that he only stayed there for twenty-four hours until he was transferred to a larger hospital because his injuries were so bad. I know it's Switzerland and they're supposed to be ultra efficient, but it's a small hospital and it was twenty years ago. Their records have been destroyed and they can't tell us where he was taken to.'

'Get everyone on the phones. Start with the local towns, Wengen and Murren, then widen the search to Bern, Montreux, Lausanne and Zurich. I want to know where he went and, if he survived, where he went from there.'

Nobody moved.

'Now people, please.'

'Why bother?' said Martin Brown. 'Why don't we just wait to see who is the last one alive and he's the culprit?'

'It's never as easy as that,' said Daykin. 'Just get on with the phone calls.'

It took them less than an hour to get back on the trail of Francis Sheppard. He had been taken by ambulance from Grindelwald to Bern where, at the Inselspital Hospital he underwent five operations in the space of two weeks. Two days after the last operation he was taken, very suddenly, by air ambulance from Bern to Newcastle. There the trail went cold again.

'Fritz,' said Daykin, 'can you get a map of the area surrounding Newcastle on your computer?'

Schmidt nodded.

'And a circle with a radius of twenty miles?'

'Yes, sir,'

'Then do it, I need seven copies.'

'What's this about, Tom?'

'There's only one reason to fly by air ambulance to Newcastle – the hospital must be near Newcastle Airport. If you were taking him to a hospital down south, or even to the Midlands, you'd fly into one of the London airports, its quicker and easier.'

Fritz Schmidt printed seven A4 maps and dealt them round the table like giant playing cards.

'Find every hospital within that circle and see if Francis Sheppard was taken there as a patient,' said Daykin. 'I'll see if I can find out who paid for the air ambulance.'

By six that evening they were no further forward. They had tried hospitals in Middlesbrough, Stockton-on-Tees, Bishop Auckland, Darlington and Newcastle itself. Then they had started on the cottage hospitals in the smaller towns, Redcar and Saltburn.

'You're all starting to look as tired as I feel,' said Daykin. 'Call it a draw for tonight and we'll start fresh in the morning.'

After the others had left, Daykin sat staring out of the window for a long time, watching the pale, watery sun cast the last of its milky rays over the horizon. He took off his glasses and polished them with the end of his tie. He had identified the person who paid for the air ambulance, a Mrs Jackson who lived in Ascot, but it was twenty years ago and there was no trace of her now.

He picked up the phone and dialled directory enquiries.

'I need the number for Belmarsh Prison.'

He dialled Belmarsh and asked to speak to the duty governor.

'You have a prisoner who is serving, but he's also there for his own protection. His name is Clive Ellington. Can you send someone to ask him the name of the man Francis Sheppard's wife married after she divorced him?'

The governor, not hiding his irritation at what seemed like a lot of trouble for a small detail, said he would send the wing officer and call Daykin back. Ten minutes later Daykin's mobile phone rang.

'Inspector Daykin? Ellington says that his name was Roger Jackson.'

Daykin thanked him.

'Come on, Royston,' he said, getting up. 'Time we went home, there's nothing that won't wait until the morning.'

Chapter Thirty-four

Ambulatio

'Private hospitals, research laboratories with hospital facilities, charities, hospices and military hospitals,' said Daykin as he walked into the incident room the following morning.

'Sorry, Guv?' said Bob Davies.

'If you'd tried all the hospitals, contact any organization that might have a hospital attached to it. The Regional Health Authority should be able to help.'

'Are you still looking for Mrs Jackson?' asked Terry Hudson, folding the *Racing News* and putting it into his jacket pocket.

Daykin nodded and went to sit in front of a telephone at the nearest table.

It took him three hours to fill in the gaps in Mrs Jackson's life. She had been born Melissa Maycroft into a wealthy family who had made their money in textiles. When she was twenty-one she inherited a large fortune from her grandfather's estate. She met Francis Sheppard when he was working at his first job after going down from Cambridge. Two years later they married and eighteen months after that a daughter, Colette, was born.

When Colette was three years old the couple separated and they divorced the following year. It was not a bitter divorce, just two people who realized that they had grown apart and no longer wanted the same things. They stayed on friendly terms, and not just for Colette's sake. He listed his wife as his next of kin on his insurance policies.

When the authorities at the hospital in Switzerland notified her of Francis Sheppard's accident she arranged for him to be flown back to Newcastle by air ambulance. There was no record of where Sheppard was taken when he left the airport.

There would be no help in finding him from Francis Sheppard's former wife. Five years after her divorce, she married Roger Jackson, a Ph.D. working as an administrator for Oxfam. He divided his time between England and Africa and when Colette was sent away to school his wife would often go with him on his trips to Africa. They loved the warm sunny days, the wildlife and the endless dry, dusty, magical landscapes. They drank cocktails watching deep red sunsets and they talked a lot of buying some land, building a home and retiring there. Four years ago Dr and Mrs Jackson were on a flight in a small plane between Mondou and Bangui, it flew into a storm and crashed, killing the pilot and both passengers.

Daykin finished his notes and put them into a file. He stood up and walked to stand behind Fritz Schmidt.

'Where are we with the hospital?' he said.

Terry Hudson, who was sitting next to Schmidt, turned round in his chair.

'We think we've covered all of them. The guys have been busy on the phone. No one called Francis Sheppard was admitted twenty years ago. There are only three hospitals left that we haven't been able to contact.'

'Are their phones ringing, or is there no signal?'

'No signal.'

'Check with the phone companies, find out why that is. I'm going to talk to Superintendent Wainwright.'

The meeting with Wainwright did not go well. Daykin had to admit that they didn't have a suspect, let alone know where the suspect was. Wainwright was under pressure from above and he transferred that pressure to Daykin.

'Results, Tom, and fast,' he said, as Daykin left his office, 'or heads will roll and they could be both yours and mine.'

'Listen up,' said Daykin as he got back to the incident room, 'the chief constable is getting restless. That means that unless we come up with some answers in the next twenty-four hours he's going to start moving specialist units in here to replace us. That won't look good on anyone's record, so let's push harder today and see what we can come up with. Fritz, stay on the computer, start collating everything we've got so far. Bob and Sarah, go back through the files, see if we've missed anything. Martin and Bridget, look again at what we know about Lucas and Sheppard – there may be a link we haven't seen. Terry, you and I will find out what happened to Francis Sheppard after he left Newcastle Airport. What have you got on the hospitals?'

'It wasn't that hard, Tom. One of them was part of a small company that ran three private cottage hospitals around Darlington. They were bought out by one of the large medical insurance companies who decided that Darlington didn't need three cottage hospitals and they closed two of them down. This was one of them. To add insult to injury, they then built a brand new facility in the country towards Richmond and then closed the last of the three down too.

'The second was in Bishop Auckland, run by a local charity. There was an amalgamation with another charity, based in North Lancashire and they moved, lock, stock and barrel, to Clitheroe.

'The last is still a bit of a mystery. It's some sort of research facility, with a small hospital, only the size of one large ward from what I can gather. The phone company says that there's a fault on the line, that's why we can't get through to them. They're working on it and should have a line up and running' – he looked at his watch – 'about now.'

'What do they call this place?'

'The Institute of Toxin Research.'

'See if they have a website, Fritz.'

Fritz Schmidt started typing on his keyboard and five seconds later a picture of a one-storey building appeared. Down the left of the screen was a menu. Daykin looked down the list of the institutes aims, its history, funding and personnel.

'See who's in charge,' he said.

Schmidt moved the cursor to the personnel logo and pressed a key. Five passport-sized head-and-shoulder photographs appeared on the screen. Beside each was a short biography. The man in charge was Professor Duncan Jackson, a man with more letters following his name than there are in a Welsh railway station.

'You're a betting man,' said Daykin, 'what are the odds that his name of Jackson is just a coincidence?'

'About the same as you winning the next Olympic marathon.'

'Let's see if those telephone engineers are any good.'

They were and lines had been restored. Five minutes later Daykin was speaking to Professor Jackson.

'Professor,' said Daykin, 'do you have a hospital attached to your laboratory?'

'Hospital is glamorizing it but, yes, we do have three private rooms with medical facilities.'

'For what purpose?'

'We are a privately funded facility, investigating the effects of poisons. We need the ability to treat volunteers who may suffer unexpected side effects.'

'Who funds you?'

'Is that important?'

'It may be.'

'A charitable trust and several drugs companies.'

'Has the charitable trust anything to do with Melissa Jackson?'

'You're very well informed, Inspector. Yes, she gave money to the trust while she was alive and left a large bequest in her will.'

'What was your relationship with Mrs Jackson?'

'What's the point of all these questions?'

'I wouldn't be calling you if it wasn't important, Professor. Your relationship?'

'She was my sister-in-law.'

'So Roger Jackson was your brother?'

'Yes.'

'So you knew Francis Sheppard?'

'Fran? Yes, very well.'

'Professor, I'd like you to listen carefully to what I have to say. We're coming up to talk to you face to face. We should be there in about an hour to ninety minutes. I believe you may be in danger. If you can, lock yourself in your office, I'll send some local officers to look after you until we get there.'

'A bit dramatic, isn't it, Inspector?'

'No, sir, it's not.'

Daykin put the phone down.

'Fritz, get an armed response unit from the Durham Force to that address. Tell them to look after Professor Jackson, say it's an emergency. Terry, you and I are going to' – he looked at the computer screen – 'somewhere near Barnard Castle.'

Daykin headed for the door. Royston, who had been pretending to be asleep in the corner, got to his feet and barked.

'We're not taking the dog, are we?' complained Terry Hudson.

'He now thinks we're the three musketeers,' said Daykin.

It was nearer to ninety minutes than an hour when Daykin drove his car into a parking space in front of the building they had seen on the computer screen. It was the sort of structure the government built in the 1950s. One-storey, mainly concrete, small, metal framed windows and a flat roof. It had been built to last for thirty years and had long ago grown grubby, tired and outdated. If it wasn't so cheap to run it would have been demolished years ago.

They left Royston in the car and walked to a front door, mainly glass, with The Institute of Toxin Research across it in faded gold letters.

If the outside of the building had seen better days, money had been spent on the interior. The reception area was bright and clean with a high, semi-circular beechwood reception desk manned by a young woman with glasses, scraped back chestnut hair and a ready smile.

'Professor Jackson,' said Daykin, holding his warrant card out to her.

'You're the second lot of police officers we've had to see Professor Jackson today, is he in trouble?' she said, as she reached for the phone.

They followed her directions down a narrow corridor lit by concealed spotlights to an office door at the far end. An armed officer stood outside the door. He nodded to Daykin after looking at his warrant card and opened the door, calling through it, 'Officers coming in, Ryan.'

Inside the office, Professor Jackson was sitting at his desk. A second armed policeman sat in a chair in the corner of the room that gave him a good view of the door.

'Professor Jackson,' said Daykin as he entered the room, 'I'm Tom Daykin, this is Terry Hudson. We'd like to talk to you about your extended family.'

'So I gather, Inspector. Is there any real need for me to be a prisoner of these armed men?'

'We had one potential witness murdered recently, I didn't want you to be the second.'

'I see,' said Professor Jackson. He sounded as if he did.

He was a softly spoken man with red hair cropped very close to his scalp. He wore an old-fashioned pair of tortoise-shell glasses, a striped shirt with a polka dot bow tie and a stained white laboratory coat.

'You said you knew Francis Sheppard,' said Daykin.

'Yes, I do. You're talking about him in the past tense. He's still alive.'

'Do you know where he is now?'

'Yes. He's just down the corridor. Would you like me to introduce you?'

Daykin shot a look at Terry Hudson.

'Yes, please.'

'Follow me,' said Professor Jackson, getting up from his chair.

The armed police officers got up at the same time.

'Thanks, lads,' said Daykin, opening the door, so the constable outside could hear, 'I just wanted to make sure Professor Jackson was still breathing when we got here. Sergeant Hudson and I can take it from here.'

They left the two officers calling their station and followed the professor. He gave them a guided tour, pointing out the laboratory, the kitchen, dining room, rest area and changing rooms. Past reception he opened a door on to what Daykin guessed was a wing that had been added long after the original building. It was a light area, with large picture windows and sky lights in the roof.

'This is where the volunteers come to recuperate after their tests,' said the professor. 'Fran should be in here.'

He opened another door at the far end of the wing.

It was a white room with a laminated, imitation wood floor. All the linen on the bed and the curtains, were spotlessly white and, apart from the floor, the only colour in the room was a vase of mixed flowers on the window sill. On a tall rack by the bed, stacked one over the other, were medical monitoring machines, connected by wires to the man lying on the bed.

He lay motionless, his eyes closed, and the only sign of life was a small black rubber balloon, connected by a tube to the clear plastic mask over his nose and mouth, that inflated and deflated as he breathed the slow, steady breaths of deep sleep.

'He's been like that since we took him off the air ambulance at Newcastle,' said Professor Jackson.

'Is there any chance he'll ever recover?' asked Daykin, looking at the pale almost deathlike face and thinking that someone must take the trouble to shave him every day.

'Almost certainly not but, with the advances of science, who knows? Melissa didn't want us to turn off the life-support machinery and, as her money pays for Fran to lie here, so he will until one day he'll die of natural causes.'

'She must have loved him very much.'

'I think it was something Roger came to accept. She was married to him, but she never stopped loving Fran.'

'Colette Sheppard,' said Daykin, 'can you tell us where she is now?'

'You seem to be asking the right questions, Inspector. I can tell you that, too. But she's not Colette Sheppard, she insisted on being called Jackson from an early age. I know it rankled her mother who wanted her to carry on the name of Sheppard.'

'A young woman called Jackson,' muttered Daykin.

'What was that, Inspector?'

'Nothing, just something someone said to me. Where is she?'

'Her mother had a bungalow built for her in the grounds here; she spends a lot of time there, on her own.'

'Not something you'd expect of a wealthy young woman of twenty-four?'

'Twenty-five. No it's not, but I'm afraid Colette marches to the beat of a different drummer.'

'Can we go somewhere so I can get some of this down in writing?'

'Lets go to the dining room, it should be quiet now.'

They each pulled up a chair to a round table and Daykin took his diary out of his battered briefcase.

'Colette was a very bright child but I don't think she took too well to being sent away to school. Melissa used to say that after the massive injuries to her father and her mother's remarriage, perhaps she thought of being sent away to boarding school as a form of rejection. That's probably why she was so badly behaved at school, she was expelled from two of them.

'She seemed to settle down a bit in her last two years at school and got a place at Imperial College reading economics. She graduated with a first and, after a gap year in Asia, she decided to study for a doctorate. She chose international finance, specifically the development of software to predict the movement of futures markets. She's done all the groundwork and I believe she is finishing off her thesis before it's typed.'

'Is she any good with computers?'

'Strange question but, yes, she's that generation and she is very good. Why do you ask?'

'She may have been in our police station, using a computer.'

They both sat silently, thinking about this possibility.

'What's she like?'

Professor Jackson looked hard at Daykin, as if trying to decide how much to tell him.

'She's very promiscuous. But, there again, she's a very attractive, single young woman in her twenties and maybe the world has moved on since I was that age.'

'Any psychological or physical problems?'

There was another pause, longer this time.

'She had certain psychotic difficulties in the past, but those are now being treated by medication and we keep an eye on her, just in case.'

'What do you mean, "psychotic difficulties"?'

'It was first noticed while she was at school. Everyone put it down to not being able to settle into her new environment. She attacked another pupil with a pair of scissors. There were other incidents, which gradually got worse. When she was fifteen she was admitted to a psychiatric ward. After they stabilized her with drugs she was released back to a school nearer to her mother. Things settled back down again, that's when she started her A-Levels. There were a few problems in university, but nothing that reached court, in one case because her mother paid the boy off.

'Now she does some low-grade preparatory work in the laboratory in her spare time, so she knows most of the staff. They keep an eye on her and she has an effective curfew at her bungalow. She has to be indoors by midnight.'

'Every night?'

Jackson looked uncomfortable.

'There are evenings when she doesn't come home, but those are fairly few and far between.'

'How often?'

'Perhaps once a fortnight.'

'Has she ever been away longer than one night?'

'You have to understand, Inspector, we can't keep an eye on her every second of the day.'

'The bungalow, can you show us where it is?'

'Certainly, it's very easy to find. Go out of the main doors and turn right. You will see a path. Follow that path for about three hundred metres and the bungalow is on your left.'

They followed his directions and found the bungalow. It was the sort of building a wealthy woman would commission. The roof tiles, woodwork, doors and rendering all looked expensive. There was a neatly kept garden surrounded by a low chain-link fence in front of the property. Daykin opened the gate and they walked between the two closely cut lawns to the front door. He pressed the doorbell and heard it ring somewhere in the building. He had just rung the bell for third time and they were about to leave, when a voice said, 'She's not in.'

They both turned and looked back at the gate. A tall young man with a bad hair cut and worse acne was standing in front of a small cartful of gardening tools. He was dressed in a pair of dark green overalls and brown boots.

'How do you know?' asked Daykin.

'I saw her leave about half an hour ago. She had a suitcase with her.'

'Do you know where she was going?'

'No,' said the young man. He took a hoe from his cart and started moving it along the nearest flowerbed.

Terry Hudson watched him work on Colette Jackson's garden.

'From what I've heard of her, she didn't seem like the gardening type,' he said.

'She's gone somewhere overnight,' said Daykin, reaching for his mobile phone, 'and I'm getting some very bad thoughts.'

He dialled the station and asked to speak to Fritz Schmidt.

'Fritz, that back door trojan horse, did you ever close it?'

Schmidt gave a long humming sound he used when he didn't know what to say.

'If you didn't, could a remote computer still get into our information?'

'I tried to close it, but couldn't. So, yes, sir.'

Daykin snapped the phone shut.

'Come on,' he said to Hudson, 'she's got the address of the safe house.'

Chapter Thirty-five

As they started their journey south, dark black thunderheads appeared from their right and rolled steadily across the sky until it was one dark and grey ceiling above them. Then the rain started, a steady downpour of heavy drops that drummed constantly against the windscreen and ran in tiny rivers diagonally across the side windows.

The spray from the lorries, the caution of other traffic, the poor visibility and the occasional accident slowed and frustrated them and, as they drove into Harrogate, the dark clouds had made an early dusk.

Daykin parked on the opposite side of the road from the house and they both looked through the rain-streaked side window at the three-storey grey stone Victorian building, shining as its damp walls reflected the street lights.

'Seems peaceful enough,' said Terry Hudson.

'So is death. Let's take a look.'

Daykin tried the front door. It opened.

'Bloody great,' he said, and pushed it fully open.

At the opposite end of the short hallway was a kitchen. Through the door they could see a young woman standing by the sink.

'How did you get that door open?' she demanded.

'We didn't have to try very hard. Who's in charge of security?' asked Daykin.

'Who are you?' she countered.

Daykin pulled out his warrant card and held it up to her.

'Sorry, sir,' she said, 'there's a sergeant upstairs, he's in charge.'

She was an attractive young woman with a good figure that her tight jeans and low-cut sweater didn't hide. She looked at Daykin with large brown eyes, framed by long dark lashes and the calm assurance of someone who knows she is good-looking. Her black hair, bobbed and curled in at the neck, was well cut and her clothes, although casual, were expensive. She saw Daykin staring at her and smiled,

219

mistaking his reason for staring.

'Go and take a look upstairs, Terry,' said Daykin.

They both turned and watched Terry Hudson climb the stairs.

'I was just asked to make a cup of tea for the others, sir. Would you like one?'

'It's been a bad car journey. Yes, please, and I think my sergeant will have one too.'

'How do you take it?'

'Just milk for me, milk and three sugars for him.'

She filled an electric kettle from the tap and switched it on. She opened three cupboard doors before she found a shelf full of mugs.

'Don't you make tea much here?' asked Daykin.

'Sorry, sir, I've just been posted here. Today is my first day.'

'You didn't say what your name was.'

'Dawson. Nicole Dawson. Detective Constable, sir.'

'Can I see your warrant card?'

'Yes, of course.'

She started to reach for a black designer handbag hanging by its strap from the back of one of the kitchen chairs.

Terry Hudson's voice shouted urgently from the top of the stairs, 'The guys' up here say they don't have a female officer with them, Tom!'

Daykin leaned back slightly and kicked the chair hard. The chair and the handbag separated in mid air, the chair ricocheting off two base unit doors and the handbag vomiting its contents across the wooden floor. In the middle of the compact, purse, make-up bag, mirror and mobile phone was a steel blue Remington semi-automatic pistol with a cross-hatched wooden grip. With speed that surprised the young woman, Daykin stooped and grabbed it. Terry Hudson appeared in the doorway and Daykin tossed the handgun to him. Then he turned to the young woman.

'Colette Jackson?'

She was so calm that Daykin felt uneasy. She casually picked up the fallen chair and sat down on it at the kitchen table. She ignored the handbag.

'Not a lot of use denying it, is there?'

'Colette Jackson, I'm arresting you for the murders of Christopher Van Meer, Robert Miller and Darius Moore. You need not say anything but it may harm your defence if you do not say something now which you later rely on in Court. Anything you do say will be taken down and used in evidence. Do you understand?'

'Why don't you tell me how you found me, Inspector, and I'll fill in the gaps.'

'You know that Sergeant Hudson will be writing down what you say and we could both give evidence against you?'

'It doesn't matter,' she said flatly.

'OK, we started by going down the wrong road, we thought that it was a woman's revenge.'

'Men! You always think it has something to do with sex.'

'We had a dancer who had been raped and had sworn revenge. When we finally located and interviewed her we knew it was nothing to do with her.'

'Tell me from when you decided that the motive was money.'

'I couldn't get my head round the fact that the last one standing would be the only suspect. It was too stupid, too simple. Then I thought about your father. Suppose he wasn't dead? I thought that the person who killed Darius Moore was a woman and what if your father had a relative, a sister or a daughter, who would inherit if he was the last one alive.'

'Very good. So now you think he's alive, what then?'

On the breakfast bar at the side of the kitchen Terry Hudson scribbled frantically in his diary.

'I thought, suppose the person who killed Bishop Moore, the woman who saw Cunningham, a woman by the name of Jackson or some similar name, and the woman who came to the station pretending to be Ilona Mancini were the same person, that meant it had to be Francis Sheppard's daughter. Now all I had to do was find her. As soon as I found Professor Jackson I knew I was near. I knew it was you who came to the station as soon as I walked into this room. You could disguise your appearance, but you wear a very distinctive perfume, only one other person I've ever known has worn it. What bothers me is why, when you had a comfortable style of living, a free house and money paid into your bank account every month, you wanted to kill people for money.'

'Have you any idea what it's like to live a life where money is no object, then be reduced to a few thousand pounds a month?'

She leaned sideways, stretching out for something on the floor. Hudson stopped writing and stepped forward, but Daykin motioned with his hand to relax. She picked up a small eelskin pouch, opened it and took out a packet of cigarettes and a gold lighter, inlaid with lapis lazuli. She lit a cigarette, inhaled deeply and blew the smoke so that it spread out like a tiny bomb blast across the kitchen table.

'I think you found out about the tontine trust when you went to see Dominic Lucas,' said Daykin.

'You're not as stupid as you look, are you, Inspector? Yes I decided to read for a doctorate and settled on a thesis on the prediction of the futures markets. My mother had told me that my father was at university with a man called Lucas who was a genius in the market. She also said that Cunningham kept in touch with everyone. It didn't take long to find him, the Bar List is published on the Internet. I went to see him and he told me how I could contact Lucas.'

'Did you kill Dominic Lucas?'

'No. I would have done, eventually, but someone saved me the trouble.'

'Lucas told you about the tontine?'

'It was right at the end of our conversation. I went to see him and he spent over three hours explaining how he identified investments and moved money around. A lot of international finance involves buying and selling quickly, before the markets have time to react, so you have to move money to places where you can use it efficiently. He finished his lecture when he told me about the tontine. He said it was a pity my father didn't get the chance to inherit the fund. I asked him how much it was worth. He said he wasn't sure to the penny, but it was somewhere just over five million pounds. He told me how much he liked my father and he was sorry he died, but at least it was doing something he enjoyed. I realized that he didn't know Dad is still alive. That's when I first thought of getting my hands on it. I didn't know how many of them were still with us, so I set about finding out. Merchanto, Swanson, McDonald and Hastings were dead, so that left only seven. Then a burglar topped Lucas and it may be that the knowledge of how much was in the fund died with him, so now I was the only one who knew. It was just getting easier.'

'Did you try to run Patrick Freeman down?'

'Yes, that was me. He was the first, he was a sitting target on that stupid bike of his. Only I didn't quite get it right, I only winged him. Still, it would make him easier to take out later.'

An odd look had come into her eyes and Daykin saw for the first time that she was totally insane.

'You'll want to know about Van Meer,' she continued, as calmly as if discussing a menu.

'The strychnine was easy to get hold of and after I found out he drank gallons of tea a day there was an obvious place to put it. Then all I had to do was wait for him to use the packet I'd laced with the poison.

'Miller was even easier. I told him who my father was and that started the conversation. Then I told him I had just been given the job as a yacht broker. He couldn't wait to tell me he had a yacht, or to show it to me. He even took me out for a trip round the bay! I told him I thought I'd heard someone struggling in the water and as he leaned over to see, I hit him over the head with the weight he used to hold the cabin door open. He made such a splash as he went into the water I thought that they'd hear it in Scarborough. When I was sure he wasn't coming back up to the surface I slipped over the side and swam to shore.

'I enjoyed killing Moore, he was an arrogant, chauvinist pig. Once he thought I might sleep with him it was easy. He couldn't take me home and a hotel would be too obvious, he was too well known, so I suggested an afternoon of passion on the sofa in his office. He smuggled me into the compound in that gas-guzzling off-road machine of his. Do you want to know how passionate he was when it came down to it? He sat down at his desk to listen to the voice messages on his answer machine before we started. That's when I stuck the knife through his neck. Then I hid in a broom closet while those bovine security guards went into panic mode and, in the confusion, I slipped out through the main gate.

'I was coming to put a bullet through the two upstairs, then that would only leave Ellington and I was finished.'

'How the hell did you think you were going to break into a high security prison, murder an inmate and walk out?' asked Terry Hudson.

'I wasn't,' she said sharply. 'There's a drug baron in Belmarsh called Finlay. I had arranged to get half a kilo of heroin in a small flour bag into the prison kitchen supplies. Once he had the heroin, he'd have someone take care of Ellington.'

'What about the two officers upstairs?'

She gave a short derisory laugh.

'Obviously, they'd have to go as well. It's strange how men, even trained men, seem to think that a pretty young woman won't be any danger to them.'

'And when you'd taken care of Clive Ellington?'

'That's when I'd contact Rosenthals with the proof that the other eleven were dead and my father was still alive. I was wondering how I would prove the deaths, but your records have all the death certificates, so I took copies.

'I suppose you've guessed what would happen when my father got the money. I was his only child and, anyway, Uncle Duncan told me that he made a will a couple of years before his accident, leaving everything to me, not that there was much then. So, after a reasonable time, I would turn off his life support machine.'

'Another one wouldn't make any difference,' said Terry Hudson from the breakfast bar.

She looked at him with an icy gaze of pure hatred, but said nothing.

'And now it's time to go,' she said.

Hudson stopped writing and took a pair of handcuffs from a small pouch at the back of his belt.

'You won't need those, Sergeant,' she said, reaching into the small change pocket in her jeans. She took out a capsule and put it into her mouth.

'What's that?' said Daykin carefully.

'The Institute has all sorts of poisons. Cyanide is the most difficult to get hold of, or I'd have used it on Van Meer. I offered to put their stock-taking on to computer and managed to lose this capsule in the process. I've kept it in case things went wrong, just like they have now.'

Daykin moved fast. He threw the table to one side and grabbed for her face, trying to keep her jaws open. He wasn't quite quick enough, he could hear the capsule break as she bit down on it. She smiled at him gently, her eyes turned up in her head and, as he gripped her shoulders, he felt her go limp as the life ebbed out of her.

'Call an ambulance, just in case,' he said to Terry Hudson, 'but I think she needs the pathologist.'

They knew that a death in lawful custody would mean an enquiry and, as a prelude, at least half an hour of Wainwright shouting at them. They watched as the ambulance crew came into the kitchen and pronounced Colette Jackson dead. They watched as the pathologist's assistants zipped her into a plastic body bag and wheeled her on a trolley out to their hearse. They watched the armed officers escort Cunningham and Freeman, pale and tired, out of the building. They listened while Superintendent Wainwright shouted at them for ten minutes and told them he had a lot more to say later.

'I wish that was the end of it,' said Daykin, when everyone had gone and they were left alone in the house, 'but now we've got to make a start on the paperwork. But before we do, why don't we go and get a couple of pints? I'm buying.'

'Have I ever told you, Tommy, how much I enjoy working with you?'

'Don't call me Tommy.'